UNRAVELED SLEEVE

Monica Ferris

BERKLEY PRIME CRIME, NEW YORK

This is a work of fiction. Names, characters, places, and incidents are either the product of the author's imagination or are used fictitiously, and any resemblance to actual persons, living or dead, business establishments, events, or locales is entirely coincidental.

UNRAVELED SLEEVE

A Berkley Prime Crime Book / published by arrangement with the author

PRINTING HISTORY
Berkley Prime Crime edition / July 2001

All rights reserved.
Copyright © 2001 by Mary Monica Kuhfeld

This book, or parts thereof, may not be reproduced
in any form without permission.
For information address: The Berkley Publishing Group,
a division of Penguin Putnam Inc.,
375 Hudson Street, New York, New York 10014.

The Penguin Putnam Inc. World Wide Web site address is
www.penguinputnam.com

ISBN: 0-425-18045-X

Berkley Prime Crime Books are published
by The Berkley Publishing Group,
a division of Penguin Putnam Inc.,
375 Hudson Street, New York, New York 10014.
The name BERKLEY PRIME CRIME and the BERKLEY PRIME
CRIME design are trademarks belonging to Penguin Putnam Inc.

PRINTED IN THE UNITED STATES OF AMERICA

10 9 8 7 6 5 4 3 2 1

Acknowledgments

There really is a Naniboujou Lodge, and I wish to thank the owners and staff for allowing me to set this mystery there. And without the aid of Joan Marie Verba, the details, symptoms, and treatment of severe allergies would not have been so realistic. The many members of RCTN, an Internet newsgroup, have again proved themselves invaluable in keeping me on track with the esoterica of needlework. I would also, and again, like to thank my editor, Gail Fortune, for finding cracks in the original plot of this novel and making me mend them.

1

Through a ring of uniformed police officers, Betsy glimpsed the body of a very fat man. A ruby ring twinkled on the hand that loosely gripped a matte black gun. A beautiful young blonde draped in furs stood nearby, looking at Betsy slantwise through narrowed eyes. Beside her was an unshaven man in old-fashioned prison stripes. Next to him was an elegantly dressed man with a gray goatee, and clinging to the elegant man's arm was a bosomy woman in a white silk blouse unbuttoned nearly to the navel.

Officer Jill Cross, Detective Mike Malloy, and Godwin DuLac appeared suddenly, apparently from behind the circle of policemen. Mike barked, "All right, Betsy, who did it?"

Godwin said cheerfully, "Come on, Betsy, you're so *clever! Tell* him!"

Betsy looked at the suspects, but nothing clever occurred to her.

Jill said, "Mike needs to shoot the murderer. It's important." She began to shout, "Let's go, tell Mike who did it, so we can all go home! It's cold, Betsy, and we want to go home!"

Everyone began shivering. Except Betsy—and the corpse. Betsy looked between the cops' elbows, hoping the corpse would start shivering, which would mean he wasn't really dead. Then she could tell them it was a joke. That would be clever. But he didn't move. Betsy wanted to go home, too, but she had to answer them first. Who killed the man?

In a rising panic, she realized she had no idea.

"Maybe it's you, Betsy," said Godwin.

Jill and Mike exchanged surprised looks that turned suspicious and then gratified.

"I knew it, I knew it!" said Mike.

"No!" said Betsy. "No, no!"

"Why sure," said Mike, and added something incomprehensible that convinced Jill and Godwin.

"Wait, wait—" said Betsy, trying to think.

"Now *I'm* the clever one," said Godwin.

Jill came to take Betsy by the arm. "I'll hold her while you shoot her, Mike."

Mike drew a snub-nosed revolver and pointed it at Betsy, who couldn't think of something clever to say to save her life.

Just as the gun went off, Betsy sat up in bed with a gasp. Her heart was thumping painfully against her ribs. She was suddenly wide awake and breathing hard.

It was a sunny March morning, the temperature already approaching thirty. Betsy went down the stairs from her second-floor apartment, through an obscure back door beside the stairs, and down a short hall that led to facing doors, one to the parking lot and the other into the back room of her shop. She unlocked the shop door and Sophie slipped through.

"Goooooood morning!" chirruped a light tenor voice. "On time this morning, aren't we?"

"In body, if not in spirit," said Betsy.

"Are you awake enough to give me an opinion?" Godwin, a slim young man in a clingy cocoa brown sweater and black wool slacks, was striking a pose in front of the checkout desk. "What do you think?" he asked, doing a model's turn.

Betsy gathered her wits for a look at the sweater. Godwin had knit it himself of silk yarn. It had a barely raised pattern of diamonds across the middle of his chest that continued across his back, and the drape of the thin, soft material on his gently buffed arms and shoulders was exquisite.

"It's beautiful," said Betsy honestly, "and the fit couldn't be better."

"John says if I gain three ounces, it will show."

"That's why I would never own a sweater like that," said Betsy, who was sure she could lose five pounds without it showing.

"You're slimmer than you were back in December," said Godwin, giving her a judicious look. "You're dressing fatter than you are. You'll be surprised when you buy that new wardrobe."

"You think so?" Even the thought of shopping for an entire new wardrobe could not brighten Betsy's face.

Godwin had two remedies for gloom. If Betsy's spirits couldn't be raised by shopping, then, "You need a change. Take a trip to a nice, warm place, get a tan, meet some fun new people."

"Yes, well, I've got to finish up some things here, first."

Betsy's sister's estate had finally been closed. As of nine days ago, Betsy was officially wealthy. She hadn't done anything with the money yet except pay some overdue bills and take a few baby steps toward closing on the building her needlework shop and apartment were in. The current owner was a careful man, anxious not to give away anything more or sooner than necessary, so buying property from him was a slow process.

Betsy had never been rich before, but she had heard of people who won a big lottery prize only to be worse than broke a year later. She was determined to not to make that mistake herself. But in her current state of chronic exhaustion, she was in no condition to make wise choices.

When her sister died, Betsy had found herself sole proprietor of Crewel World, and had been struggling with the two steep learning curves of needlework and owning her own business. But she found she enjoyed the challenges, and especially liked being her own boss. So far, the shop had stayed in the black. But now there was the added burden—a surprise to find it was actually a burden—of being sole inheritor of three million dollars. It would be so wonderful to just close everything down for a month, get really far away, think about what she wanted to do, where she wanted to go.

Or would she go anywhere? She liked Crewel World. Her customers were such nice people, most of them, loyal and patient. Besides, while needlework wasn't what Betsy would have chosen as a hobby, much less a career, it was surprisingly engrossing and created such beauty that she was no longer sorry it had been thrust upon her.

She looked around the shop. It had a big front window, splashed with counted cross-stitch patterns and needlepoint canvases—mostly in green because St. Patrick's Day was near, but also tulips and other spring flowers, and Easter-themed projects and patterns. Back here it might have been dim, but well-placed track lighting put light everywhere it was needed. A dividing set of shelves cut off the rear portion and disguised the long, narrow shape of the shop.

Then she noticed the warm smell of coffee. Betsy went to pour herself a cup. "Did you put up the canvases that came in yesterday?" she asked, and was surprised at how slow the words came out. She was tired. Actually, more than tired, she was exhausted.

"Not yet. Look, why don't you take the morning off? Go back upstairs and sleep some more."

She shuddered. "No, I don't want more sleep. The problem is not getting to sleep, it's the nightmares." She went to the big desk that was the shop's checkout counter.

"Pretty bad?"

"Awful," she said frankly. "Terrifying. I might have known this would happen; I'm not cut out for murder investigations. Twice now, people I knew and liked have turned out to be murderers. And another one tried three times to murder me. I don't want to do this anymore—" Betsy turned away from Godwin's look of compassion. It wasn't sympathy she was after. She thrust her fingers into her hair. "Have you vacuumed yet?"

"In a minute. I'm sorry sleuthing is making you so miserable, because I *love* it when you prove you're so much more clever than everyone else, even the police. And I love it that you're so good about telling me first. In a gossipy town like Excelsior, that makes me Queen."

Betsy couldn't help smiling. "You mean King, don't you?"

"No, honey, *you're* the King. Queen is my place, and *much* more my style." He winked at her and strolled to the back room to get out the Hoover.

Still smiling, Betsy took the deadlock key from a desk drawer, went to the front door to unlock it and turn the needlepointed sign around so OPEN showed through the window. She paused at the white-painted old dresser just inside the door. Ads for stitching retreats, classes, and conventions were tucked into the frame of its dim mirror. One was for a stitch-in to be held in Fort Myers, Florida. *Don't I wish,* she thought.

Thrust out from the opposite wall was an old, white, glass-fronted counter. On top were three sample sweaters with patterns next to them, and a plastic chest with little transparent drawers filled with beads of every size, shape, and color, along with threadlike beading needles. There were two books on beading leaning against it, but the woman who had loaned Betsy her beaded purse had picked it up on Friday and Betsy hadn't managed to borrow another beading project to replace it. She was not remotely skilled enough to do beadwork worthy of inspiring a customer.

However, that forest green sweater was hers. One of her customers, Rosemary, was an excellent teacher, and Betsy was especially proud of the cable stitching. Betsy gave it a little rearranging tug as she went by. The glass-fronted cabinets held back issues of stitchery magazines, the more expensive and fragile wools that couldn't bear the repeated touch of fiber fondlers, and unperused needlework books for customers who insisted on extra-fresh editions.

Betsy went back to the checkout desk to put the key away and place the forty dollars opening-up money in the cash register.

The shop's front door opened with an electronic *bing* and Betsy turned to her first customer of the day. It was Mrs. Savage, who hoped to match a tomato red shade of needlepoint wool. Betsy directed her to the triple row of wooden pegs on the long wall, hanging with loosely knotted skeins in what only seemed like every possible color.

Betsy took a thin stack of painted needlepoint canvases from the desk to the rack of fabric doors hanging on a wall and began to attach the canvases with drawing pins.

Bing went the door again and Betsy turned to see a hearty-looking man with an outsize attaché case grinning at her. "Ms. Devonshire?" he said, and when she nodded faintly, he came forward, hand extended. "I am very, very glad to meet you!" he said in a deep, rich voice that ran up the scale to *glad* and then back down again, shaking her hand with a grip that stopped just short of painful.

He swung the case up onto the desk and opened it. Inside were eight-by-ten color photographs of houses. Big houses. "I'm sure you must be thinking about moving out of that small apartment of yours into something much more suitable for a person of your income," he began.

"No, I'm not," said Betsy.

His surprised chuckle started high and ran steeply down the scale, and Betsy smiled, not because she liked it, but because it reminded her of Throgmorton P. Gildersleeve—old-time radio's most famous pompous ass. "Very nice, you have an interesting sense of humor," he said. "I almost believed you there for a second. Now, I have a house—not too large, but a beautiful house, built just over a year ago, right on Lake Minnetonka, not ten minutes from—"

"I am not interested in buying a house. I like living over my shop."

"You can't possibly mean that."

"Why not? My sister lived upstairs, and the money I inherited came from her."

The woman seeking tomato red wool came over to the desk. "What do you think, Betsy? Is this a match? Or is this one closer?"

"I beg your pardon, but Ms. Devonshire and I are discussing—"

But Betsy interrupted him, saying to her customer, "Let's go stand by the window, Mrs. Savage. We can tell better in natural light." She said over her shoulder to the salesman, "Please go away, can't you see I'm busy?" Anger put steel in her tone, and by the time she and Mrs. Savage agreed that one of the skeins was a near perfect match to the sample Mrs. Savage had brought in, the salesman had gone.

"He must be new to the real-estate business, quitting that easy," remarked Godwin after Mrs. Savage had also left. "I thought that fellow on Saturday was going to set up camp."

The phone rang, and Betsy answered it. The caller mispronounced Betsy's name ("Devon-shyre" instead of "Devon-sheer"), and wanted Betsy to know that another American Family would become homeless every minute they talked, and would Betsy care to make a substantial contribution to an organization whose goal was to build a tent city on the grounds of Minnesota's state capitol building—

Betsy kept a lot of American Families in their homes by hanging up at that point.

By noon the shop, while crowded, had exactly two paying customers. The other people were there to sell Betsy a Lincoln, a Chrysler, land in Arkansas, Florida, and Mexico; to collect for crippled children, blind adults, homeless horses, and women whose emphysema was caused by secondhand smoke; to double Betsy's inheritance in six months or six weeks; to reminisce about how she and Betsy had been best friends in grade school, where they had promised that if one ever got rich she would share it with the other; and to sign Betsy up for cellular phone service, cable television, satellite television, and a professional interior decoration of the new house this gentleman with him wanted to build to

Betsy's specifications on land he was also prepared to sell her.

Staring around wildly, Betsy began to cry, which caused Godwin to lose his temper and chase them out with a steel knitting needle.

"That decorator I think I could've taken," Godwin said with a snort when the shop was empty of all but the woman walking her fingers through the counted cross-stitch patterns in the half-price box. Betsy's tears turned to laughter at that, but the laughter died instantly when she heard that infernal *bing* that meant someone else was coming in. She turned a stony face to the front door.

Shelly Donohue was standing there, looking startled. "Wow, something's got your underwear in a knot," she said, a half-formed smile fading.

Shelly was a medium-sized woman who worked in the shop part-time. She was about thirty-five, with long hair pulled into an untidy bun at the nape of her neck. She wore a full-length, down-filled coat and boots that looked suitable for walking on the moon. In honor of the sunshine, the coat was open.

"It's all right for me to be here," she said, because school was in session and she taught fourth grade. "My students are on a field trip to the Minneapolis Art Museum this afternoon. What's wrong, anyway? You don't look well."

"I'm just tired," said Betsy, shoving her fingers into her hair, a gesture she was afraid might become habitual.

"And every sales rep on the planet is on the phone or here in person, trying to cut himself a slice of Betsy's inheritance," said Godwin. "I've been telling her all morning she should go to Cancun for a week, get away from all this. She could soak up some rays by day and party by starlight. Enough strawberry margaritas will scare away the nightmares while she gets a break from the money mongers."

"Nightmares?" echoed Shelly, coming to put a hand on Betsy's arm. "How awful! I just hate it when I have a nightmare." A smile with a trace of envy in it appeared. "What are you dreaming, the IRS is after your money?"

Godwin said, "This is serious! She's dreaming about death and corpses—"

"Oh, ish!"

"Hush, Goddy," said Betsy, adding to Shelly, "They're about what you'd expect after what I've been through lately. Kind of a delayed reaction to December, I guess." Around Christmas, someone had tried to murder Betsy. "I'll be all right pretty soon. I'd take Godwin's advice, but we're shorthanded as it is, and Joe is being difficult about selling me this building, and anyway I've got some ideas for changes I want to make in the shop, so I need to talk to an architect or—" Shelly and Godwin exchanged swift glances of dismay. "What?"

"What kind of changes?" asked Shelly.

"Nothing drastic," said Betsy. "I was thinking of replacing that dresser up by the front door—"

"No, no, you can't do that!" said Godwin.

"Why not?" asked Betsy. "The drawers don't go back far enough to hold the bigger canvases, some are curled up in there. And the veneer on the top is lifting."

Godwin said, "Honey, there are people who, if they walk in here and don't see that dresser, will think they've come to the wrong place."

"Okay, we can find a carpenter who will build us a dresser just like the current one, only two inches deeper front to back."

Shelly turned and walked to the dresser. "But don't you see? If you push out two inches into the walk space

here, then you'll have to cut two inches off the counter."
She turned and put a hand on the counter. "You can't
do that; I just love this old counter."

"So do several antique dealers who have offered me
enough to pay for both a new counter and a new
dresser."

"Oh, Betsy, please don't sell this counter! Don't
change anything! This place is perfect as it is!"

"I agree," said Godwin, nodding sincerely.

Tired as she was, Betsy understood what was really
going on. Betsy's sister Margot had founded Crewel
World, had brought in the counter and the dresser, had
put the wooden pegs on the wall and the curious set of
canvas doors. She had been a compassionate but driving
force in this town, with countless friends. So long as
these things remained, Margot was, in a way, still here.

Shelly looked a little ashamed. "I know, don't say it,
we don't have the right to make demands like this.
Crewel World is yours now, so you get to do whatever
you want with it." She looked around, her smile upside
down. "At least you didn't close it."

"For which there are a lot of grateful people," added
Godwin. "But you shouldn't make any decisions about
changes right now. You should go away for a week,
even a couple of weeks, then you'll see the place with
new eyes, and be better able to decide what you really
want to do."

"But don't go anywhere Godwin suggests," said
Shelly. "His favorite places are like Animal House every
night. In fact, go farther away than Mexico. Have you
ever been to Spain?"

"No, just England and France."

"Well, I went to the Costa del Sol one winter, and it
was marvelous. It's warm and sunny, it has sleepy little
towns with winding narrow streets, and there's the Med-
iterranean Sea to bask beside. Barcelona is nearby, with

a cathedral you have to see to believe, and there's a castle called Montserrat—"

"Spain's too far!" objected Godwin.

"But that's the attraction," replied Shelly. "It's far from here, way over on the other side of the Atlantic. And the Costa del Sol has these lovely little shops, nothing like here at home. I bought an alabaster statue of a medieval saint for about twenty dollars, very crudely done, but powerful, his eyes just glower at you—"

Godwin said, "Yes, the very thing for someone haunted by bad dreams. Cancun is just as warm and it's lively and never boring. Their beaches are really nice, and there are dolphins who will come and play with you." He sighed. "Wish I could go there now myself."

"But Spain's so exotic, and full of history, with—"

The conversation, which was bordering on argument, cut off when the door sounded, marking the arrival of three members of the Monday Bunch. A group of women stitchers who met every week at Crewel World to work on projects, the Monday Bunch gave advice and support to one another, and indulged in Excelsior's favorite pastime, gossip.

Within a few minutes two more arrived, making six, counting Shelly. Stout Kate McMahon, with her graying red hair and broad smile, was finishing up a hardanger project. Betsy had thought to take up hardanger, and so she came to stand behind Kate and watch.

"What is that, a satin stitch?" she asked.

"Not exactly. I push the needle in here, coming up here, four threads up. You have to watch carefully, because this square has to match exactly the square across from it, and also line up with this square and this square. See, here or here is wrong."

Betsy leaned closer and felt her eyes cross. She couldn't quite see what the difference was. "I think I need to be more nearsighted to do hardanger."

Kate laughed. "Yes, I take my glasses off when I do this."

Betsy went back to her chair and took out the needlepoint project she was working on, a pillow with rows of geese in various poses alternating with the heads of daisies. If it went on as well as it had begun, she planned to display it in her shop.

Godwin, working on a lush and colorful counted cross-stitch pattern of a medieval castle, said, "Betsy's thinking of taking a vacation. March in Minnesota is the pits, don't you agree?"

Alice Skoglund, a broad-shouldered woman with a strong chin and a tendency to verbal faux pas, agreed. "I hate early spring. That's when the snow starts to melt and uncovers all the little animals that died during winter."

"Mercy, Alice!" exclaimed Martha Winters.

"Well," she said, only a little abashed, "it is."

Bing! went the door to the shop.

"That's why I like to fly away to Cancun," said Godwin, consulting his pattern and grimacing at the number of half stitches in the section he was working. "I've suggested Cancun to Betsy." He glanced up toward the door. "Oh, hi, Jill. We're talking about a getaway for Betsy. She really needs one. Can you join us for a while?"

They all looked at Officer Jill Cross standing just inside the door, big in her uniform, her smooth pale face looking back placidly. "For half an hour," she said, lifting a bulging plastic bag with the Crewel World logo on it.

"I think Betsy should go to romantic Spain," said Shelly.

"Too far," said Godwin. "Go to Mexico—you don't have to worry about your internal clock getting all wonky."

"I think she should go to Hawaii," said Kate. "It's tropical, but it's also America."

"There are Minnesotans who winter in Mexico," noted Martha, around the end of a piece of floss she was moistening in her mouth. "You might find yourself in the middle of Old Home Week down there. That would be nice."

Betsy frowned at the thought of Minnesota sales reps on a vacation won by never missing an opportunity. Suddenly distant Spain seemed more attractive.

Shelly spoiled that by saying, "Liz and Isobel are going to Spain. Actually, so is Father Rettger—but I think he's going to Compostella, not Costa del Sol."

Godwin, seeking to change the subject, said, "Martha, some people think it's *not nice* to lick your floss."

Martha, complacently relicking her floss before threading her needle, said, "Some people should find more important things to worry about."

Jill came to the table with a small sheet of paper in her other hand. "Here," she said, putting it in front of Betsy.

Betsy picked up the sheet of paper. It was an announcement for a stitchers' retreat. "Where did you get this?"

"Off the mirror on your dresser." Jill gestured with a minimal nod of her head toward the front of the store. "I saw it when Godwin put it up there a couple of weeks ago, but it got covered up by that announcement about CATS." CATS was a big convention for stitchers coming to Minneapolis in November.

"May I see that?" asked Kate, and Betsy handed her the flier. "Oh, Naniboujou! I've heard of that place." She twisted around to look up at Jill. "But it's way up on the North Shore, isn't it? Practically on the Canadian border."

"Brrrr!" Godwin shivered dramatically. "It's still the dead of winter up there!"

"It's still the dead of winter down here," said Betsy, surprised.

"No, it isn't," said several women, equally surprised. Pat said, "Why it's only March and there's bare spots on the ground already, and if you look at the branches of the trees, you can see the buds are swelling. I'm expecting a crocus any day now."

"I've been to Naniboujou," said Martha Winters, working her needle under some finished stitches on the back of her linen before starting to stitch—she might be a floss licker but she would never tie a knot at the end of her floss. "Only in the summer, of course. But it's a beautiful place, a lodge with a big dining room that serves wonderful food, right across from a state park with miles of hiking trails. Lake Superior is right outside your window, and they have these old-fashioned Adirondack chairs down on the shore, so you can sit with a glass of iced-tea and watch the waves."

"Just the thing to do in March on the North Shore," said Shelly. "Wade a mile or two through six feet of snow in a state park, and rest afterwards on the lakeshore with a glass of iced tea while watching the next blizzard blow in from Canada."

Even Martha laughed at that.

"Did they have a band on Saturday night?" asked Godwin.

"No band, no bar, no television," said Martha. "Not even a phone in your room."

Kate handed the flier back to Betsy. "The application is still on this. Which isn't surprising, nobody we know would want to head north this time of year, would they?"

There was a murmur of agreement.

Betsy looked up at Jill. She was a tall woman, strongly built—though most of her bulk was from the bulletproof vest under a heavy shirt and winter-weight jacket. She had ash blond hair and equally pale eyebrows on a face that rarely showed what she was thinking. She was looking at Betsy now with that calm, unreadable face.

The calm transmitted itself to Betsy. *Nobody I know, no television, and no phones, no phones, no phones,* thought Betsy. "If the stitch-in is this weekend, can we still get a room?" she asked.

"I called in my reservation six weeks ago," said Jill. "And got the last room. I had to take one of the expensive ones, with a fireplace. It's also a double. The stitch-in is just for the weekend, so you can move into your own room on Monday. I'm staying a week; I had to take some vacation or lose it, and I thought I'd get in some cross-country skiing." Jill was made for Minnesota; Betsy was sure she considered summer to be a sad break from winter sports.

Betsy looked again at the brochure. The room had knotty pine walls, the bed looked comfortable. One whole week—She looked at Godwin. "Can we get enough part timers for you to manage a whole week?" she asked.

Godwin sighed dramatically—but he did everything dramatically. "Well, I don't know if I should try to help you, if you won't take my advice and go someplace warm and fun." Then he smiled and said, only a little less dramatically, "All right, Cancun won't go broke because you don't go there this year. And of course we'll manage. Didn't two of our part-timers complain last week that they weren't getting enough hours? We'll manage just fine."

2

They left early Friday morning. Betsy, still wan and heavy-eyed, was also helplessly annoyed as she walked to Jill's car. She was being followed by a tall, redheaded woman in a chartreuse coat who wanted Betsy to buy a portfolio of Internet stocks. The woman had a fistful of documents as vividly colored as she was, and was talking very rapidly about e-this and dot-that.

Jill, though not in uniform, got out of the driver's side of the car and said, "Eh-hrrrum!" The woman glanced at her, stopped in her tracks for a second look, then turned and hurried away.

"How do you do that?" asked Betsy, putting her two suitcases down. "I actually snarled at her, but she kept on talking. All you did was clear your throat."

"I look at them like I think they may resist arrest," replied Jill placidly. She went to the trunk of her car, opened it, and put Betsy's suitcases in beside her own.

There were other things in the trunk: a Dazor light, a sewing frame, a box marked WINTER SURVIVAL KIT, snowshoes.

Betsy pointed to the snowshoes. "What are they, antiques?"

Jill smiled. "Well, I did make them back when I was sixteen."

"What, you liked to make reproductions of old things?"

Jill frowned very slightly. "No, people still use them. When you want to walk over deep snow, there's nothing as good as snowshoes." She closed the trunk. "That state forest right across the road from Naniboujou has an interesting waterfall. I thought I might walk back in to see it."

"What's so interesting about it?"

"Half of it disappears into a rock."

Betsy couldn't think what to ask about that, so she looked at the cross-country skis fastened to the rack on top of Jill's car. There were two pairs, she noticed. Jill said, just a little too casually, "Grand Marais has some very easy cross-country ski trails."

Betsy let her face reflect her thought: *As if.* She went to get in the passenger side of the big old Buick. She'd tried cross-country skiing with Jill and been surprised and disappointed at the exertion required. Like her cat, Betsy was not keen on exercise.

The wide, comfortable seat of the car welcomed her. Betsy fastened her seat belt and relaxed with an audible sigh as Jill pulled away from the curb. "Say, Jill," she said, "would you consider being my bodyguard when we get back? Easy job, you'd just stand behind me clearing your throat at all those dreadful people who insist on a share of my money."

"You don't need a bodyguard. Going off for a week to an unannounced destination will discourage most of them. When you're not there to hound, they'll go hound someone else. You're going to have to be firm and persistent with the rest. Which I've seen you being, when you're in your detective mode."

Betsy grimaced. "I hope you got a good look, because those are going to be mere memories from now on. I'm resigning my commission and turning in my badge. Neither of which I was ever issued, by the way."

Jill gave Betsy a faintly surprised look. "I thought you liked detecting."

"No, not at all. I certainly didn't go looking for cases, they just sort of happened. And I didn't know what I was doing. Clues more or less fell out of the air right in front of me."

"Huh," remarked Jill, then went wordlessly back to driving.

They went past the beautiful Victorian Christopher Inn, then over the bridge and onto Highway Seven, heading toward Minneapolis. Betsy looked out the window at trees and houses passing by. The road was clear and dry, white with dried salt—whiter than the crunchy honeycombed snow pulling its filthy skirts away from the verge. The sky was a light, cloudless blue.

"But that only means you're a natural," said Jill, suddenly picking up the topic again.

"Yes, but I'd have to harden my heart too much to keep doing it, dealing with crime and criminals, and I wouldn't even want to know how to do that."

"Do you think my heart is hard?"

That surprised Betsy. "No, of course not! But you—you're—" Betsy had to think for a moment. "You don't let things hurt you. You have this . . . I don't know, a kind of imperviousness. You don't get angry or scared."

"I was raised to—not to let things get to me," said Jill, and from the way that was wrenched out of her, however cleanly, Betsy knew it was a confession. Jill was as reticent about her upbringing as about her feelings. "But just because I don't break into tears or fall into a rage every time I'm sad or angry doesn't mean I don't feel those emotions."

Betsy, embarrassed, had to think a few moments before she could reply. "How do you deal with the ugliness you face every day?"

"It's not every day—this is Excelsior, after all, not Chicago or DC. And what I do is, I don't take it personally. I think of myself as a street sweeper or garbage collector, taking the crud off the streets. The rotten egg isn't stinking just to annoy me. And somebody has to clean it up."

Betsy nodded. "I'm glad you can do it. The world would be impossible without police. But with me, it's different. I get involved at a personal level, because it involves people I know. And I can't do that anymore. Not when I dream all night about friends who turn out to be murderers."

"Not all of us do."

"But in a recent dream you were at the front of the pack, shouting at me to tell you whodunit. And I had no idea." Betsy frowned. "That was probably the oddest part, you shouting. You have never shouted at me, ever. In fact, I don't think I've ever heard you shout at anyone." She smiled. "But you clear your throat real good."

Jill chuckled softly, then said, "See how unreal the dream was? In your dream you couldn't solve it, but in real life you can."

"Please. I'm absolutely sure that next time I'm faced with a case, it will be just like what I dreamed: I won't have the first clue."

"I take it you never solved a mystery before you came here and figured out who murdered your sister?"

"Absolutely."

Jill fell silent. Betsy sighed and closed her eyes. The car was warm, the seat comfortable, Jill the kind of driver who inspires confidence. Before she realized it, she dozed off.

She was on a train at night, looking out the window into utter darkness. Suddenly a man wearing a Richard Nixon mask slammed through the door into the car, and shot the woman in the first seat with a silenced gun. The woman slumped sideways, and the man ran away, but everyone else in the car immediately turned to Betsy. One said, "Who was that masked man?" in a serious voice, which at first terrified Betsy because she had no idea, then amused her so much she started to giggle, which woke her up.

"What?" asked Jill.

"Stupid dream. Tried to be a nightmare, didn't quite make it." Betsy yawned and looked out the car window. They were on a section of freeway lined with concrete walls, some striated, some smooth. The marked sections had remnants of vines clinging to them, demonstrating the purpose of the striation. "Where are we?" she asked.

"Six-ninety-four East, about to cross the Mississippi. Not even out of the Cities yet."

"How do we get to the North Shore?" asked Betsy. "Follow the Mississippi? It originates in Lake Superior, doesn't it?"

"No, it starts as a brook you can step across in the upper central part of the state. But the North Shore does refer to Lake Superior. We drive about a hundred miles north to Duluth, then follow the Superior shoreline northeast to Grand Marais, then sixteen more miles to Naniboujou."

"Grand Marais," repeated Betsy. "That's a beautiful name. Is it a big city?"

"It's sometimes called the Scandinavian Riviera." Jill smiled, as if at a joke.

"What?" asked Betsy.

"You'll see."

"What happens at a stitch-in?" asked Betsy.

"It's like the Monday Bunch, only it goes on for two days. There's usually a class on some aspect of needle-work, a time for show-and-tell, lots of friendly advice from people sitting near you, and plenty of time to make some real progress on a project."

Betsy looked out the window. The land was nearly level, the pastures outlined with trees and shrubs, with shaggy farmhouses and newer suburban models tucked among more trees, their chimneys smoking faintly.

After a while she slept again. No dreams this time, or when, after a period of looking out the window, she dozed off. Again she woke, this time to a landscape only a little whiter than near the Cities, with small, well-kept houses, their chimneys steaming, set back among crowds of naked gray trees. She yawned. Was she never going to stop feeling sleepy?

Jill said, "It must be frightening to find that sleuthing is the talent God gave you, rather than one for counted cross-stitch or finding a good man. And you can choose to bury this talent if you like. But I'm not sure that will give you the peace you're looking for."

Betsy, annoyed at Jill for nagging but too tired to argue, watched a long row of billboards approaching, advertising a casino. "Where are we?"

"Hinckley. About halfway to Duluth."

She closed her eyes—really, this seat was almost too comfortable—and immediately fell back into a dream-troubled doze.

With a start, she asked, "Are we nearly there?" and was dismayed at the whiny-child tone of her voice.

"No, we're still half an hour out of Duluth," said Jill.

They were passing a lake dotted with what looked like old-fashioned outhouses. Ice fishermen, she knew, were huddled inside them, poised over a hole chopped in the ice, holding a miniature fishing rod. "Do ice houses ever fall through?" she asked.

"Once in a while. They're supposed to take them off the ice pretty soon—they're already off down in the Cities." Jill glanced over at the lake. "I see they've ordered the cars and trucks off up here."

Betsy said, "I remember somewhere in Wisconsin they used to put an old car out on a frozen lake and you could enter a raffle to bet when it would fall through."

"They used to do that up here, too. Look, I was thinking while you were asleep, and I think I understand why you feel you shouldn't feed the dream-maker any more real-life crime. And I'll support you if you choose to do that. It's a shame, though; I've met exactly one other person with your talent for solving criminal cases."

"Was he another cop?"

Jill nodded. "She, actually. A Saint Paul detective. But she wasn't like you, she's one of those people who operate at a whole different level than us humans. Another cop told me once that all she has to do is walk into a room and the perp will start sweating, and pretty soon the truth comes out of his pores, too. You're not like her because you're amiable, and because you solve these things like it's a game. But like her you're seriously good."

"If this were a game, I wouldn't mind going on with it, because I wouldn't mind losing once in a while. But murder is serious, peoples' lives are at stake. If I accuse someone falsely—" She sighed and put her head back, closing her eyes. "I could not bear that."

After a minute or two of silence, Jill said quietly, "All right, I promise I won't ask you to go sleuthing again, and I'll discourage others from coming to you."

"Thank you," Betsy murmured. Having received the support she felt she badly needed, Betsy relaxed—and suddenly didn't feel quite as exhausted.

Jill said, "Did I tell you Lars is selling his hobby farm?"

Lars was Jill's boyfriend, a fellow police officer and a workaholic. That he'd give up a source of hours of backbreaking labor surprised her. "No, you didn't. What's he going to do with the money, invest in something that's even more work?"

Jill laughed, and Betsy asked, "Does he ever take a vacation?"

"Not since I've known him. Oh, he takes time off, but it's just so he can concentrate on some major project, like refinishing every floor in the house that went with the farm he's about to sell."

They were coming into Duluth, a city set on a broad and high terraced hill overlooking a magnificent harbor. I-35 swooped in a big curve down the hill, then ran near the lake. The overpasses had silhouettes of Viking ships carved into them.

North of the city, bluffs stood with their feet in the icy water of Lake Superior. I-35 ended and they picked up Highway 61, which ran through tunnels in the bluffs. Then the land opened out again, though now Betsy noticed something stressed about it, something very opposite from the lush farmland farther south. The snow cover was deeper, but Betsy sensed the soil under it was thin, as if bedrock were just a few inches below that. Naked granite poked up here and there, dark brown or rust red, ancient stuff, worn smooth between the creases. Trees, fewer in variety, looked to be struggling. Betsy told herself not to be foolish; for all she knew, the trees were young, the soil rich.

But knowing that in Mississippi and Georgia the azaleas were blooming, and in Maryland the tulips were nearly finished, while here one could still go ice fishing, troubled her adopted California soul. She was not bred to be icebound despite her youth in Wisconsin.

The towns north of Duluth were small and looked as stressed as the land. Small houses, some merely cabins, shabby bars, and unkempt gas stations lined the road. Here were nothing approaching the beautiful mansions in the northern suburbs of Duluth. Of course, these buildings weren't flimsy, like the shacks Betsy had seen on a trip through the Deep South years ago. Up here, a person couldn't live in a house with thin walls or broken windows.

How did the people manage to survive in Minnesota before insulation and storm windows? Betsy wondered. And what on earth did the pre-Columbian Indians do when winter set in?

But she didn't ask Jill; she only gazed out at the tall pines and clusters of aspen—or were they birch? She didn't know. The trees thinned out and there was Lake Superior on her right, a beautiful, restless slate blue. *DMC 824,* thought Betsy, absently comparing the color to a floss number. *Wait a minute,* she thought, *the lake ice is out already. I guess there are signs of spring up here after all.* That thought occupied her happily the rest of the journey.

3

"Look for the entrance sign for Judge Magney State Park," Jill said, so Betsy looked.

They had gone through Grand Marais a few miles back and Betsy had seen why Jill smiled when she called it the Scandinavian Riviera—it was a pretty little town, especially in contrast to the hardscrabble villages they had gone through. Like Duluth, it was on a steep hill that stepped down to Lake Superior, but just as this hill was much more modest, Grand Marais couldn't hold a candle to Duluth, much less the Riviera. And therein lay the joke: Scandinavians, who dominated Minnesota culture, were presumed to be an unassuming people who would find this modest little town just their speed.

Highway 61 ran alongside the lake. The trees were mostly pine, with the occasional cluster of birch. The snow cover was deep and fresh, and by the plumes of exhaust coming from other cars, the bright sun hadn't managed to raise the temperature anywhere near freezing.

The sign was easy to spot; it was one of those green billboards the federal government puts up. A dozen yards past it was a commercial billboard with an American Indian feather headdress on it, announcing the entrance to Naniboujou.

Jill slowed, signal blinking, and made a right turn onto a narrow, snow-packed lane. A hundred yards away was a two-story rustic building covered with black wooden shingles under a gray roof. A scatter of trees marked the broad lawns beside and behind the lodge. A shingled tower marked the front of the building, and all along the wall beside it were tall, many-paned windows rising to peaks, framed in red.

The car crunched to a halt in the parking area, and Jill shut off the engine. "All out," she said. Betsy, very stiff, stood a moment outside the car and took a deep breath of the still, bitter-cold air.

As they walked to the lobby door—which wasn't in the tower, but alongside it—Betsy saw the restless surface of Lake Superior barely twenty yards away. No beach was visible, just a shallow drop-off at the edge of the lawn to blue water. She could hear little waves shushing.

"Come on," said Jill, and Betsy saw her standing beside an open door.

The lobby was very small and strangely shaped. Shelves between the door and a single double-hung window were full of sweatshirts in various colors. A shelf under the window held collectibles and books, a theme that continued on more shelves. The rest of the room was mostly a check-in counter, with a wooden staircase and a door marked PRIVATE beyond it, amid a whole collection of odd angles.

The dark-haired man behind the counter greeted Jill warmly by name, and Betsy wondered how often Jill had been here. Betsy glanced to her right, through an open doorway, and her eye was startled by a large open space painted in primary colors. She went for a look, stepping into a room forty feet long and two stories high, full but not crowded with tables draped in midnight blue. There was a man in a brown uniform sitting alone at one of the blue tables, lingering over a cup of coffee.

There was a huge cobblestone fireplace at the far end, with a small fire burning brightly. A pair of cranberry couches faced one another in front of it. A row of French doors marched down each side of the room. One row looked out over the parking lot, the other looked into a sunlit lounge.

Betsy took another step into the room. Every inch of wall and ceiling was painted from the smallest box of Crayolas in unshaded blue, yellow, red, green, and orange. Squiggly lines, jagged lines, and rows of the pattern called Greek keys covered every surface—except between the French windows, where there were big faces, with Aztec noses and tombstone teeth and half-moon ears. It was startling, bold, amusing, wonderful.

"Come on, we'll drive around back," said Jill.

"What?"

"Our room's easier to get to through the back door."

"Oh. Okay." Betsy, trying to look at the room and follow Jill at the same time, stumbled, and Jill caught her by the arm. "Who painted that room?" Betsy asked as they went out into the cold again.

"Antoine Goufee, a Frenchman. It was back in the twenties, and I hear they haven't so much as touched it up since."

"What was he smoking, I wonder?"

Jill laughed. "It is interesting, isn't it?" She started the engine. They drove around the side of the building, which stood at a more-than-ninety-degree angle to the front portion. Jill pulled up at the far end. There were four other cars already there, like their own, crusted with road salt. "Let's unload."

The back door was unlocked. It let into a plain wooden stairwell that smelled faintly of age. At the top was a landing with a couple of fold-away beds. Through a door there was a richly carpeted hallway paneled in golden knotty pine. Prints of nineteenth century Native Americans punctuated the walls.

Their room was at the other end of the hallway, through a door set at an angle. *This place is just full of angles,* thought Betsy.

It took two trips to bring up the luggage and needle-working equipment. The room was small, and seemed smaller because its walls and ceiling were also paneled with planks of knotty pine. The bed was a four-poster, its cover forest green, and the two windows had narrow blinds behind forest green drapes. There was a fireplace with a dark metal surround flush against the wall, a small desk, a closet. The bathroom was little, too.

"See?" said Jill. "No phone, no TV."

"Uh-huh," said Betsy, looking at the one bed. It was queen-sized, but she had not shared a bed with another female since she was nine. Still, the bed looked as inviting as it had in the brochure. Despite all her dozing in the car, she craved a nap.

Then she looked at her two big suitcases. Oh, why had she brought so much? The task of unpacking seemed overwhelming.

Jill said, "You look all tired out. Care to trust me to unpack? You take your knitting and go down to the lounge. It's really pretty down there."

"No, I couldn't, really . . ." Betsy began to sigh, then stopped. If she couldn't nap, not having to unpack was a very pleasant second choice. "Well, thanks," she said. She picked up her canvas bag and went out. There was a staircase right across the hall, and Betsy went down it to find herself in a short passageway that led to that amazing dining room. This time she was at the fireplace end. The big smooth stones, she saw, were matte ovals of granite, probably taken from local rivers. The small fire was still burning cheerfully, and the cranberry couches looked very inviting. The room was empty; the man in the brown uniform had gone away. On the far wall, a large Indian's head was thrown back in laughter.

Betsy went for a look into the sunlit lounge. It ran the length of the dining room, but its ceiling was low and it was painted a soft, warm cream. Six pairs of windows lined the room, and groups of couches and chairs with deep cushions and wicker arms invited one to come in and be comfortable. Sunlight picked out the polished surfaces of low tables and deep windowsills, the narrow green and blue stripes of the cushions, and the fuzziness of the leaves on the potted geraniums.

Betsy picked a couch about halfway down, angled so she could lift her eyes and see the lake. She had grown up in Milwaukee, on the shore of Lake Michigan, and had lived many years in San Diego. She found views of big expanses of water homey and comforting. The clean white snow had only a pair of ski tracks across it. A dead birch, its trunk black and white, its limbs lopped short, stood near the shore. A quartet of birds, too far out to be identified, wheeled and turned over the water, which had gone from DMC 824 to a pale blue-gray— DMC 799, perhaps—scattered with golden coins of sunlight. The lawn outside the window wasn't very broad, and edged with the brown and red stems of leafless bushes. Beyond was a mix of evergreen and birch trees, here and there a narrow pine thrusting itself high above the other trees. There had been a vogue for narrow artificial Christmas trees, but Betsy hadn't realized there actually was such a variety. She wondered what it was, and a phrase from an old book with a Canadian setting

came to her: lodgepole pines. Were these lodgepole
pines, so tall and straight?

She opened the canvas bag of needlework. Though
she called it her knitting bag, it actually held counted
cross-stitch and needlepoint projects, too. But when she
was tired she liked the soothing rhythm of knitting. She
took out the sweater she was making. She was doing the
cuff of one sleeve, and she liked deep cuffs. Knit one,
purl one, across and back again, nice and easy. She was
doing the sweater in a heather mix of blue wool on number seven needles.

Across and back, across . . . and back. The room was
warm and quiet. Betsy wasn't a lazy person, but she was
physically worn out as well as sleepy. She caught herself
nodding and shook her head. Knit, purl, knit, purl, knit
. . . Perhaps she should have changed out of her sweatshirt, she was getting very warm. She looked out the
window at the immaculate blue sky, the gray branches
of the trees.

Something large floated into view over the trees. A
hawk? No, look at that, it was an eagle—and its head
was snow white, it was a real, live bald-headed eagle!
As if responding to her wish, it curved toward her in its
flight and glided down, lower and lower, until it was
crossing the lawn nearly at ground level, scarcely six
yards from the window and startlingly large. It rose
abruptly near the lakeshore to land on top of the dead
birch, settle its wings, and look out over the water. In
that moment it seemed to become part of the tree; she
might never have realized it was there if she had not
seen it land. She watched it awhile, but it sat still, so
she returned to her knitting.

Knit, purl, knit, purl, then turn the needles around and
do more of the same back across. Knit, purl . . . knit . . .
purl . . . Her head was heavy, her eyes closed of their
own accord. She laid her head back for just a minute . . .

"Hello?" said a soft voice.

Betsy opened her eyes and saw a woman had come to sit across from her. The woman was very fair, dangerously thin, with short, pale blond curls. The sunlight made them gleam like a halo. She was wearing a powder blue-and-white Norwegian sweater with elaborate pewter fastenings, the cords and voice box of her neck prominent above it. She had her own canvas bag with her, a light blue one with dark blue wooden handles, and had brought out a counted cross-stitch pattern of a Victorian doll wearing a lace-trimmed dress. Her fingers were very slender, separating two threads from a cut length of lavender floss with tender delicacy. Betsy was sure she didn't know her, yet the woman looked vaguely familiar. "Hi," Betsy said.

"Are you here for the stitch-in?" asked the woman. She opened a Ziploc plastic bag and took out a damp blue sponge, bent it in the middle until it resembled an open mouth, then closed it on a section of floss—some women declared that floss was less liable to knot or tangle if dampened.

"Uh-huh," said Betsy. "I'm from Excelsior."

"That's down near the Twin Cities, isn't it? But I hear we've got people coming from as far away as Chicago. I'm only from Duluth."

Since she didn't introduce herself, perhaps Betsy was supposed to know her. Seeking a clue, Betsy said, "This is my first time at a stitch-in."

"Really?" The woman put the tip of the dampened floss in her mouth—Betsy smiled; here was another floss licker, and never mind that she'd already moistened her floss. "This is the first time I've come to one at Naniboujou," she continued, deftly threading her needle, "though I've been to lots of others. And of course I've been here many times. I just love this place, even though they make us stand outside to smoke nowadays. Maybe it will help me quit."

Betsy nodded, remembering how she had decided to quit the day she found herself standing outside in a chill downpour, damp and shivering, shackled to Mistress Nicotine. How much worse it would be in this frigid climate! But she did not say what a friend always said, "Smokers of the world, unite! Throw off your chains!" Because it was no laughing matter and teasing only made things worse.

So instead, Betsy said, "I can't get over that dining room."

"Yes, it's just amazing, isn't it?" The woman picked up her fabric—a cotton evenweave, Betsy noted. "I first came here twenty-seven years ago, on my honeymoon—" She bridled just a little, obviously thinking Betsy would be surprised to learn she was old enough to have been married twenty-seven years ago.

So Betsy politely said, "You don't look old enough to have been married twenty-seven years," though that was not true. Sunlight can be cruel, and it clearly showed the tiny lines of a woman in her midforties, at least. Face lifted, too, Betsy thought, noting the oddly placed creases in the woman's cheeks when she smiled. Though very thin people's faces creased differently when they smiled.

"Oh, yes, I have two grown-up children. My daughter still lives at home, but my son is out of college now and looking to work in environmental protection. Do you have children?"

"No," said Betsy. "We tried, but it turned out I couldn't get pregnant."

"How sad. They do give you a link to the future, I think. What are you working on?"

"A sweater. I've learned to like all kinds of needlework, but knitting I find most soothing."

"I like counted cross-stitch best for relaxation. It takes my mind away from my troubles."

As if reminded, the woman stopped stitching to look a little downcast. Impulsively Betsy asked, "Is it something you want to talk about?"

"Well, people will see us together, I suppose. And wonder. You see, my husband and I are divorced, but we're trying to get back together. Since we honeymooned here . . ." She blushed and looked away, out the window. Betsy smiled; that someone less than eighty years old could actually blush when mentioning her honeymoon was as charming as it was silly. "I wonder . . ." The woman paused again. "This is just too stupid," she said, drawing a deep breath. She put her stitching away with swift efficiency as she murmured very quietly to herself, "I must go get Eddie, then." And she stood and strode out.

Betsy frowned after her. Who was Eddie? Oh, of course, her ex-husband. And Betsy thought she recognized the lure of a nicotine fix, too. Probably wants to borrow a cigarette from him, or ask him to join her in one. *Poor thing,* Betsy thought, remembering her own struggle against the habit. Maybe that's how she stays so thin. Though the woman didn't look just fashionably slender, she looked emaciated. Perhaps she was ill. Maybe this attempt to reconcile was triggered by a serious illness, perhaps something caused by smoking. Betsy tried to think who she knew, or should know, who was ill with cancer or emphysema. But no name came to her, perhaps because she was still a little sleepy.

She looked down at her knitting and picked up her needles. Was the next stitch knit or purl? Knit. She set off again on the cuff, but the cozy silence made it difficult to concentrate. Not that it was hard, or anything, just knit one, purl one, knit one, purl . . . No good. Yawning, she let her hands descend into her lap.

This lounge was so beautiful. Beams rising between the pairs of windows leaned gently inward, leading the eyes up, to where the ceiling beams were painted the same color as the walls. So long as her head was already leaning back, she let it fall against the back of the couch. Her eyes closed . . .

She struggled awake. She'd been having a dream about a sinister blond woman who wanted her to have a cigarette, and for a moment or two she wasn't sure she was awake yet. The couch was unfamiliar. She was in a long room full of odd shadows.

The dream about the thin blond woman had been set in a long room full of sunlight. Or had there really been a woman? The dream had been in two parts, she thought, and only in the second was the woman sinister.

And she actually was in a long room. But she was alone, and it was dusk outside. Was this part three of the dream?

Her nose twitched. No, the room was real, she was at Naniboujou Lodge, and there were some very delicious smells coming from the dining room, accompanied by the sound of quiet talk and the clinking of silverware on porcelain.

She shoved her knitting into her bag, but left the bag on the floor. Was Jill eating dinner without her? She got clumsily to her feet and went to the door at the end of the room, walked into the dining room, and paused to look around. There was a small crowd of perhaps thirty or thirty-five women and three men seated at the tables, eating, talking, laughing. The stitchers-in had arrived. But none was Jill.

Betsy turned, went past a long and broad counter, behind which was an old-fashioned circular red velvet couch with a red velvet pillar sticking up out of its middle, and into the lobby.

There was no one at the check-in desk. A wooden

staircase, not wide, with a carpet runner, stood ahead of
her. A stylized bird, a crow or an eagle, was carved on
its finial post. She remembered that bird from when she
had come down last time. Betsy went up. Her room, she
remembered, was at the end of the corridor near the
staircase, its door set at an angle. She came to the top
of the stairs and paused. The stairs turned completely
around, going up, emptying into a short hallway, and
she had to wait till her head turned itself back around
again. Through there was the corridor, and there was the
angled door.

Her key was in her pocket, right? Right. Funny Jill
hadn't come down, if it was dinnertime. This was one
of these package deals, the meals included in the price
of the weekend, so missing a meal wouldn't save her
any money. Maybe she was taking a nap.

The dumb key wouldn't turn in the lock. Betsy pulled
it out and turned the knob—and the door opened. There
was no light on in the room, but there seemed to be
someone on the bed. "Jill?" said Betsy, but softly, in
case Jill was asleep.

Betsy found the light switch, and a lamp came on.
There was, in fact, someone on top of the comforter, but
it was the thin blond woman. Her complexion was
blotchy and her lips were blue. And she didn't seem to
be breathing.

The room was small. In three steps, Betsy was beside
the bed. She looked around. The suitcases had been put
away, though something dark was draped across a chair.
There was no one in the room.

Except for the woman on the bed. Betsy reached out
to touch her.

No pulse, no breath, skin eerily cool. This was too
dreadful, this was nightmarish.

Betsy turned and blundered out, yanking the door
closed behind her. She more stumbled than ran down

the twisting stairs. There was still no one behind the counter in the lobby. What kind of place was this, where the front desk was unmanned and people came to die on other people's beds?

The feeling of unreality was so strong that Betsy didn't want to run into the dining room, yelling about a dead woman. A dark-haried man in a white shirt and navy trousers was standing at a lectern halfway down the room. He looked a lot like the friendly clerk who had been behind the check-in counter earlier. Betsy hurried to him to say in an urgent undertone, "There is the body of a dead woman on the bed in my room."

He stared at her for a long moment, then said, "Are you sure?"

"Yes."

"Who is she?"

"I don't know. I talked to her earlier, but I don't think she told me her name. She's here for the stitch-in, I know that."

"What room are you in?"

Betsy couldn't remember, but thought of her key. She brought it out. "Twenty," she said, reading the number off it.

The man said, "Come with me," looked around, and started toward the fireplace end of the room. There, he took the elbow of a young wait person with braids wrapped around her head and a coffeepot in each hand and said in a low voice, "Billie, I have to go with this woman to her room. Take over for me?"

"Sure."

Since they were at the fireplace end, he went out the door that let onto a short passageway, and up the back stairs she suddenly remembered she had come down originally. He didn't ask for her key, but used a pass key of his own to open the door. Betsy, unwilling to see that still face again, hung back.

"Hello?" said the man.

And Betsy heard a sleepy reply, "Hello?"

Betsy peered around the man's elbow to see a figure sitting up on the bed. It was Jill.

4

Jill struggled to awaken. Recognizing the man's voice, she asked, "What's wrong, James?"

His voice was strained. "I—I'm not sure, Ms. Cross. Your friend said—"

"Betsy?" Jill said sharply. "Where is she?" She realized it was dark out. "Say, what time is it?"

"Seven thirty-five," said James.

"I'm right here," came Betsy's voice from behind James. "But, I don't understand. I came up here just two minutes ago and there was a dead woman on the bed."

"What?" Jill sat the rest of the way up. "Come in, come in. What happened?"

James went to the fireplace to give Betsy room to come in. He turned and looked with Jill at Betsy for an explanation.

But Betsy didn't have one. Not a coherent one, anyway. "I was in the lounge knitting, and this woman came in and sat down across from me. She was very pretty but very thin. Blond hair, curly, cut short. She had a blue and white sweater, one of those Scandinavian sweaters." She gestured at her shoulders, describing the starburst pattern with her fingers.

Standing just inside the doorway, Betsy looked bewildered. She was wearing what she'd worn on the trip up, an old blue sweatshirt one size too large; and leggings, unflattering on her short, plump figure. Betsy looked anything but commanding normally, and now she looked ruffled and scared.

But she didn't lie.

Jill said, "Go on."

"I don't know what's going on. I was asleep, you see, then I came up here to find you, because it's dinnertime, and instead I saw her, on this bed, and she was dead. So I ran back downstairs to tell someone, and James came up with me, only it was you on the bed."

Jill looked over at James to see if he could shed more light on Betsy's story.

He shook his head. "No one matching that description has checked in while I was on the desk—and I'm the only one on the desk this weekend." Trying to be helpful, he asked, "What time did you see her in the lounge, Ms. Devonshire?"

Betsy shrugged helplessly. "I'm not sure. I came down there right after we got our luggage up to our room—"

"That was a little after three," Jill put in.

Betsy continued. "I brought my knitting down, but I dozed off, and this woman spoke to me, woke me up. It was still daylight, the sun was shining on her hair, I remember how it shone in the sun. We talked just a little while. She said she was here for the stitch-in and to reconcile with her ex-husband. Then she said she wanted to meet him for a cigarette and went out, and I went back to sleep, and when I woke up it was dark."

"You fell back asleep?"

Betsy nodded. "I had a dream about her, then I woke up again, and I wondered if you'd come down to eat without finding me. You weren't in the dining room, so I went up to our room. Only when I opened the door there she was, that same thin woman, dead."

"Are you sure it wasn't me you saw? It was dark after all," said Jill.

"Oh, yes. I turned the light on, and I touched her. Her lips were blue, and she wasn't breathing at all, and I couldn't find a pulse. I didn't know what to do, I couldn't think what she was doing in our room, or where you'd gotten to. I came right down and got you"—Betsy nodded toward James—"and you brought me up, only it was Jill asleep on the bed."

Betsy looked as if she didn't expect to be believed, as if she wasn't sure of her story herself.

"So this woman appeared to you between naps," said Jill.

"Yes," agreed Betsy reluctantly. "But it wasn't a dream, Jill. I mean, dreams are kind of vague, and this woman wasn't vague, not the first time. The pattern of that sweater, one of those starburst kind, I could draw it for you, you know how I'm getting about knitting patterns. And the sweater had fancy pewter fasteners, not buttons. You don't dream details like that."

"No, I guess not." Jill scooted to the edge of the bed and hung her legs over. She rubbed her eyes with her fingertips, trying to pull her thoughts together. She said, "You're sure you didn't go to some other room by mistake?"

"No—well, there's only one room right at the top of the stairs, at an angle, not flat along the wall, right? With a fireplace?"

"That's right," said James. "But here we are, in your room, and there's no dead body in here, thank God. I don't know what else to say. Except that I've got to get back. You'd better come down soon, if you want to eat."

"We'll be right down," said Jill. "Just let me wash my face."

A dash of cold water helped. Jill came out of the bathroom to find Betsy, looking half ashamed, waiting by the window.

"Lighten up on yourself, Betsy," Jill said. "Everyone has dreams that seem real. I've done it myself. And this is just another one of the kind of dreams you've been telling me about. More realistic than the others, but your unconscious had to get it right at least once, right? Come on, let's see if a hot meal makes you feel better."

Betsy said, as they went out the door, "Is James related to the check-in clerk? They look a lot alike."

Jill laughed. "They are the same person. He's James Ramsey. He and his wife Ramona own this place. Very fine people."

Most of the other guests had either finished or were eating dessert by the time they got down, so they sat alone at one of the small tables along the outside wall. Heavy sheets of clear plastic were hung on the French doors to keep out the cold.

"The idea was," said Jill, "to open these doors and set up tables under an awning along this wall and serve food and drinks out there—in the summer, of course."

"But they never did that?" asked Betsy.

"I don't think so. Well, maybe the original owners did. This place began life as a very large and exclusive private club. People like Ring Lardner and Babe Ruth signed up as members. It opened in July, 1929." Jill paused, one pale eyebrow raised just a bit.

Betsy frowned at her, then said, "Oh! Of course, October 1929, the Crash, followed by the Depression."

Jill nodded. "Naniboujou never really got off the ground as a private club. This building was supposed to be bigger, there were supposed to be tennis courts on that lawn between here and the lake, all sorts of things never happened. Most of the land was sold—some of it became the state park across the road—and the lodge kept changing hands. It was even a nightclub for a while, and a Christian retreat. Now the Ramseys run it as a public lodge. But they refuse to apply for a liquor license."

"They don't need a liquor license if this is the usual kind of food they serve," observed Betsy, lifting her fork.

The salad had been mixed greens with purple onion slices, strawberries, some kind of soft cheese—brie, Betsy thought—with a dressing made of raspberry vinegar and poppy seed. It was followed by a spinach lasagna so light it was apparently made with eggs as well as cheese. With the lasagna came carrots glazed with brown sugar, orange juice, and ginger. The bread was fresh-baked sourdough. Jill, sighing happily, said the food was always wonderful. Dessert was lemon-flavored ice cream with tiny, chocolate-coated chocolate cookies.

Over coffee, Jill said, "Tell me some more about the woman you dreamed you saw."

"Why? I'm starting to agree with you, it was probably a dream," she said. "I was so tired, I'm still tired, I've been tired for weeks." But Jill only waited, so Betsy said, "Okay, the woman was like an angel, kind of. Inhumanly thin, like something that lives on manna or ambrosia, not spinach lasagna and ice cream. A golden angel—except she didn't have a message for me. Don't angels generally come with messages?"

Jill didn't reply, but kept her face still, waiting.

So Betsy continued. "After she left, I went back to sleep. Or the dream ended. And I had another dream, where the thin woman wanted to do something wicked, I don't remember what, but she kept whispering about it. And she wanted me to smoke a cigarette with her.

Then I woke up again and smelled delicious food and it was getting dark, and you hadn't come down, so I decided to come up and get you. I went through the lobby—Why do they have two staircases going up to the second floor?"

"Because it's easier to get luggage up to the second floor the back way," said Jill. "They don't want guests dragging luggage through the dining room."

"No, not the back door, I mean two staircases up to the front of the hallway, one off the lobby and the other off the dining room." She frowned. "How come I only saw one staircase when I came down?"

Jill said, "The staircase off the lobby goes to the wing that faces the lake. The staircase off the dining room goes to our wing."

"There are two wings?"

"Sure, didn't you know that? We've got the wing that overlooks the west lawn, it's got the knotty pine paneling. The other wing has painted walls."

Betsy half closed her eyes, remembering something. "Uh-oh," she said. "The stairs off the lobby go to the wing without the paneling, right? The stairs off the dining room go to the wing with knotty pine—our wing?"

"Yes."

"Well, it's the room at the top of the lobby stairs where the body is, because I went up those stairs."

"Are you sure?"

"I'm sure I went up the lobby stairs. And if there's a door up there set at an angle, and there's a fireplace in that room, too, then yes."

Jill put her cup down. "Wait here," she said. She went out to the lobby, where James was checking in a late-arriving couple.

When he'd finished and the couple went up the hallway beside the staircase, she said, "The room at the top of the stairs from here has a fireplace, right?"

"Yes, why?"

"Is it painted green?"

"Yes."

"Who's in there?"

James checked his register and said, "Frank Owen."

"By himself?"

"Yes."

"Come with me a minute," she said, unconsciously using her cop voice, and started back into the dining room. James, frowning, hustled to catch up.

"What's this about?" he asked, and she explained Betsy's mistake.

When they got back to their table, Jill said to Betsy, "The fireplace room in the east wing has been reserved by a man as a single. No wife or significant other along."

James said, "Mr. Owen used to be married to a woman who might match the description Ms. Devonshire gave, but—"

Betsy interrupted, "They came here on their honeymoon."

James's eyebrows lifted in surprise. "Yes, that's right. That was before we bought Naniboujou, but they told me about it, said they were glad we could take it over and keep it open."

"This woman I saw was his ex-wife. She's here, or she was here. She said they were going to try for a reconciliation. She's the woman I saw dead."

"But he didn't reserve for two," James said.

"Maybe she came to surprise him here," said Betsy.

Jill asked, "How did she know he was here to surprise?"

"How should I know?" demanded Betsy, exasperated. Heads at nearby tables turned toward them, and Betsy said, more quietly, "Maybe he always comes here this time of year."

They both looked at James, who shrugged and said,

"He comes up two or three times a year, usually in the summer, but yes, also in winter. They used to do a lot of cross-country skiing, until his wife got sick. I think he's taking it up again, in fact."

"Sick?" echoed Betsy, and Jill remembered Betsy's description of a very thin woman.

"She's got a lot of allergies," said James. "It started with something she came in contact with as a nurse, and it kind of spread in every direction. She's allergic to pollen, dog dander, pork, dairy products, wheat, and I don't know what all else. She had to give up all her sports. And he gave up doing them, too, to take care of her. But eventually they divorced, and so now he's going back to skiing, at least."

Jill said to Betsy, "But didn't you say she went out for a cigarette? Isn't smoke one of the big things people with allergies stay away from?"

"Yes, that's right," conceded Betsy.

"Mrs. Owen smokes, or used to," said James. "We're smoke-free, and she used to complain about having to stand outside to have her cigarettes."

"Yes, she said that," said Betsy.

James continued. "I don't know if she still smokes; after their divorce she stopped coming; she hasn't been here in years."

Jill had nothing else to ask, so he went away. Betsy said, "Maybe we should go ask Mr. Owen what he did with his wife's body."

Jill studied Betsy, her tired face with its frightened eyes. "He'll say he hasn't seen her, of course. If he's murdered her, he's not going to admit it. And if she never was here—"

"No, she was here. Too many things fit. His room is where I saw her, and the description matches, according to Mr. Ramsey. Unless I'm psychic, and I don't think I am. Maybe if we talk to him he'll say of course she was here, he found her ill in his room and took her to the hospital. I'd like that; I can stop worrying that I'm going crazy." Betsy looked around the dining room. "Maybe he's here, having dinner." Among the two-dozen or so women were three or four men.

"No, I asked James to point him out, and he said Mr. Owen wasn't in the dining room."

"What does he look like?" asked Betsy.

"Beats me, I didn't think to ask. All right, let's go."

They went out into the small lobby, and feeling James's eyes on them all the way to the first landing, went up the narrow wooden stairs to the second floor.

Again there was that feeling of funny angles as they went around a not-ninety-degree turn and across the oddly shaped landing and came into the painted hallway. There, an echo of their own hallway, was the door set at yet another angle. After a moment, Betsy became aware of Jill's questioning regard, so she nodded. This was, in fact, the hallway she had entered, thinking it led to her and Jill's room.

Jill walked to the angled door and knocked brusquely.

A man's voice inside said, "Come in."

Jill turned the knob—the door was not locked—and opened the door. She felt Betsy close behind as they went in.

The room was painted a medium green. The windows and four-poster bed were the same as in their own room, down to the paisley pattern on the comforter.

There was nobody on the bed. A slim man with thick, coarse graying blond hair and a heavy mustache was sitting at the little desk, a half-eaten slice of pizza in one hand. The room was redolent of cheese, sausage, and spiced tomato. "It's from Sven and Ole's in Grand Marais," he said, lifting the slice a little. "I always get one of their pizzas when I'm up here. May I ask why you're here?"

"Where's your wife?" asked Betsy.

"I don't have a wife," he replied.

"Are you Frank Owen?" asked Jill.

Betsy said, "Eddie Owen, you mean."

The man said, "My name is Frank Owen. Who are you?"

"My name's Jill Cross and I'm with the Excelsior Police Department."

"Kind of a long way from home, aren't you?" Owen's voice was quiet and warm, with no hint of tension and only a little puzzlement.

"I talked with your wife earlier today," said Betsy— and was disappointed when there was no guilty start, only a mildly surprised look—"and she told me she was here with you in hope of a reconciliation."

Owen's mustache shifted just a little, in either a grimace or a little smile. "She's not here, I haven't seen her."

"Has she talked to you about reconciling?" asked Jill.

He nodded. "We've tried it, several times. It never works. It took me a long time to realize it was never going to work. Are you two friends of hers?"

Betsy shook her head and Jill said, "So you did at least talk to her."

"Not today." Owen shook his head and put down his slice of pizza, accepting that he wasn't going to finish eating it anytime soon. "I wouldn't dream of telling Sharon I was coming up here, and I certainly didn't invite her to stay with me. She did call a couple of weeks ago, hinting she wanted to see me, but I wouldn't agree to that." His voice was firm, his blue eyes almost too guileless.

"Where were you this afternoon?" asked Jill.

He looked at her for somewhat longer than it should have taken him to remember his whereabouts that recently. But there was no annoyance in his face and voice when he replied patiently, "I got here around noon and had lunch in the dining room. I came up to my room and unpacked, then lay down for something over half an hour, maybe an hour. Then I got up and drove to Grand Marais. I did a little shopping—my daughter collects Inuit art, and there's a gift shop in town that sells it— but I didn't buy anything. I shopped for a new set of ski poles and then took a nice run on one of the Pincushion trails, came back to town, bought this pizza, came back here, and was having a quiet little supper when you two knocked on my door." He looked at Betsy. "Who's she, by the way?"

"She's with me," Jill said, and hoped Betsy wouldn't add anything.

Betsy didn't, but Owen asked her, "What else did she say?"

Betsy shrugged. "Not much. Does she smoke?"

Owen grimaced. "Yeah. She keeps trying to stop, her doctor's all over her about it. She's allergic to damn near everything else, you'd think she'd be allergic to tobacco."

"Are her allergies serious?" asked Jill.

Owen nodded and sighed. "She lives on lamb and a special diet supplement without soy or dairy in it, she can only wear silk or cotton, and despite being very careful she's in the hospital two or three damn times a year—" He cut himself off, having grown heated and abruptly realizing it. "It's a damn shame," he said, more quietly. "When we first got married we used to go rock climbing, cross-country skiing, adventuring, and run marathons. She was great, I had trouble keeping up with her. Then she got this latex allergy—she's a nurse, it was the gloves she had to wear—and it was like dominos falling. I tried to be helpful, I tried to keep up with all the new rules, but she got to be such a witch about it—" He blew lengthily through his mustache, cooling his temper again. "It was at least partly my fault, I just couldn't go along with the constant changes in the rules." He looked longingly at his pizza. "At least now I can have things like this in the house again." He smiled up at Jill and Betsy. "And peanut butter. You wouldn't believe how much I missed peanut butter."

Betsy asked, "Does your ex-wife have a black or dark blue coat, kind of shiny? And a big black purse?"

"I have no idea."

A few minutes later, on their way up to their room, Jill said, "What's this about a shiny coat?"

"I suddenly remember seeing a shiny coat, a full-length one, draped across a chair when I came up and found Sharon's body. It was some dark color." Betsy was frowning, trying to remember. She hadn't of course, been really looking at anything but the body. "Or maybe it was the black lining I saw, like it was turned or folded so the lining was showing. And there was something else, a big black purse, I think. Both of them were on the chair Frank Owen was sitting in this time. What do you think about Mr. Owen?"

"He's mad at her, which is understandable. He married an athlete and wound up with an invalid. Tough bounce for both of them."

"I wonder how long ago they divorced. When I talked to Mrs. Owen, it sounded as if it hadn't been long, but I got the feeling from him that it's been a while."

Jill asked, because Betsy had an uncanny feel for such things, "So what do you think? Did he murder her?"

"I don't know. I don't know if it's Sharon Owen's body I saw—though whose else could it be? Did you notice he didn't slip once?"

"Slip on what?"

"He always referred to her in the present tense."

5

The bed was big, so each woman had enough room to spread a little without danger of encountering a leg or something even more intimate. Nevertheless, Betsy lay on her side close to the edge and told herself firmly not to sprawl.

She composed herself to sleep, but it wouldn't come. The napping in the car, and the nap in the lounge, combined to make her wakeful. Plus there was the uncomfortable thought that she might wake in the night, become aware of someone else in the bed, and think it was Hal, her ex-husband. And forgetting all that had happened the last few months—no, that was ridiculous. Still, it had been a long time . . . Whoa! Where that might lead had her very wide awake indeed.

Jill, on the other hand, was already asleep. *Must have a clear conscience,* thought Betsy with a wry smile. She slipped carefully out of bed, but stood a moment, unwilling to turn on a light. It was dark in the room, and there was no noise out in the hall. Betsy thought, *I'll get my knitting bag and go into the bathroom—Oops.* She'd left the bag down in the lounge.

She pressed the button on the side of her Indiglo watch. It was ten-thirty, not very late. On the other hand, things were scheduled to begin early tomorrow morning. Perhaps everyone had gone to bed. She stepped carefully across the room, feeling her way with hands and toes. Finding the door, she leaned against it, listening. Silence.

She felt her way back to the bed and the robe at the foot of it. She loved her robe, a real antique of gray flannel with broad maroon stripes. It was much too big for her, covering her ankles and crossing deeply in front. She liked to think it had once belonged to Oliver Hardy. She tied it on, pushed her feet into her felt slippers, then went on noiseless feet to the door again, and out.

The hallway was dimly lit, the stairs down to the dining room a little brighter. The dining room itself was an immense dim cavern, its sole source of light the lounge, which was brightly lit. There were about twenty stitchers at work in there. Betsy paused outside the doorway. The stitchers were all dressed, and here she was in night-clothes.

No, wait, there was a woman in a velour nightgown. And there, another woman in a lovely peignoir. So now Betsy felt frumpish.

And then she felt annoyed. She wanted her knitting, it was in that room, she wasn't naked, so why shouldn't she go get it? She straightened her spine and walked in.

Some of the women smiled at Betsy, but most just gave her an incurious glance and continued with their work and talk. "I call them CASITAs, Can't Stand IT Anymore," one woman with flashing blue eyes was say-ing. "You know, an acre of blue or sixteen yards of backstitch. I keep them in a big drawer."

The woman she was talking to laughed. "CASITAs, I like that, Melly! I keep mine at the bottom of the pile of UFOs, hoping I'll never work my way down to them."

Betsy found her bag sitting on one of the coffee tables. She retrieved it and made her escape.

Back upstairs, she opened the door to the room as quietly as she could, and found the light on and Jill sitting up with a magazine. "If you weren't back in another two minutes, I was going to come looking for you," she said.

"I'm sorry," apologized Betsy. "I didn't mean to wake you."

"You couldn't have helped it, I'm a light sleeper," said Jill. "What's up?"

"I couldn't sleep, and then I remembered I left my knitting downstairs. I was going to sit up awhile in the lounge, but there's a whole group holding a session."

"Well, this *is* a stitch-in. There are women in attendance who will get maybe an hour of sleep a night. James will probably lose money just on the coffee. But I'm glad you're back, I want to show you something." Jill closed the magazine and handed it to Betsy. "Here, look at the cover."

It was *American Needlework Magazine,* and the cover featured a piece of linen with a bouquet of cross-stitched pansies surrounded by hardanger squares. "I brought it because I've been thinking of trying hardanger," Betsy said. "Kate does it, you know."

"Yes, but that's not what I mean. Look at the designer, her picture is up in the corner."

There was an inset in the upper left corner of the cover, a head-and-shoulders photo of a painfully slender blond woman wearing a blue and white Scandinavian sweater with silver fastenings. The cover announced an interview with Kaye of Escapade Design, and an original pattern designed by her for the magazine's readers.

"Oh, my," said Betsy.

"She's even wearing the same sweater you described, down to the pewter fasteners."

"Yes, I see that," said Betsy. She opened the magazine and found the interview with Kaye and skimmed the first few paragraphs. A larger photo of Ms. Kaye in a sunlit room accompanied the article—the cover shot had been cropped from this photo. Betsy said, "I read this article. When I read about the mystery teacher, I remembered Kaye lives in Duluth and was hoping it would be her." The literature had announced a class but, hoping to stir up interest, said the nature of the class and its teacher would be revealed at the stitch-in.

"See? You were hoping she'd be here, and so you dreamed she was. And because you've been having bad dreams, you dreamed she was murdered."

Betsy sighed and closed the magazine. "Now I do feel like an idiot. Poor Mr. Owen, what he must have thought of us! I'm sorry, Jill, dragging you into this—but it seemed so real!"

"I'm sure it did. Well, don't worry about it. I'm going back to sleep. You?"

"Yes, all of a sudden I'm tired."

And this time, despite her concerns, despite the naps, despite a fear of nightmares, she'd barely closed her eyes before she was asleep.

But no matter how many times she fled up the stairs, she always found herself in the lobby. James was behind the counter, his friendly eyes gone cold and his smile evil. Betsy would make some feeble excuse and flee up the stairs, only to step back into the lobby at the top. She knew she'd been going up these stairs for a while. And she knew that one of these times he was going to bring out a great big knife and stab her with it.

But there was nothing else she could do but run despairingly up the stairs.

Here she was again—and there was James, and this

time he had a Crocodile Dundee knife in his hand. He put it crosswise in his mouth, like a pirate, so he could use both hands to climb over the counter. She turned toward the stairs. But her legs were moving slowly, as if mired in molasses.

She yelled and struggled, but he was beside her, saying her name.

He grabbed her by the arm, she struggled to pull free—and someone had taken her by the shoulder and was saying her name.

"No! Help, no, leggo!" Betsy said, or shouted.

"Betsy, Betsy, wake up, wake up!"

Jill's voice.

It was all right, it was Jill.

"Oh! Oh, my goodness, wow! Gosh, what a nightmare! Thank you, Jill!" Betsy sat up. Her hands were trembling, her heart was racing. "I thought . . . I thought James was going to get me that time."

"James?"

"Yes, he was behind the counter in the lobby, and the lobby was at the top of the stairs, or the bottom, it didn't seem to matter."

"I see." Jill's tone was very dry.

Betsy shook her head. "Well, I guess you had to be there." She lay back down. "Whew!" she said. Then, "Sorry about that. Was I very loud?"

"More thrashing than noisy. You mentioned stairs, so I guess that's what it was, climbing stairs."

"Yes, lots and lots of stairs, but none of them got me away."

"That's the way it is, sometimes," Jill said. In a firm tone Betsy thought of as her "cop voice," Jill said, "But now you'll go back to sleep and dream only slow, quiet, pleasant dreams."

"Yes, ma'am," she said obediently—and to her surprise, she not only went right back to sleep, she slept the rest of the night in peace.

She was wakened the next morning by a pleasant alto rendition of "Let the Punishment Fit the Crime." She thought for a moment she was in her own bedroom, listening to KSJN's zany *Morning Show,* then realized the tuner wasn't a little off station. The hiss was the rush of a shower.

No need to drag herself out of bed to get down to the shop. Today she would sit among stitchers and get some real work done.

The thought startled Betsy. She hadn't felt her growing interest in needlework was anything other than an honest attempt to learn enough to be an intelligent help to her customers. She had inherited the shop. At first, she kept it open because there were customers waiting to give her money for things already in the shop, and she needed to support herself while the money portion of her inheritance worked its way through probate. She had good employees already on board, and running a needlework shop with them seemed more interesting than any temporary job she might otherwise have found.

But she had come to like needlework for its own sake—and why not? It was beautiful stuff. There were counted cross-stitch patterns as exquisitely detailed as any painting. It took patience, and an eye for detail, to make one of those big pieces. And if they were challenging to work, what an eye it must take to design the patterns! Betsy vowed one day to go to a needlework show and meet some of these amazing people.

Betsy's own natural talent seemed to be in the area of needlepoint, where a couple of mistakes didn't screw up the whole doggone piece, and where you could get creative with stitches, fibers, and colors.

The shower and voice cut off together. Betsy, not wanting to be caught lazing in bed, hastily climbed out.

She went to the closet and found her clothes in something like the order she would have chosen herself, if Jill hadn't done it for her. She settled on a brown wool skirt and an ivory sweater.

Jill came out of the bathroom wrapped in a thick terry robe, her pale hair only slightly darkened by being wet. "Good morning," she said. "Did you sleep all right?"

"The second time, yes, thank you. Where'd you put my underwear?"

"Bottom drawer, on the left."

Drying off after her own shower, Betsy's stomach growled. Wow, she was hungry. She hadn't been really hungry since back in December, when a dose of arsenic had ruined her digestion for what she feared was forever. But here she was, wondering if breakfast would be as good as last night's dinner.

It was: waffles with a delectable orange-rum syrup, and the bacon just smoky enough. There was a side dish of peeled grapefruit sections that had never seen the inside of a jar.

Jill didn't mention the too-real dreams Betsy had been having, for which Betsy was grateful.

They were savoring second cups of coffee—robust without being bitter—when a tall, heavyset woman with a very short haircut walked to stand in front of the fireplace. She wore an unflattering purple knit dress.

"Good morning!" she called, with laughter in her voice, and called it several more times, until the room quieted down. Betsy looked around. She thought at first that here was a nice cross section of young, old, slim, fat, tall, short, and everything in between—even a woman in a wheelchair—then she realized everyone looked prosperous. Of course, nobody poor would spend three hundred dollars for a weekend of stitching.

Including Betsy.

Betsy felt a little guilty about that, but only for a moment. After all, not everybody could be poor.

The woman said, "Good morning," one last time, then went on. "As most of you know, I am Isabel Thrift, treasurer of the Grand Marais Needlework Guild. Welcome to the First Annual Naniboujou Stitch-In. I am so pleased at this wonderful turnout for this first time. But . . ." Her tone was suddenly very sober, and a soft, portentous groan went around the room. Obviously rumors were about to be confirmed. "But, as some of you know, the organizer of this event hasn't been feeling well lately. Two days ago the doctor diagnosed walking pneumonia, and going to her car after leaving his office, she fell and broke her leg. The pneumonia isn't the walking kind anymore; she's at St. Luke's in Duluth. But the hard work is done, and the stitch-in goes on. Charlotte Porter is, of course, also president of the Grand Marais Needlework Guild. And she's the one who arranged for our mystery guest, who, I'm pleased to announce, is going to teach two classes, one on hardanger and a beginner's class on designing counted cross-stitch patterns." There was a pleased murmur. "Charlotte wouldn't tell me the teacher's name; she was very mysterious about it." Isabel's tone was again humorous and the ladies laughed.

Betsy sat up straighter. Wow, she was going to get an actual glimpse of how designing was done!

Isabel continued. "So, will our mysterious instructor please stand up and introduce herself? Or himself?"

There was a rustle as everyone looked around. But no one stood up.

"Maybe it was Charlotte herself who was going to teach the class," someone suggested.

But another said, "No, Charlotte doesn't do hardanger well enough to teach it."

Isabel forced a smile and said, "Well, this *is* mysterious!"

There was brief, uncomfortable laughter, then a quiet murmur moved around the room as Isabel frowned and tried to think what to say next. A slim woman with a deep tan at the next table said, "Who?" to the table beyond hers, and repeated the name to the others. "Kaye of Escapade Design."

Betsy said to Jill, "I see I wasn't the only one thinking it might be her."

Isabel said, "Well, maybe she's not here yet. While we wait for her, let's get started. Come on into the lounge."

The room filled with pleased, anticipatory murmurs as the guests began to stand and move.

Jill and Betsy returned to their room to load up with the paraphernalia of needlework. Betsy took a moment to tuck the magazine into her knitting bag.

Back downstairs, the women—and two of the men—had just about filled the sunlit lounge. There was a sign-in sheet on a clipboard displayed on a table; Jill and Betsy signed it.

Jill said, "I see two seats there," nodding toward the middle of the room. As they moved toward them, Betsy glanced out the big windows and halted in amazement. The lake steamed as if it were coming to a boil. A light breeze bent the steam this way and that, uncovering small areas of dark blue water and quickly covering them again.

"Oh, pretty!" said Betsy.

"Yes," Jill said, "the air is colder than the lake. As soon as it warms up a little, the steam will quit."

Jill followed Betsy to a pair of facing couches. Isabel was sitting on one, the strong sunlight putting lavender highlights on her purple dress, and on the other was the tanned woman who had repeated the name "Kaye of Escapade Design."

Isabel said, "Sit down, sit down! I'd introduce you to Carla, but I don't know your names."

"I'm Jill Cross," Jill said, sitting next to Carla, "and this is my friend Betsy Devonshire. We're from Excelsior, where Betsy owns a needlework shop."

Betsy sat next to Isabel, smiled, and said, "Hello."

Carla, whose short hair was salt and pepper, smiled back and said, "I'm Carla Prakesh, from Duluth and Fort Myers, Florida. What kind of needlework do you sell?"

Betsy said, "Needlepoint and counted cross-stitch, knitting yarn, and patterns, some crochet supplies. I carry only a few Penelope canvases, as not many people care to do both petit point and needlepoint on the same piece." She mentioned that because the brown canvas Carla was working on was called Penelope.

"And isn't that a shame?" drawled Carla. "I mean, trame is the original, isn't it? This is how the medieval noblewoman applied her needle. Cross-stitch was done by the peasants."

Betsy didn't know what to say. While she really liked needlepoint herself, she didn't think it was because she carried the genes of a medieval noblewoman.

Isabel had made a sound in her throat, and Betsy glanced over to see she was working on a cross-stitch pattern of roses.

"Where do you find your trame canvases?" asked Betsy. Only a few months ago she would have pronounced it "trame." Now she knew it was pronounced "trah-*may*." In trame, the pattern is first painted onto the canvas, then floss is basted horizontally across the pattern in colors to match, and the result sold to a stitcher who stitches over the basting. It is an expensive form of needlework, but allows complex and beautiful patterns, often based on medieval and Renaissance patterns or the paintings of old masters.

"I buy them from a sweet little shop in Fort Myers,"

Carla replied, with an archness that encouraged her listeners to deduce that "sweet little" meant very upscale. "Perhaps you've heard of it? C. Chapell is the name."

"No, but I'm new to the business," said Betsy. "I inherited the shop from my sister, and I still have a great deal to learn about it."

Carla drew a deep breath to expound further, but Isabel had simultaneously drawn a shallower breath and so got in ahead of her with, "What are you working on this weekend, Jill?"

Jill had set up her project, a large painted canvas of an elegant tiger sitting on a green silk pillow, looking over his shoulder at the viewer in a grand and aloof way. She had a set of stretcher bars and was preparing to stitch the needlepoint canvas onto the bars.

"I love the way he sits alone in all this space," said Jill, "and I'm tempted to just fill the background with basketweave stitch."

"Oh, I think it would be boring to do that much basketweave," Carla said. "Don't you, Isabel? Well, maybe not you; you do all your pictures with lots and lots of little x's."

Isabel's roses were highly detailed, in at least six shades of pink and six of green on very fine, snow white linen. "I don't find counted boring at all," she said with hardly any rancor.

"But with just plain basketweave and all in the same color, the slightest flaw would just jump out at you, Jill," remarked Betsy, the voice of experience.

"Now if it were trame," pounced Carla, "there would probably be a pattern of jungle leaves and flowers in fifteen or twenty colors all around that tiger. Very lovely and elegant."

"But leaves and flowers wouldn't look as good as this vast plain," said Jill, smiling at her subtle pun. "Maybe I won't even stitch over it, just have it finished with a white backing. Or maybe a lighter shade of green than that pillow he's sitting on." She held it out at arm's length by the top stretcher bar, her head cocked a little.

Jill was rarely forthcoming like this, especially among strangers. Betsy sat back, watching, sure Jill was up to something.

Jill said, "I wonder what our mystery instructor would suggest."

"Who can guess? No one knows who she was supposed to be," said Isabel, making a single cross-stitch in a deep shade of pink on a rose petal.

Jill said, "But didn't Carla here say it was Kaye of Escapade Design?"

Carla said, "No, I heard someone else say that. I don't know for a fact who it was supposed to be."

Betsy said, "Do you know Kaye?"

"Yes. She's from Duluth, as am I. So naturally our paths have crossed a few times."

"Is she a good teacher? I'm thinking about hardanger, and it might be helpful to take a class."

Carla grew thoughtful. "Well, she's all right, I suppose. Of course, her specialty is counted." The drawl was very apparent. But apparently realizing she'd gone a little too far, she amended, "Now she is a very talented needlewoman, she really is. Her hardanger is amazing. And with beginners she can be sweet. But if anyone comes to her with an idea of their own, she's not . . . sympathetic. Not actually rude, just not . . . sympathetic." She looked at Isabel for confirmation.

And, reluctantly, Isabel nodded. "But we don't know that she was supposed to be the mystery teacher."

"Who was the first person to suggest it was Ms. Kaye?" asked Jill.

Isabel said, "Oh, it was probably several people getting the same idea at the same time. She was the obvious choice."

Carla said, "I don't even know who it was I heard saying it was her, but as soon as I heard the name, I thought that was probably who it must be. She and Charlotte have been friends forever."

Isabel looked up from the paper pattern clipped to the edge of her hoops and nodded. "I think that's why her name was suggested. She only recently started selling her designs, but I know she's been designing for several years. Charlotte's the one who encouraged her to submit her designs to catalogs and teach classes. Her designs are good, and some are very clever."

"And they're selling well," acknowledged Carla, with what Betsy was sure was as much envy as fair judgment.

"Do you design?" Betsy asked her.

"Goodness no. I prefer the classic models and am quite happy in my humble place as faithful stitcher." She smoothed a section of her work over her lap. It was of a medieval woman standing outside a pavilion set up under stylized trees. Betsy was sure she had seen that same design in a book on medieval and Renaissance tapestries.

Betsy was reaching into her knitting bag for her own project when James called her name. "Ms. Devonshire?"

Betsy raised a hand. "I'm over here."

James came to her and said quietly, "Ordinarily I wouldn't do this, and if you like, I will say I was unable to find you. But there's a phone call for you in the office, from someone named Godwin. He says he's sorry, but it's very urgent."

"All right, I'll come." Godwin had a tendency to panic, but he knew how much she needed this break. It probably really was important.

James led her to a door in the far end of the lobby, which he had to unlock. Behind it was a tiny, cluttered office. He handed her a heavy black receiver from a very old telephone. "Hello?" said Betsy.

Godwin said breathlessly, "Oh, thank God they found you! I'm *so* sorry to take you away from your weekend, but this is an *emergency*! You won't believe what's happening here, it's just *awful*!"

"Take it easy, Godwin, slow down, what's the matter?"

"There's water coming through the *ceiling*! It's ruining *everything*!"

"Water? What, is it raining there?" That was a silly question; there were apartments over the shop, rain would have to leak through the roof, the upstairs ceiling and then the floor of Betsy's apartment.

"No, it's *not* raining! That's the *point*! It's *not* raining!"

"Then where is the water coming from?"

"That's what I'm *talking* about! It's coming through the *ceiling*! It's not dripping, it's *dribbling*! And it's ruining *everything*!"

James made an excuse-me gesture at Betsy and left, closing the door behind him. "Where is it coming from?"

"The *ceiling*!"

"For heaven's sake, Godwin, make sense!"

"I *am* making sense! There is water, *water* simply *pouring* through the ceiling of the shop, and it's getting *all over* everything! There's a *huge* puddle right in the middle of the floor!"

"Where is it—no, never mind, it's coming from my apartment, obviously."

"Oh," said Godwin, "is *that* what you were asking?" He giggled. "Silly me! Yes, it *must* be coming from your apartment, mustn't it? Did you leave the water in your *bathtub* running?"

"No." Betsy thought. "And I didn't leave the water in the kitchen running, either." She thought some more, trying to picture various possibilities and a cure for each. She said, "How bad is the water damage in the shop?"

Godwin sounded calmer now. "It's coming through in *two* places, actually, one where the library table is, where it seems to have *killed* the cordless phone and wet down the basket of loaner tools. And it just *soaked* the spinner rack of perle cotton floss; it's standing in a puddle, a *big* puddle, you could go *splashing* in it. And the *ceiling* is kind of *bulging down*, like it's going to *crack open*—"

His voice was starting to sound panicky again, and Betsy said hastily, "All right, all right, something needs to be done immediately. You're there, you know where I keep the spare key to my apartment, you go up and see what's going on. Shut off the water supply to whatever's running over, if that's the problem. Then fix it— or get it fixed, whichever. I'll reimburse you when I get back. Or, if you're maxed out, use the shop's credit card. Then contact our insurance agent, who is going to have a cow." Back in December Betsy had made a claim for smoke damage.

There was a brief silence, then Godwin said without any italics, "You're so good in an emergency, Betsy! I suddenly feel much better. All right, I'll summon a plumber or a roofer or whatever, as soon as I find out what the problem is. Then I'll call Mr. Reynolds. Are you going to start back now? How many hours are you from here?"

"No, I'm not coming back. Why should I? You're a trustworthy, competent person, you've steered me through enough problems in the shop for me to know that. Of course, if you get upstairs and find there's a gaping hole in the roof that's pouring melting snow into my apartment, then maybe you should call me again."

Godwin's laugh this time had more assurance in it. "Yes, all right, but I don't think *that* will be the problem. And you're right, I can take care of it otherwise myself. Now I think about it, we had a waterpipe break one time, it made an even worse mess, but there were no fatalities, so I don't suppose there will be any this time, either. But let me add, Joe Mickels was landlord then, too, and he was a real stinker about it. But I suppose, since you've started dating him, he'll be much sweeter."

Betsy said, "But I'm not dating him anymore. Didn't I tell you? He thought because I was so clever about maneuvering him into selling the building to me that I was his kind of person, a little too interested in making money. We went out three times, and every time, all he wanted to talk about was all the clever ways there are to make money, and hinting that no one knows how rich he really is. Which makes it all the more ridiculous that he's the cheapest date I've been out with in my life."

Godwin laughed. "I can believe that. He made an ass of himself at an all-you-can-eat buffet once, eating till he waddled, and insisting on a doggie bag. But I wish you'd strung him along for a while. It would make this problem a lot easier to deal with."

"No, friendly doesn't work on Joe. Better he still thinks I'm too clever for him, so when you call him, tell him I've already been notified. That may keep him from trying to get cute. Whew, I'm glad we haven't signed the final papers yet." Betsy had been going round and round with Joe about the sale, trying to bring him to the closing, but he was apparently determined to hang on to those rents as long as possible.

"All right. Are you having fun up there? Is that why you don't want to come home?"

"Not yet. But soon, I think."

"Well, get lots of rest. Take at least one nap a day. 'Sleep knits up the raveled sleeve of care,' you know. That's Shakespeare."

"Yes, I know. And I think you're right. Now, go show me my confidence in you is not misplaced."

"Yes, ma'am. And, Betsy . . . thanks."

Betsy hung up. But not wanting to return to the lounge, where Carla waited, she sat for a bit, looking around. The office was not only tiny, it was oddly shaped and without a window. A computer took up most of the desk space, but it sat on a very old desk, possibly original to the building. The walls were papered with cheery yellow roses, one section almost hidden behind Post-It memos, lists, and other reminders. The door was old and ill-fitting—another reason to think the office was a retrofit. Light could be seen at the bottom where there was an inch or more of space.

How wonderful to be the owner of Naniboujou, with its beautiful lounge and magnificent dining room, but how sad to spend the wakeful hours in here, struggling with maintenance, heating, insurance, the wait staff, the kitchen, without even a window to look out of at the lake. Of course, what with changing bed linen, serving meals, chopping wood for that fireplace, and coping with guests who complained of dead bodies in their rooms, perhaps the owner didn't spend all that much time in here.

Betsy was reminded of a sign she'd needlepointed back in February: THE ONLY THING MORE OVERRATED THAN NATURAL CHILDBIRTH IS OWNING YOUR OWN BUSINESS.

But at least she wasn't going to be the one shelling out big bucks to do the repairs back home. The thought of Joe's greed doubling back to bite him in the butt made her smile suddenly, and she lolled back in the chair, tipping ash off an imaginary plutocrat's cigar. But the chair, an executive model, dropped backward so sharply she thought it was going over. She threw herself forward and the chair slammed upright, throwing her onto the dark hardwood floor.

"Ouch, dammit!"

After a second, she rolled onto her backside, and sat

quietly for a minute, gently rubbing her left knee, squeezing her eyes shut to keep tears from flowing.

As the ache subsided, she took a deep breath and dared to look for injuries. The knee, while painful, didn't have broken bones poking out. It didn't look bruised. In fact, there wasn't even a run in her pantyhose. She brushed at her skirt, which wasn't very dusty, and leaned forward to start getting up. Her eye was caught by something grayish white on the floor near the back of the knee well of the old wooden desk. It looked like one of those fat markers for a whiteboard, or maybe a highlighter, probably dropped and kicked out of sight.

Awkwardly, favoring the painful knee, she crawled forward to retrieve it.

It wasn't a marker. It was a translucent tube with black and yellow printing on it, filled with a colorless liquid. And clearly labeled: EPIPEN.

Betsy reached up to grab the front edge of the desk with her free hand and got her feet under her. She pulled the chair forward and sat down. There was liquid inside the object and what looked like a very big-bore needle. Instructions printed boldly on it said to remove the gray safety cap, with an arrow pointing to the other end. The cap was a flat thing, with a gripping edge like the milling on the rim of a quarter. The instructions continued that one was to put the needle end against the thigh, and "using a quick motion," push "until injector functions." *Ouch,* thought Betsy.

Smaller printing described the pen as an auto-injector which would deliver a "0.3 milligram intramuscular dose of epinephrine," and noted it was "for allergic emergencies (anaphylaxis)."

Did the owner of this place suffer from allergies? If so, he would be pleased to know where this device had gotten to. She put it in the center of the desk, and would have reported finding it, but the lobby was unmanned, so she returned to the lounge.

"What's up?" asked Jill.

"Godwin says there's water leaking into the shop from the ceiling. I told him to handle it."

Jill raised her pale eyebrows in surprise.

"What?" said Betsy.

"You think the boy is up to it?"

"Sure, don't you?"

"I'd rather it was Shelly working this weekend. She's calmer in an emergency."

"Oh, Godwin's already over the vapors. He'll be fine." Betsy rummaged in her knitting bag for her own project, a counted cross-stitch pattern of a rose window, to be stitched on black Aida cloth. She found the round plastic box in which she kept her floss, the Aida cloth, and spare needles. She unfolded the cloth on her lap, and her eye was caught by a finished section of Carla's trame. "You do really excellent work," she said, trying to keep the note of surprise out of her voice. People as rudely opinionated as Carla were often less than talented.

Jill leaned forward for a look. "You did the faces in petit point," she noted. "Nice." Petit point stitches are half the size of needlepoint ones, and enable the stitcher to get lots of detail on faces and hands. That's why there was Penelope canvas, which was double woven to make both petit point and needlepoint stitches possible on the same canvas.

Betsy said, "How long does it take you to complete a project this large?"

"About four months, if I get to work on it steadily," said Carla. "Of course, that rarely happens. One is so busy nowadays, with travel and committees and all." She heaved an overburdened little sigh.

Betsy noticed a tiny movement and glanced at Isabel, who was heaving a sigh of her own and rolling her eyes

at Carla. Betsy barely suppressed a giggle, and bent over
her canvas bag to look for her scissors and the paper
pattern, lifting and moving her knitting aside, hiding a
grin. But honestly, the way things curled down and out
of sight in this thing—*The American Needleworker*
magazine she had tucked in was lifted with her knitting
and fell out.

"Oh, did your *Needleworker* come already?" asked
Isabel. "Mine's probably in my mailbox then, waiting
for me to come home."

Betsy pulled out the pattern, handed the magazine to
Isabel, and continued to root in her bag for her scissors.
"I pay extra for first-class delivery, because it's so annoying when a customer comes in with a question about
something she saw in a needlework magazine or catalog,
and I haven't read it yet."

Isabel didn't answer. Betsy found her scissors in their
little case on the bottom, hung them around her neck on
a braided cord, and looked over to see Isabel staring at
the cover of the magazine as if she'd never seen a
counted cross-stitch pattern of pansies before.

"What?" asked Betsy.

"Well, look who's on the cover!"

"Who?" asked Carla.

"It's Sharon Owen."

Betsy frowned and said, "No, that's Kaye of Escapade
Design."

"Well, sure, Sharon Owen and Kaye of Escapade are
the same person. No way for you to know that, I suppose, but Sharon Kaye Owen is her full name." Her sigh
this time was authentic. "I really was hoping she'd be
our surprise instructor. We do like to support local talent." She saw Betsy was staring at her and said, "Is
something wrong?"

6

Jill reached for the magazine, turned it so its cover faced Isabel, and said, "I bet she wears this sweater a lot."

Isabel said, "She does. It's knitted of silk, because she's allergic to wool, so it's unique. But how did you know that?"

Jill said, "Because she was wearing it when Betsy saw her here yesterday."

"You mean she *is* here? Why haven't we seen her?"

Betsy said, "Yesterday afternoon Sharon Owen sat down across from me right in this lounge. We talked a little bit about how great Naniboujou is; she said she's always loved it, and that she had come up here on her honeymoon. She also said she was here to meet her husband—"

Carla interrupted, "She's not married."

Betsy said, "You're right, *ex*-husband. She said she was here to try to reconcile with him."

"Never happen! She's been divorced from Frank for eleven years."

Betsy said, "Is Frank also called Eddie?"

Isabel replied, "No, of course not. Why?"

"I thought she said at one point she was going to meet Eddie."

Jill said, "None of the three men here are named Eddie?"

Isabel shook her head. "No."

Betsy said, "Maybe he's an employee here."

Carla said dryly, "Maybe it's Eddie she wants to reconcile with."

"What do you mean?" asked Betsy.

"Now, Carla," warned Isabel.

But Carla said, "She's always running off with some boyfriend or other." She frowned and added with a faux air of thoughtful frankness, "Well, actually, she never tries to reconcile with the boyfriend once she leaves him, at least as far as I know. She just dumps him forever when she decides to give Frank another try. But of course she can't stick with Frank, either."

Isabel, frowning at Carla, said, "It's kind of sad, really. One of those cases of can't live with him, can't live without him."

But Carla said, "That's strictly on her part. He's done with her, no chance in the world he'll take her back. He finally realized she's one of those people who make promises they have no intention of keeping. All she ever did was get the children excited and hopeful, then she'd abandon them again. He should never have let her come back after she left the first time, because then and every time after, she'd be nice to everyone for about a month, then get bored and unhappy and be out the door, on to bigger and better things."

"That might have been true once about the children getting hopeful," said Isabel, "but they aren't exactly children anymore. Beth must be twenty-two or-three, and Douglas is what, twenty months younger than she is?"

"Eighteen," Carla said, adding with an air of quoting an authority, "It doesn't matter how old the children are, they still suffer when there's a bad divorce. Besides, Beth never really left home, she just took over the mothering chores from Sharon Kaye. Frank's done all he can, more than he should, really, but Sharon is a perfect witch with a capital B."

Isabel said firmly, "This is all very interesting, but wandering off the point. The point is, was Sharon Kaye actually here? Ms.—Devonshire, is it?—"

"Betsy," said Betsy.

"Betsy seems to think so. And as I said, it would make sense if Sharon Kaye was the mystery teacher. She does beautiful pulled thread and cutwork. And her latest cross-stitch pattern is amazing. Even that very first one in her series, the 'When I Grow Up' teddy bears, is adorable. I've been stitching them on an afghan for my granddaughter. I know she can be impatient with people—"

Carla sniffed pointedly.

"But, I'd give her a chance, if it were up to me. And Charlotte is, after all, her friend. If she was here yesterday, why isn't she here now?" Isabel stood and put her project on the cushion where she'd been sitting. "I'm going to ask if anyone else has seen her."

As Isabel stood and began working her way from group to group down the room, Carla said to Betsy, "What's that you're working on?"

Betsy's pattern was a counted cross stitch pattern from a booklet called *Rose Windows,* by Sue Lentz. She had taken the book to Kinko's and after a copyright discussion with the man behind the counter paid for an enlargement of the pattern labeled "Traditional." Like the others, the pattern was a circle cut into rows of wedges around a central medallion. Because the cover showed it stitched on black, she'd cut a length of sixteen-count Aida from her shop's supply, added a spool of Kreinik Confetti blending filament, and selected antique DMC colors. Though the pattern wasn't for a beginner, Betsy had gotten used to color changes, doing a set of Christmas tree ornaments, and had surprised herself by working a snowflake pattern that called for careful counting. She'd heard black was difficult to stitch on, but sixteen-count wasn't tiny. And these glowing colors would look especially nice on the matte black of Aida. If it came out well, she'd frame it and hang it as a model in her shop.

Betsy unrolled the black cloth and said, "I'm better at needlepoint than I am at counted, but my shop sells both, so I thought I'd better at least try something more advanced." She showed the pattern to Jill. "Not that this is really advanced."

Jill snorted faintly.

Betsy said, "What, Miss I Only Do Needlepoint?"

"That's not as easy as it looks. You have to really pay attention to your counting on circular patterns."

It was Betsy's turn to snort. "You have to really pay attention to any counted. Isn't that the point?" She ran her fingers down the ribbon pinned to the fabric to where her needle threader was attached. "Anyway, all I brought to work on besides this is my knitting."

Knitting was Betsy's therapy. It freed her mind to ponder, to wonder, to connect things. But Betsy didn't want to think—not about finding a woman's dead body on a bed, or worse, that her bad dreams had become so realistic she could no longer tell them from reality.

She found the center of the fabric. The one-inch medallion in the center was old gold, and she threaded her needle and set to work. "Count twice, stitch once," was the advice given by counted cross-stitchers, and Betsy was careful to obey. Still, Isabel was gone long enough that she came back only as Betsy was putting in the last three stitches. "No one else has seen Sharon Kaye," she reported.

"Perhaps we should call Charlotte in the hospital," suggested Jill. "Ask her if Sharon Kaye is, in fact, the surprise guest."

"Why?" asked Carla. "It isn't important, is it? Sharon isn't here now, and neither is our mystery teacher. That is, unless Isabel takes my earlier suggestion. What do you think, Isabel?"

Isabel said, "I don't think so, Carla. For one thing, hardly anyone here is interested in trame, and for another, you don't have enough supplies with you to give everyone a chance to try it. Merely talking about it won't satisfy."

Carla tried to take that in good grace, but there was a snappish emphasis to the next few stitches she took on her canvas.

Betsy kept her eyes on her work, threading her needle with the soft pink of the first wedge and counting carefully before taking the first two stitches. But when the silence went on and on, she glanced up to see Carla, her embarrassed cheeks overriding her artificial blush, smiling apologetically at Isabel. "I'm afraid I do ride my hobbyhorse hard," she said.

"It's all right," said Isabel stiffly.

Betsy smiled, too, relieved the tension was not because of her and her strange story. "There seems to be something obsessive about needlework. I don't know if it draws the kind of person inclined to obsess, or if doing the work brings out the obsession. I have customers who seem to suffer withdrawal if they have to stop stitching for as long as a week." Betsy's smile deepened a bit. "Such a delicate, dainty art, needlework," she continued, her own needle flashing. "Created with fibers twisted tight, and sharpened, highly polished steel."

Carla's eyebrows lifted in surprise, then she laughed. "I like that!"

Isabel said, "I don't feel obsessed. When I pick up my needle, I remember my mother doing needlework by lamplight, and my grandmother, and I can sense her grandmother under an oil lamp, and hers, and hers, and so on, until we are back sitting by the fire, trying a new pattern on doeskin and keeping an eye out for the sabertooth that took a neighbor's child last night."

Jill remarked, "We are bloody-minded today. I wonder why."

Carla said, "I think we're disappointed and angry. All that hinting, and no surprise."

Isabel said, "I think the idea of a mystery teacher was always a bad one. Everyone had a secret wish for what the class should be on or who the teacher should be, each one different, so most of us were doomed to disappointment even if the instructor showed up."

"That's true," said Carla.

Isabel said, "Who would you have liked it to be, Betsy? I mean, if it could have been anyone at all."

"Anyone? Joyce Williams. I'd love to sit and watch how she knits those Latvian sweater patterns. Or Kaffe Fasset. I hear he's a wonderful teacher. How about you, Jill?"

Jill said, "Susan Porta, maybe. Or Jean Hilton. They both do exotic fibers, and that's what I like to use in needlepoint."

Isabel said, "I'd like Charley Harper to come by. Not because I think he'd have something to teach me, but because, judging by his designs, he has a terrific sense of humor." She added, more darkly, "And I'd like to have a word with him about the way he designs his patterns."

Betsy said, "I like Charley Harper, too. I especially

love the one of the brown pelican sitting on a brown piling in silver rain. The pattern's in my stash, along with the cobblestone Aida cloth and floss. I picked a thin silver braid for the rain, and the Aida is a nice big fourteen-count . . ." Her voice drifted off as she began to think about the project. Then she laughed. "I already have more projects than I can finish in a year. Now that I have a little money, it's going to be really hard not to buy lots more."

Jill said, "When you no longer resist temptation, you will know you are officially a stitcher."

Isabel said, "I have a T-shirt that says, WHOEVER DIES WITH THE BIGGEST STASH WINS. I'm definitely in the running."

Betsy said, "I sell a T-shirt that says, WHOEVER DIES WITH THE BIGGEST STASH IS DEAD. WHEN'S THE ESTATE SALE?' "

The women laughed. Carla said, "I don't think I've heard of Charley Harper."

Jill said, "Counted cross-stitch," and Betsy looked for and saw the very slight raising of Carla's upper lip.

Honestly, she thought, *why there has to be this split between the counted cross-stitch and needlepoint communities, I cannot understand. It's worse than dog people versus cat people.*

Betsy and her sister Margot had had both cats and dogs, often simultaneously, while growing up. So it was no surprise that Crewel World carried cross-stitch, knitting, and needlepoint supplies.

There was a period of silence while everyone settled into their projects. Betsy finished her first wedge in DMC, then got out the Kreinik metallic filament and snipped off a foot of it. It changed colors every couple of inches from gold to blue to green to silver. She consulted the pattern and began the first stitch. Pulling it through, the ultra-fine stuff, twisted and crinkled around a very thin thread, caught on the cloth, and slipped out the eye of her needle.

"That should look very pretty," noted Isabel.

"Yes. This will be my first try at a blending filament." Betsy took another stitch, holding the filament in the eye with her fingers, and this time the filament knotted without warning, and when she tugged experimentally, it broke.

She glanced at Jill, who was smirking subtly. Betsy stuck her tongue out at her, teased the filament loose, cut off the knotted portion, rethreaded her needle, and set off again. But with almost every stitch, when the filament didn't twist and knot, it slipped out of the needle or snagged and broke. It was impossible for Betsy to lose herself in a stitching pattern when the thread was being difficult. Despite herself, thoughts of Sharon Kaye began to intrude. At last she growled, stuck her needle in the fabric, and asked, "What hospital did you say Charlotte Porter is in?"

Isabel said, "What a good idea! I think it would be a nice thing if we bought a get-well card and everyone signed it. She's at St. Luke's in Duluth."

But Betsy wasn't thinking about a get-well card. She stood and said, "Excuse me, I'll be back in a few minutes." Then she remembered: No phones in the rooms.

Jill murmured something and Betsy bent to hear it said again. "Pay phone in the lobby."

She nodded and went out into the lobby, where she found James on duty and got him to break a five-dollar bill into coins. She sat down in a dark corner near the office where the pay phone lurked. In a few minutes, the heap of coins considerably diminished, she sat frowning.

Charlotte Porter was feeling quite, quite comfortable, thank you, and thanks so very, very much for the sympathy expressed by the stitch-in people, weren't they nice, and she was sooooo sorry she couldn't be there. She had her stitching with her and had thought perhaps to join the stitchers in spirit, but the pain medication was making it sooooo hard to work on her Celtic Christmas angel. Mystery guest? Oh, wasn't she there? How strange, Charlotte had talked to her day before yesterday and she had assured Charlotte she'd be there. Her name? "Kaye of Escapade Design. Sharon Kaye Owen, yes, yes, yes, you know her? Wonderful lady, terrific friend, good teacher. I can't believe she's not there yet. She's going to teach an advanced class on what-is-it, hard-anger, and a beginner's class on designing a counted stitch pattern, cross-stitch. She was sooooooo excited about it."

"Did she say anything to you about her ex-husband being here?"

"Oh, is Frank there? Let me think, she does go on about him, doesn't she? She thinks she's still in love with him, though of course she isn't, she just can't bear thinking that someone else might get him. Though she hasn't got him anymore, I've told her that lots of times. I shouldn't be talking like this about her, she's a very good friend and a very, very fine woman, talented and very, very, very patient with beginners especially. That's why I agreed when she volunteered to teach at Nani-boujou. Isn't that a lovely, lovely name? Some people call it Nanny-*boo*-zhou, but it's pronounced Nanny-boo-*zhou*. So Frank is there? He and she used to go up there all the time, until the divorce. Which was all her fault, I suspect. The divorce was. I shouldn't say that, either, should I? It's the pain medication, I suppose. It makes me feel sooooo very nice, but a bit talkative. Do you suppose they gave me truth serum?" The idea amused Charlotte, and she giggled in a slow, strange way.

"I believe some truth serums are actually pain medications," said Betsy.

"Oh, my dear, you mustn't take what I'm saying as the truth," said Charlotte, giggling some more. "I'm just saying whatever comes into my head, speculating out loud." She lowered her voice to a whisper. "Gossiping."

"I understand," said Betsy. "But I think you've talked enough for now, and I should let you get some rest."

Since it was nearby, Betsy made use of the restroom and then went back to the lounge, where, in a pretense of looking at Jill's project, she murmured that Sharon Kaye Owen was, in fact, the mystery teacher and had talked with Charlotte about teaching at the stitch-in as recently as Thursday.

Betsy sat down and took up her needle, but after about ten minutes, Jill said, "I want a cup of coffee," and looked pointedly at Betsy, who obediently said she'd like one, too.

Carla said, "They leave a pot out, but it's probably awfully strong by now."

Jill said, "Maybe we can get them to make a fresh pot. Come on, Betsy."

Betsy followed her across the chromatic dining room to a pair of doors on the other side of the fireplace. Jill pushed through the one with the marks of people shoving on it, Betsy on her heels, and they were in the kitchen.

"Hi, Amos!" Jill called, and a trim, gray-haired man looked up from a big pot he was stirring on an eight-burner stove.

"Hi, Jill!" he said. "Arrested anyone lately?"

"No, but that doesn't mean there isn't someone who needs arresting." She walked to the big stove at which he stood.

Amos laughed, then saw something in Jill's face and said, "What's wrong?"

"We're not sure." She turned slightly and said, "This is my friend Betsy Devonshire, who owns a needlework shop in Excelsior. Betsy, this is Amos Greenfeather, chef here at Naniboujou for the past six years."

He had the broad face and black eyes of a Native American, but not the usual impassivity Betsy had come to expect. He made a little French-style bow in her direction, and Betsy said, "Your meals are delicious."

"Thank you." He smiled broadly.

Jill said, "Would you know Sharon Kaye Owen if you saw her?"

"Never heard of her. Is it important? Maybe the wait staff would."

"Are they around?"

"Most of them." He turned the heat down under his pot and went to the back of the long, narrow kitchen. Like all places not frequented by paying customers, it was a little shabby. The big stove was elderly, the stainless steel pot on it was scratched from countless scrubbings, and ceiling tiles over it were warped by heat and steam. But everything was spanking clean, and the only smells were the fabulous ones of bread baking and stew stewing.

Amos came back with four women and a fresh-faced young man. All wore clean white shirts. The women were in dark skirts well below the knee and comfortable shoes, the young man in navy twill trousers. No multiple piercings, no Kool-Aid-red hair. How quaint, thought Betsy. How refreshing.

"Would any of you recognize Sharon Kaye Owen if you saw her?" asked Jill.

"I would," said a woman with short, dark brown hair and beautiful light brown eyes. She looked a little older than the others, and she spoke with the authority that marked her as their senior in rank, too. "She used to be a frequent guest at the lodge."

"I don't think I ever saw her," said the young man, and the other women also shrugged.

"She's a little taller than I am," said Betsy, "very thin, with blue eyes and very light blond hair, short and curly. She was wearing one of those Norwegian sweaters, blue and white with a starburst pattern around the neck, and pewter fastenings."

"Did any of you see her today?" asked Jill.

Shrugs and negative shakes of heads.

"Yesterday?"

Same response.

"I saw her yesterday afternoon," said Betsy. "I came downstairs from our room and went into the lounge. She came in and sat down across from me. We talked for a bit and then she said she wanted to go see Eddie, and I think, to have a cigarette." Betsy looked at the young man. "Is your name Eddie?"

Looking slightly alarmed, he shook his head. "No."

Betsy asked, "Is anyone working here named Eddie?"

The senior woman said, "No."

Betsy persisted, "Didn't any of you see her going out? Or standing outside smoking? This would have been after four o'clock."

"Not me," said a woman whose dark blond hair was in braids wrapped around her head.

"No," said the young man. The other two shook their heads.

"We were pretty much on break from the dining room," offered the woman in braids. "Around three, everything's cleaned up from lunch, and dinner is a ways off."

"But suppose someone comes in and wants a meal?" asked Betsy.

"Too bad," said the young man with a regretful smile. "The kitchen's closed except at mealtimes."

"But I saw someone in the dining room yesterday afternoon about three," said Betsy. "He was wearing a brown uniform."

The wait people all looked at one another, then at Betsy. "We don't serve meals except between eight and nine-thirty in the morning, eleven and one-thirty in the afternoon, and six-thirty and eight in the evening," the young man explained patiently.

"Well, there's generally coffee," said the senior woman, the one with the light brown eyes. "Guests can come and serve themselves as long as it lasts."

"Yes, but by three o'clock that stuff's pretty rancid," remarked the woman with braids.

"Coffee's coffee to people who need a caffeine fix," said the chef.

"So you don't remember seeing him, either?" asked Jill.

"Nope," said the third woman, and everyone agreed that they hadn't seen him.

Betsy's heart sank. Such a small, telling detail—and it was false, too? But Jill said, "I remember him, he was sitting at a table in the middle of the room."

Heartened, Betsy asked, "Does anyone know about a company hereabout whose employees wear brown uniforms? Chocolate brown, not tan."

The young man said, "Park rangers."

Jill said, "And there's a state park ranger station right across the road."

"But it's mostly closed in the winter," the woman in braids said.

"What does 'mostly' mean?" asked Betsy.

The young man said, "Well, a ranger comes by once in a while to see if the box they leave out for admittance fees needs emptying, and to fill up the tray with more maps of the trails. And they have this guy, he's not a real ranger, go back on a snowmobile once or twice a week to see if a hiker broke a leg and froze to death."

The wait staff sniffed quietly, whether at the lack of

more frequent patrols or the silliness of winter hikers, Betsy couldn't tell.

"Does this man on a snowmobile wear a park ranger uniform?" asked Betsy.

"No," the senior woman said.

Betsy closed her eyes. She'd only glimpsed the man sitting at the table. Maybe he wasn't wearing a uniform, only a brown jacket and trousers. Why had she been so sure it was a uniform?

Her eyes opened again. "Do the park rangers have patches on their sleeves? White or maybe buff?" She sketched a good-sized triangle on her shoulder.

"Yes, they do." The older woman nodded. "Did the man you saw have a patch?"

"Yes."

There was nothing more volunteered from them, and there was an air of impatience as they waited to see if Betsy had more questions.

"Okay," said Jill, "let's understand this. There was a park ranger having coffee in the dining room yesterday afternoon. Betsy and I both saw him, but none of you did. So the fact that nobody else saw Sharon Kaye Owen, who sat across from Betsy in the lounge and said she was here to reconcile with her husband, doesn't mean she wasn't just as real. She was here."

Betsy said, "And she's dead."

7

There was a shocked silence. Then the senior woman said, "How do you know that?"

"Because I went up the stairs from the lobby instead of the dining room, and into Frank Owen's room, thinking it was mine. She was lying on the bed, and she was dead."

"Oh, you're the woman!" said the senior woman. "James told me about you. But there wasn't a body in either of the upstairs fireplace rooms, was there? So we decided it was some kind of . . . peculiar mistake." She was being polite to a guest.

"We're assuming somebody moved it, Ramona," said Jill. "There was plenty of time to do that between when Betsy first saw it, and when we figured out what room she had seen it in."

Ah, so this was James's wife, co-owner of the lodge. Ramona knew who, and what, Jill was; and Jill's acceptance of Betsy's story put a new complexion on things. *How incredibly valuable to have a police officer backing you up,* thought Betsy.

Ramona asked, "What do you want us to do?"

Betsy was surprised at the lack of rancor in her voice. Rather than jumping to a denial that such a thing could possibly happen in a quiet and happy place like Naniboujou, or expressing concern about Betsy's sanity (options very much on Betsy's own mind), Ramona wanted to know what the next correct step might be.

Jill said, "I think the police should be called at this point. Grand Marais Police are the controlling authority, right?"

Ramona said, "No, the person to call would be the sheriff. But what would be the good of that? There's nothing for him to investigate. All we have is the unsubstantiated word of a guest that a stranger no one else saw came and is now gone."

"There's some substantiation," said Jill. "The person Betsy saw was supposed to be here. She was the 'mystery teacher' Charlotte Porter invited, her name is Sharon Kaye Owen of Escapade Design. Isabel Thrift can confirm that."

"Sharon Kaye Owen? Is that who we're talking about? Oh, my, I know her! But she hasn't been here in years."

"Car!" exclaimed Betsy.

"Car?" echoed Ramona, looking slantwise at Betsy.

"She didn't ride up here with someone, so she must have driven herself. What kind of car does she drive?"

"I have no idea."

Betsy went out the swinging door into the dining room and crossed it to the lounge, to where Isabel was sitting.

"What kind of car does Sharon Kaye drive?" she asked.

"I don't remember."

Carla said, "It's blue, a Saab, I think." She frowned and reiterated, "I think."

Betsy straightened up and called for the room's attention, then asked, "Does anyone here know what kind of car Sharon Kaye drives?"

"A gray BMW," said someone.

"No, I think it's light green," disagreed someone else.

"It's blue," said Carla firmly. "Kind of a medium shade."

"Thank you, never mind," Betsy said.

She went back into the dining room, where Jill waited. Betsy said, "We need to get a list of what everyone's driving, so we can eliminate possibilities. Let's ask Isabel—"

Jill interrupted, "What makes you think the murderer left her car here?"

The excitement of the chase cut off as if someone twisted the faucet, hard. Betsy sat down. "That's right, that's right. In fact, he probably drove her away in her own car."

"Not far," said Jill. "If you're thinking he came back here afterwards." She sat down across from Betsy.

"I am?"

"Well, Frank Owen's the one you suspect, isn't he? The obvious one."

"I suppose so."

"Well, who else could it be?"

"I'm not sure. Did you notice how Carla leapt to Frank's defense?"

"Carla?" Jill turned that over in her mind. "Okay, I think I did, on reflection."

"If there's something between Carla and Frank, and Sharon Kaye tried to put a stop to it . . . Or, it could be Eddie. Since he's not here, maybe he drove here with Sharon Kaye and drove off with her body."

"Who's Eddie?"

"That's a very good question. Let's go talk to Frank."

•   •   •

Frank Owen was dressing to go out, in wool knee pants, argyle stockings, and a forest green sweater with cable stitching, a cross-country ski outfit. He opened the door to his room with the sweater around his neck and down one arm, the rest of it gathered on his other shoulder. He frowned at Betsy, looked beyond her at Jill, then frowned back at Betsy again.

"What kind of car does your wife drive?" asked Betsy without preamble.

"Ex-wife."

"What kind of car does your ex-wife drive?"

"I have no idea." He shoved his other arm into the sweater and pulled it down.

"Have you tried to call her today?"

"No, why?"

"To find out if she's all right."

He twisted his shoulders impatiently. "Of course she's all right. She was never here, that's all."

"Well, she was supposed to be here, to teach a class to the stitch-in people."

He frowned at Betsy, then Jill, who nodded. He said slowly, "I suppose that does make a difference, doesn't it?"

"Do you have her home phone number?"

"Yes," he said, and got it from a big black notebook that zippered closed.

She started to turn away, but Jill said, "Wait a second. Just because she's not here doesn't mean she's at home." She asked Frank, "Do you know where else she might be?"

"I don't have her current boyfriend's number, if that's what you mean."

"Is his name Eddie?"

"No, Tony. Why?"

"Maybe she's at your place?"

"I very much doubt it, Liddy knows how I feel about

Sharon. But my daughter sometimes goes to have lunch with her." He added, "Maybe Liddy knows where she is."

"Might your daughter know what she's driving?" asked Jill.

"I don't know. Possibly. Why, what's so important about her car?"

Jill said, "May we have Liddy's phone number? Is that your daughter's name, Liddy?"

"Yes, Elizabeth, called Liddy." He recited the phone number; Betsy wrote it under Sharon Kaye's home phone number.

"Well, thank you, Mr. Owen," said Jill.

He started to close the door, then opened it again. He said, his voice showing the same mild concern on his face, "I think I'll come down with you."

Down in the lobby, Betsy got out her quarters and dimes and dialed the number Frank had given her. After four rings an answering machine began, saying in a crisp, competent voice, "You have reached Escapade Design. At the tone, leave a message."

Betsy said, "Hello, I'm calling from Naniboujou Lodge. Are you there, Mrs. Owen? Please pick up if you are there." No one did, and Betsy hung up.

"Which doesn't prove anything," said Frank. "She's the only person I've ever known who can ignore a ringing phone."

Jill said, "But surely, if she heard the name Naniboujou Lodge, she'd be reminded she was supposed to be here and take the call."

Frank's mouth thinned. "Not if she doesn't want to hear a critical voice."

"Is your daughter at home?" asked Betsy.

Frank checked his watch. "Probably."

Betsy dialed the number. "Hello, is this Elizabeth Owen?" she asked when a woman answered.

"Yes?"

Betsy said, "I'm calling from Naniboujou Lodge. We're trying to locate your mother. She was supposed to teach a class at a stitch-in here."

Elizabeth said, "Oh, yes, I knew Mama was going to teach a class. Was that this weekend? Isn't she there?"

"No, and we're wondering if you know where she might be."

"Not at home?"

"No, we tried that."

"Then I'm sorry. I didn't know the class was this weekend, or I would have warned Daddy. He is there, isn't he?" A note of anxiety crept into this question, and she added, "Is he all right?"

"Yes, he's fine," said Betsy. "I'll let you talk to him if you like. But your mother seems to have gone missing."

"Missing? I don't understand. You mean she never arrived?"

"No, she was here, I talked with her yesterday. But she doesn't seem to be here now."

"How . . . peculiar. Well, maybe she left again. She's been known to do that."

"Do you know her boyfriend Tony?"

A note of wariness crept in. "Yes, why?"

"Could she be with him?"

"No, he's in Chicago for some kind of training, won't be back till next weekend."

"What kind of car is she driving?"

"A blue Volvo, brand new. Vanity plates, of course, 'escapade' spelled S-K-P-A-Y-D. Among other things, that was a poke at our last name, Owen."

"Thank you, Ms. Owen. Here, your father wants to talk to you."

Betsy handed the receiver to Frank, then she and Jill

hurried up to their room and put on coats, then went down the back stairs to the parking lot.

A sky blue Volvo with the vanity plates described was the third car from the end of the row, its fenders white with salt. Through a back seat window they could see a wicker basket with the lid fastened down.

"No," said Jill.

"No what?" said Betsy.

"That basket isn't nearly big enough."

"No," agree Betsy. Not even for an extremely thin woman, folded small.

The car was locked. They walked around to the back. Betsy said, "Could—could she be in the trunk?"

Jill said, "It's probably locked. Let me see." She fumbled with a mittened hand for the release under the edge of the trunk lid. She found it, pulled, and with a tiny creak, the lid lifted. There were two suitcases in the trunk, but no body.

"I was scared she'd be in there," said Betsy.

"I was afraid she wouldn't be," said Jill. She lowered the lid again, latching it. "I don't understand why this car is still here."

Betsy said, "Maybe because she's still around here somewhere, too."

They heard footsteps crunching and turned to see Frank approaching, hatless and pulling his fists up inside his sleeves like twin turtle heads. "This it?" he asked, his breath smoking in the cold air.

"Yes," said Betsy. "Are you sure she didn't come knocking on your door?"

"She might have. I was out most of the time. Actually, I don't see how she knew I was going to be here in the first place. I sure didn't tell her."

"Who did you tell?"

"My daughter and—" He paused, obviously struck by something. "A couple other people," he finished lamely, but added more strongly, "I don't think any of them would tell Sharon, they knew how I felt about her. My daughter says she didn't, and is sorry she didn't warn me Sharon was coming."

"If Sharon didn't know you were here, where did she think she was going to stay?" asked Jill.

"I don't know." said Frank. "I didn't know anything about her or her plans." The sun went behind a cloud and he shivered. "Look, it's too cold to be standing around talking. I'm going back inside." He set off for the front of the lodge. Betsy and Jill went with him. He said, "I still think there's some kind of logical explanation for all this. She's probably gone off with some friends."

"Is that like her to behave so irresponsibly?" asked Betsy.

"Oh, hell yes. Since her life got so limited by her allergies, she grabs at any kind of pleasure she can have, whenever she can, and damn any promises she made. It makes sense, I suppose, but it's frickin' annoying to anyone who thinks he can rely on her."

They followed him back inside, where he excused himself and went from the lobby into the dining room, and headed for the fireplace. Betsy, watching him go, asked Jill, "If he'd gone to his car instead of back in here, would you have arrested him?"

"For what? First, he's not standing there with a knife in his hand and Sharon Kaye's body at his feet; second, I'm out of my jurisdiction and not here on official business; and third, without a gun and handcuffs, I'm not sure I could have taken him. He looks pretty wiry." She was smiling faintly. "Why, is he back on your list of suspects?"

"He was never off. But anyway, we really can call the sheriff now, right?"

"Oh, yeah, with that car sitting there, I'm sure they

can get a search warrant for both it and Mr. Owen's room."

The front desk was unmanned. But the door to the tiny office was open. James was sitting inside, and Betsy could see the ruled lines of a bookkeeping program on his computer monitor. As they headed that way, Betsy said thoughtfully, "I wonder who was the other person he told?"

"Beats me."

James agreed that the presence of Sharon's car was concrete proof that Sharon had been here, and that a thorough search of the building and grounds was the obvious next step. "I'll call Sheriff Goodman," he said.

Fifteen minutes later a salty, dirty white car with a five-pointed star on its door pulled up. Sheriff Gregory Goodman, a short, brisk man with slicked-back dark hair and a rough-edged voice, was more indignant on behalf of the lodge than its owners.

"I still can't believe what you're telling me!" he barked at Betsy when she told him her story of seeing Sharon dead in room 10 for the second time. "Things like this just don't happen to decent folk like the Ramseys!"

"Yes, they do," said Betsy sadly. "Not often, and it is terrible, but they happen."

Goodman frowned at her. "You sound like you been in a mess like this before."

"I have," said Betsy. "More than once. I came up here to get over the last one, and now I seem to be involved in another one. Of all the things in the world, this is what I wanted least."

Her sincere tone brought a sharp look from James, and the sheriff asked, "How do you know the person you saw on the bed is Sharon Kaye Owen? Have you ever met Mrs. Owen before?"

"No. But her appearance is striking, and her picture

is on the cover of a magazine I subscribe to. That's why, for a little while, we thought perhaps I'd only dreamed I saw her. Because when I saw her, she was wearing the same sweater she's wearing in the photo."

"So how come you think now you didn't dream the whole thing?"

"I told you: Because her car is here. And she was supposed to be here to teach a needlework class." Betsy knew from previous encounters with law enforcement people that they made every witness tell his or her story at least twice, and then asked questions.

Goodman, frowning, went back a page in his notebook, read something, and nodded. "How sure are you that when you saw her on the bed she was dead?"

"I went close to her, and I could see she wasn't breathing. Her lips were blue, and her face was discolored in places. I pressed the carotid artery in her neck, but couldn't find a pulse." Betsy shivered. "I was sure she was dead."

"But you're not a doctor. Or a nurse."

"That's right."

"So it's possible she had passed out, then woke up after you left and walked out under her own steam."

"Yes, that's possible. The question is, since she didn't take her car, where did she go?"

Jill and the sheriff exchanged a look, and suddenly Betsy felt a chill. It would be horrible if she woke and, sick and confused, wandered out in the cold, perhaps into the surrounding woods, to become another body found too late by that part-time forest ranger.

Maybe, Betsy thought, *I should have stayed with the body. I could have opened the door and yelled for help, couldn't I?* She shook herself out of that thought, having learned long ago that "shoulda-woulda" regrets were the most useless.

"Show me the car," Goodman said, and Betsy and Jill

walked out with him. He walked all around it, peering in the windows, but didn't touch the door handles. Betsy, noticing that, was glad she had refrained as well.

"The trunk was unlatched so we opened it," said Jill, and he gave her a disapproving glance.

"There's two suitcases in it," said Betsy. "But no dead body. We pushed it closed."

Goodman went back to his squad car to check the vanity plate, and when it proved to belong to Sharon Kaye Owen of Duluth, he asked a deputy to swear out a search warrant for the car and for a search of the lodge and its outbuildings. When Jill offered to assist, he told her to go stand guard on Frank Owen's room, allowing no one in. "Is he here?"

Betsy looked into the dining room. "He's over there, by the fireplace."

The sheriff looked as well. "Who's that with him?"

"Carla—what's her last name? Prakesh. One of the stitchers." Carla had left her Penelope canvas to sit on the couch opposite Frank, listening intently while he spoke to her.

The sheriff started across the room. Betsy watched to see if he would arrest Frank. When the two glanced toward him, Carla stood but Frank didn't. The sheriff said something, Carla replied and added something more to Frank, then went into the lounge. The Sheriff sat down and pulled out his notebook.

Betsy, feeling her work was done, decided to go into the lounge. She paused in the doorway, blinking, shifting gears from sleuth to stitcher. The sun poured full strength through the windows, its brilliance doubled by reflection off the snow-covered lawn. It came through the big windows like a barrage, ricocheting off the light-colored walls and ceiling. If it had been sound, it would have been deafening.

There were about thirty women and two men in the

room. They were all busy. The sunlight flashed on the movement of needles, laying tools, embroidery hoops, the knobs on scroll bars. Wool, acrylic, silk, and cotton colors glowed, both on the stitchers and their work. It was so womanly a scene, the quiet, cheerful voices, the peaceful bent heads, the busy hands—and not Betsy's responsibility to supply their material or cope with their wants or complaints. And now, with law enforcement on hand, there was no pressure to do any sleuthing.

Betsy looked around, thinking to sit with or near Carla, but the woman had chosen the last open place in a cluster of upholstered chairs the stitchers had rearranged.

At first disappointed, Betsy told herself firmly she was relieved; after all, she wasn't going to sleuth anymore. She retrieved her needlework bag from beside Isabel, who was describing an encounter with a "pattern from hell" to a woman nodding sympathetically, and continued down to an empty wicker chair facing a sofa on which sat a plump woman totally involved in her stitching. Her indifference was welcome; Betsy didn't feel like talking to anyone right now. Anyone else, anyhow. She looked through the glass of a French door, where the sheriff, now standing, looked about to lead Frank out of the dining room.

Betsy again firmly quashed her curiosity, and got out her stitching.

She pulled her needle from its place on the border of the Aida cloth, consulted the Sue Lentz pattern, and took a couple of stitches.

"Oooh, the rose window patterns; I worked those a few months ago," said the woman sitting across from Betsy, not so totally involved in her own work after all. She was a tall, heavyset woman, her dark blond hair given golden highlights by the sun.

"Did you enjoy it?"

"Not the stitching." The woman chuckled. "But they were beautiful once they were finished. I see you're working the one on black."

"Yes, I haven't tried doing a pattern on black before, and I guess it's time. I'm Betsy Devonshire, I inherited a needlework shop in Excelsior and I've decided to keep it running. That means I have to get serious about needlework."

"I'm glad to hear you're keeping the shop open. We treasure our independents because of the special attention and the classes—though too often we buy our floss at Michael's or Wal Mart."

"I know." Betsy sighed and the woman chuckled again. Betsy leaned forward to see what she was working on. It was a rectangular needlepoint canvas, painted with grapevines top and bottom, and a beautiful uncial H leading off a William Morris quote: HAVE NOTHING IN YOUR HOUSES THAT YOU DO NOT KNOW TO BE USEFUL, OR BELIEVE TO BE BEAUTIFUL.

"I don't think I've seen that canvas before," said Betsy.

"It's a Beth Russell kit, I ordered it from England by Internet. I'm Nan Hansen, by the way. Oops!" She had begun to reach out a hand to Betsy, but instead knocked over the bottle of water resting on the arm of the couch.

"Nice to meet you."

Nan picked up the bottle of water and put it on the coffee table. "Were you out for a walk? It's so lovely up here in the summer, but I've never been one for winter sports. Outdoor ones, anyway. You're a lot braver than I am."

Betsy was considering how to reply to this when a man's rough-edged voice called from the other end of the room, " 'Scuse me, ladies! May I have your attention!"

Betsy looked up to see Sheriff Goodman standing,

hands on hips. "Who's in charge of this sewing shindig this weekend?"

Isabel stood. "Since the woman who organized it couldn't be here, I suppose I am."

"Will you come with me, please?" Goodman said, bending a turned-back forefinger at her.

They were no more than out the door when James Ramsey came in. The lodge owner said into the staring silence, "As most of you know, Sharon Kaye Owen was supposed to be here to teach a class. She was actually seen here yesterday, but not since, nor can she be located anywhere else. The reported circumstances of her disappearance are . . . disturbing, and the sheriff is here to begin an investigation. I'm sure he'll be asking all of you some questions." A brief murmur rose and quickly died as he continued. "Her car has been found in the parking lot, so a search will be conducted of the premises. I know this is an inconvenience and I apologize for it, but of course we are anxious to have this mystery solved."

A murmur of agreement rose, but one woman asked, "Are they going to search our rooms?"

"I can't imagine why," said James. "Can you?" There was uncomfortable laughter. "Now, if you will excuse me?" He bowed slightly, and left the lounge.

When he was gone, their voices rose in varied discussion of this turn of events. But in a couple of minutes, as work resumed, the noise quieted.

"You seem to have stirred up a mystery—maybe," Nan said to Betsy.

"Me?"

"Yes, that's what you were doing outside, looking for Sharon Kaye's car, isn't it? Of course it was, you were in here asking what kind of car Sharon Kaye drove. Are you a detective? I know that woman you were with is a police officer. What's going on, can you tell me?"

"There's hardly anything to tell," said Betsy. "Did you know Sharon Kaye?"

Nan nodded, and pulled a strand of cream-colored yarn through another basketweave stitch. "Yes, I did. A few years ago, she buckled down and got really good at counted cross-stitch, after years of just fooling with it. But then she couldn't do what she really loved anymore, which was climb mountains and swim oceans. She liked doing hard things, so I suppose we shouldn't have been surprised when she recently decided to challenge herself by designing."

"Were her designs any good?"

She took another stitch. "Well . . . not brilliant or breaking new ground. But competent, and getting better with every new one."

A woman across the way cleared her throat, and when they looked at her she said, "I'm doing the flower series she designed." She held up her project, a counted cross-stitch pattern of five daffodils in a glass vase. "I'm Linda Savareid, from Albert Lea. This is the first pattern of hers I've worked, and I love it. Her design is so easy to follow." Linda had streaky brown hair and the gentle, competent air of a grade school teacher Betsy had once loved.

Nan said, "Getting on the cover of *ANW* was a real coup for her. If she ever comes up with something really fresh, she could become one of the shining lights of counted design." She looked at Betsy over half-moon glasses. "Well, unless . . ." she said.

"Unless she's dead," said Linda.

"Yes."

Having broken the subject open, the women on the couch with its back to Betsy began talking about Sharon Kaye, and soon the women across from them joined in. Betsy shamelessly eavesdropped (and so she didn't realize for some while that she was making some mistakes in counting her stitches).

"I can't imagine her dead," said a woman with an interesting white streak in her russet hair. She had finished stitching a hardanger pattern of squares and was very carefully snipping out their centers. "She sort of took over any room she was in."

"I hope nothing bad has happened to her," said one young woman dressed in a red sweatsuit. She was stitching the alphabet in bright silks on Quaker cloth. "She is so nice! When I was just starting out, she sat with me for half an hour and showed me how to grid and follow a pattern. She was so patient and so encouraging, it made me feel special."

"Well, good for you, Katy; she was rude to me every time we met," said a young woman with several earrings and a glint in her eye.

"Now, Anna," warned Nan.

"Humpf!" snorted Anna. "You know as well as I do, she could be damn rude when she felt like it, and what's worse, she always had to have her own way about everything or she'd walk out right in the middle of whatever we were doing."

"She wasn't well," said Nan.

"She was as well or as sick as she wanted to be," retorted Anna. "All that stuff about being allergic! I saw her shopping at a mall once, looking healthy as a horse, then she turned up the next morning at a stitch-in wearing a mask and whining that someone present had eaten peanut butter. She positively enjoyed making us all feel guilty for having a life. Poo!"

Linda Savareid turned in her seat to say, "I had a student in my seventh grade class who was allergic to peanuts—and believe me, it's not a guilt trip. A fellow student brought an assortment of cookies as a birthday treat one day. Some had peanut butter in them, but none of us knew it. The allergic child ate one and stopped breathing. If he hadn't had an EpiPen with him, he'd've been dead before the ambulance arrived."

"What's an EpiPen?" asked Nan.

"It's a medical device designed to be used by non-medical people," said Linda. "It delivers a big dose of epinephrine to someone having a severe allergic reaction, and can keep them alive until they get to a hospital."

Nan said, "Sharon Kaye has one."

"I didn't know she had allergies," said a young man stitching a Norman Rockwell painting of a fisherman in a small boat in the rain. "She came to our store and was a wonderful teacher. But she never said a thing about being allergic." He turned to the even younger woman sitting beside him. "Remember when she came to our store, Suzy?"

The young woman nodded, but kept her eyes on her knitting. She was making an argyle sweater in four colors of wool.

The young man continued. "Miss Kaye taught a class of six people just starting out in cross-stitch."

"When was this?" asked Betsy.

"Right after we opened, eighteen months ago. She drove all the way to Fergus Falls, and got us off to a good start. We're in our second year now, still doing pretty good." There was a note of pride in his voice, and his back straightened. "It was all Suzy's idea. I wanted to buy a farm. Right, Suz?" He nudged the woman beside him, who blushed becomingly and still didn't look up. She looked barely out of high school, and Betsy wondered at the audacity of such young people opening their own business. Betsy also wondered why such a shy woman would decide to go into a business that demanded constant customer contact.

"And you say she was a good teacher?"

"She was wonderful," murmured the young woman.

"How long did the class last, Mike?" asked another woman in somewhat absent tones. She was working on a canvas held firm with scroll bars. Rather than fasten it to a stand, she had made a big loop of ribbon, twisted it into a figure eight, ran it around her neck, and put a loop of the eight around each of the two top knobs of the scroll bar. The bottom of the frame was braced on her ample tummy, and she was using both hands, one to push the needle into the top and the other to pull it through. As a result, her bargello pattern—waves of various colors done in long, vertical stitches—was progressing very rapidly.

"All weekend," said the young man, "Saturday morning and Sunday afternoon, three hours each. Every student who signed up came to both sessions." He looked at Betsy, and she saw he had devastating green eyes.

"I'm surprised Sharon lasted the entire weekend," said Nan. Her voice was slightly squashed, as she was bent severely forward to poke around on the floor for a pair of dropped scissors. "Oof, there they are! It would be more like her to do what she did here, change her mind at the last minute. Or quit partway through. I've known her for years, and she's always been what she calls whimsical. Whim of steel, if you ask me."

"Now be goot, Nan," said a woman wearing a deep yellow cardigan. Her project was a tiny bouquet of roses being worked with a single thread of silk on fine gauze. She wore a very large magnifying glass attached to a gray headband. Her eye, then her nose, then her ear in succession were hugely magnified as her face turned past Betsy toward Nan, a disconcerting effect. When she spoke, it was fluently, but with a German accent. "She is not here to defent herself, so be kind."

"Oh, there's no defense for what she does." Nan wove her needle into a corner of her canvas so she could concentrate on this conversation. "In fact, there's generally some mischief in it. Haven't you ever noticed that, Ingrid? Charlotte's in the hospital, so here's her chance to make us all mad at Charlotte by walking out on her agreement to teach a class."

"But you're not mad at Charlotte," Betsy pointed out.

Nan replied, "You just watch, next month Sharon will come to our stitchers' meeting and be so contrite and sweet, and she'll have such a clever explanation, everyone, probably even me, will be glad to forgive her. Charlotte hasn't got that charm, and what they'll remember next year, when Charlotte tries to organize another stitch-in, is that she promised us a surprise guest teacher at this stitch-in and didn't deliver."

Betsy said, "And you think Sharon Kaye did that on purpose? To make the group mad at Charlotte?"

Nan backed down at this blunt restatement. "Well, probably not. She and Charlotte are friends, after all. It's just that's always how things turn out around her. If some project gets in trouble, no matter how thickly Sharon Kaye's involved in it, somehow she never gets any of the blame. Maybe it isn't malicious, it could be that she just does whatever she feels like doing without any thought to how it will affect others. I'm sure if she agreed to come up here and teach a class she really meant to teach it. But then she got another invitation that seemed like more fun, and it never occurred to her to say something. Or she got here and saw someone she doesn't like, and just went away without telling anyone about it."

Ingrid said, "I think it more likely she got here and something set off an allergic attack. She wouldn't haff time to tell somebody about it, she would just go, quick, off to the emergency room."

"Emergency room—are her allergies that serious?" asked Betsy. "I mean, her ex-husband told me she smokes, and I wouldn't think someone with serious allergies would smoke." Betsy was trying to pretend she wasn't really interested in the topic of Sharon Kaye's allergies by continuing to work on her cross-stitching. It was hard to see the openings in the weave of the black cloth when the background was her brown skirt, so she kept having to hold the fabric up toward the window to make the tiny openings in the weave visible.

"Oh, it's so *aw*-ful that she smokes!" Ingrid said. She had an expressive face and voice, eyebrows lifting, lip movement exaggerated, voice going up and down the scale, like the magnifying glass that caused the weave on her yellow sweater to swell then collapse again as the lens moved across it. "I haff told her over and over that she simply must quit, because she does have serious allergies that put her in the hospital sometimes, and smoking affects breathing, everyone knows that. And when she feels an attack coming on, it's important she get medical attention *immeeee*-dee-utly. I once saw her collapse from—what is the word? Some kind of shock."

"Anaphylactic," said Linda.

"That's right, anaphylactic. She has carried that device you were talking about that can inject medicine ever since that time she collapsed right in front of us, and nobody knew what to do. It was very frightening!"

Betsy said, "Did anyone ever see her use the pen? I should think if she carried it, she wasn't pretending to have allergies, because what would happen if she used that pen and wasn't really in anaphylactic shock?"

Linda said, "It's like a big dose of amphetamine, so surely it would be dangerous to use it if it wasn't a real emergency."

The EpiPen Betsy found in the lodge office had been full of medicine, unused. She said, "She didn't become ill while I talked with her, or at least she didn't seem ill. Could she tell when an attack was coming on? She

just said she had to go meet someone, not that she was
having an attack. I thought perhaps she was having a
nicotine fit."

"Trust me," said Ingrid, "she would never mistake a
nicotine, ah, what did you call it, 'fit' for one of these
attacks. It was very important to her to keep track of
those things, because first she turns red, then she turns
blue, then poof! Collapse, and perhaps she is dead."

Betsy remembered the dead woman's blotchy face
and blue lips. And the blush when she had mentioned
her honeymoon. Maybe she was starting an allergic reaction then. *Now don't make too much of that blush,* she
told herself. *Maybe she's the sensitive type. And maybe
she just got bored and walked out. Anyway, if she did
die here, they'll find her. And if not, be grateful. So don't
think about it anymore.* She looked at her stitching:
she'd gone over two threads instead of one. And trying
to unstitch it by going back through the same hole
caused the floss to snag and fray. This stupid Aida fabric! She unthreaded her needle and used its tip to tease
the floss out of the fabric. Trying not to think about
Sharon Kaye was making her head hurt.

Nan said, "Are you all right?"

Betsy squeezed her eyes shut and murmured, "Just a
bit of a headache." This part of her stitching was starting
to look really wrong. She picked up the pattern to do
some recounting.

"Say, Anna, where's Parker?" asked Nan.

"Prying agates out of the ice on the beach," said Anna.
"He's writing a paper on the geology of the North Shore.
We were here last summer and he made me hike to the
Devil's Kettle and back—those stairs!"

"Agates?" said Betsy, thinking of marbles.

"Beautiful stones you find along the shore of Lake
Superior," said Anna. "Dull brown on the outside, but
slice them with a saw and they are magnificent inside."

"Oh, I've seen them!" said Betsy. Glassy layers of delicate color, sometimes with a hollow center, agate slices were for sale in gift shops down in the Cities. "I wondered why I saw three men in the dining room and only two here in the lounge."

The talk went on to vacations and tourists and hiking. It was nearly an hour later that Jill came in.

Betsy looked up and said, "What did they find?"

Jill replied, "Nothing. No sign of Sharon Kaye." She spoke quietly, but Nan overheard her and immediately turned and passed the word along, and in a few seconds the room was abuzz with the news.

Betsy felt giddy, whether with relief or distress she didn't know. She said to Jill, "So what are they going to do now?"

"Nothing. The sheriff and his crew have gone away."

"But—" Betsy rubbed a spot over her left eyebrow, where the headache was really pounding. Why hadn't they found anything? Had they looked absolutely everywhere? Was there something else she could have told the sheriff, some other question she could have asked? No, no, no, stop it! This no longer involved her. She had done her duty. But . . . She stood. Jill said, "What now?"

"I have to ask Isabel something." A dim notion had made its way out of the thicket of pain. She stooped beside Isabel to ask, "If Sharon Kaye had an allergic attack, she might have asked someone to take her to the hospital. Is there someone who signed up for this event who isn't here?"

Isabel said, "That's what the sheriff asked me. I told him no. Everyone who signed up is here."

So even that dim light was extinguished.

"Here," said Jill from behind her, "you're looking tired. I think you should lie down for a while. I'll get our things and walk you up to our room."

As they walked to the door beside the big stone fireplace, Betsy asked, "Did they do a really thorough search of Frank's room?"

"Yes, Goodman's crew was very professional."

Betsy said, "What I don't understand is why the door to Frank Owen's room was unlocked when I went up there the first time. If I had a dead body in my room, I'd sure lock the door until I got rid of it."

"So would I." Jill nodded.

"Maybe the murderer didn't have a key." They started up the stairs, Betsy leading.

Jill said, "So you're still thinking maybe Frank Owen wasn't responsible for the body? Then what was it doing in his room?"

"I don't know. Because the murderer needed somewhere to put it and that room wasn't locked?" She stopped and turned around on the stairs. "But that would be stupid, wouldn't it? Why carry her upstairs to hide her? Why not just take her out the back door? I thought he might have planted the body in Frank's room, but if that was his plan, why come back and move it? That wouldn't make sense—but nothing about this does." She turned away and started up again, dizzy from the pain in her head. "Am I going crazy? I don't want to investigate, so why can't I leave it alone? What's the matter with me? Is this what a nervous breakdown feels like?"

"I don't think you're having a nervous breakdown. I think there are obvious questions occurring to you, as they would to anyone who found a body. I also think you need to get a little distance from it for a while. A nap may help."

In their room, Betsy took a couple of aspirin, then removed her shoes and lay down on the bed. Jill shut the blinds and folded the quilted coverlet over her.

"Jill?"

"Yes?"

"I saw an EpiPen in the little office off the lobby. Could it be Sharon's?"

Jill came to look intently at Betsy. "Was it used?"

"No. I found it on the floor under the desk."

The intent look went away. "Did you ask James about it?"

"No, he wasn't in the lobby, so I just left it in the office."

"Maybe it belongs to someone who works here."

"Yes, of course." Betsy closed her eyes—she was so very tired!—and tried to block out the thoughts vying for her attention. But in they trooped, pushing and shouting and waving their arms. Her head felt squeezed in a vise.

"I'm allergic to cigarette smoke" was a common complaint, even among people not allergic to other things. Yet Sharon Kaye smoked.

Was she one of those people who claimed to be allergic just to gain sympathy? Then what about the collapse Ingrid had described? Suppose the EpiPen Betsy found was Sharon's. If Sharon had an allergic attack, why wasn't it used? What was it doing in the office? That office door was kept locked; Sharon couldn't have put it in there herself. Was James somehow culpably involved in all this?

Or was it possible Sharon hadn't been here at all, that this had been a dream after all? No, she must have been here, her car was here. The car made it real.

If Sharon had been here, why did she leave? Someone had suggested that Sharon had left because she saw someone she didn't like. Who didn't Sharon like? More important, who didn't like Sharon? Certainly some of the stitchers had been acid-tongued when speaking of her.

Was it a coincidence that Sharon's ex-husband chose

this weekend to come here, the same weekend Sharon agreed to come and teach a class?

Maybe it was learning he was here that had sent Sharon away. Certainly Betsy would not stay in a hotel, especially in a remote location, if her ex-husband turned up.

What was Hal up to now? Thank God he'd stopped sending flowers. The pig.

Was her headache a little better?

What was the cause of that water leak in the shop? Was she right to trust Godwin to handle it?

Was Godwin taking good care of Sophie?

If he forgot to give Sophie water, could the cat perhaps turn on the faucet in the bathtub and refresh herself?

And, of course, not being able to turn it off, the water would run and run, and the tub would fill and overflow.

And Godwin was upstairs in her apartment, lifting buckets of water out of the tub and pouring them onto her living room carpet while shouting, "Get an ax, chop a hole in the floor before Sophie drowns!"

And the cat was swimming neck deep in water toward a toy motorboat whose engine was idling over by the window. Sophie was too big for the motorboat, she would tip it over and sink it if she tried to get aboard. Betsy didn't have an ax; she took a meat cleaver from the kitchen and stepped into the living room and sank in over her head, and swam down, down, reaching for the carpet, cleaver at the ready, holding her breath, but by the time she got down to the carpet, she was already in need of air, so she dropped the cleaver and started back up, kicking desperately for the surface, which was too far away, she needed to breathe, she couldn't hold her breath any longer, she would have to open her mouth and breathe water, she was going to drown.

Betsy sat up on the bed, gasping.

Then she fell back on the pillow, to inhale more deeply and less desperately while her heart slowed down.

Well, at least this bad dream wasn't about murder.

What time was it, anyway? She looked at her watch. Nearly noon. Half an hour's sleep, not enough.

But despite the brevity of the nap, and the bad dream, she felt better. Her headache was gone, anyway. Rather than try to sleep some more, she'd wash her face and comb her hair and go back downstairs to stitch some more.

She went down the stairs into cooking fragrances and found the dining room was being set up for a buffet lunch. The long, broad counter at the other end was being laden with a delectable array of salads, cold cuts, meatballs, chicken wings, marinated vegetables, and desserts. A line was forming, snaking down the long room, winding among the tables. Betsy inhaled deeply and went into the lounge to retrieve Jill, and found her almost alone and everyone else still there packing away their stitching.

They got into line. Betsy complained about her problems with the rose window pattern. Jill said, "If you put a white cloth on your lap, you can see the holes in the fabric a lot better."

"Well sure, I know that!" Betsy grimaced. "I just didn't think of it." This was certainly not one of her brighter days. Talking about the patterns painted on the walls and how they would make pretty and easy cross-stitch patterns, they chose the first table they came to with two seats available. It was already occupied by a man and a woman. It wasn't until they had put their plates down that Betsy realized the woman was Carla.

But it would have been very rude to walk away at that point, so they sat. Carla said, "Jill, Betsy, I've been having the most interesting discussion with Anna's hus-

band Parker, here. He's been out looking for garnets—
no, agates. He's a graduate student in geology, and full
of the most amazing facts about this part of the state.
Mr. Lundquist, this is Jill Cross and Betsy Devonshire,
of Excelsior, who are here for the stitch-in."

"I took a course in geology several aeons ago," said
Betsy, glad to discuss a topic that didn't involve either
crime or trame. "I enjoyed it very much—especially the
part about continental drift and earthquakes, since I was
living in California. But if I remember correctly, this
area is stable, geologically speaking. And therefore not
terrifically interesting."

"Well, that's partly correct," said Parker, with the pe-
dantic air of the becoming-learned. "The bedrock around
here is of the Keweenawan Supergroup, intrusive rocks
of dominantly mafic composition."

"Which means?" asked Carla with a little smile.

"Composed of something that looks like granite, but
isn't, not really. There was once a rift in the earth's
mantle here, and consequently lots of volcanos. The
bluffs around here are the lava flows, which were
thousands of feet thick. If you walk up along the Brule
River, you can see how the water has cut a slice in it.
The soil that overlays it is glacial drift, left behind when
the last glacier retreated about twelve thousand years
ago. This area is the North Shore Volcanic Group, which
formed approximately eleven hundred million years ago,
although most of Minnesota is part of the Canadian
Shield, Precambrian rock six hundred to thirty-six hundred million years old."

"Good Lord!" said Carla. "Older than—well, old."

"Is that what you're studying?" asked Betsy. "The
Precambrian formations?"

Parker shook his head. "I've been studying the Brule
River rhyolite flow, part of a very ancient mountain

range, the Sawtooth Mountains. The hills around Grand Marais are a remnant of them."

Betsy said, "What about the Devil's Kettle?"

"What about it?"

"Jill told me the water goes into a rock and never comes out again. Has that got something to do with the rift? Can you explain where it goes?"

"I believe the water probably flows underground and empties into Lake Superior."

Jill said, "But they put dye into the kettle, and it never showed up in the lake or anywhere."

"Oh, it will, eventually. I'm trying to prove a theory that there's a large and very slow-moving aquifer deep underground, which is fed by the Devil's Kettle."

Betsy said, "Are you saying that one of these days someone will be fishing along the shore here, and suddenly yellow dye will show up in the water?"

"It's possible," said Parker. "Though if my theory is correct, none of the people involved in the original experiment will be alive to see it. I think the water presently going into the aquifer will spill into Lake Superior in seventy-five or a hundred years."

"Have you been to see the waterfall?" asked Jill.

"Oh, yes, I went there a dozen or more times last summer—in fact, I was there again last week."

"Isn't it frozen solid?" asked Betsy.

"No, the river has a cover of ice, but the waterfall is open. I took some photographs along the riverbank, and of the falls itself. There is an interesting mix of boralfs and udipsaments along the top there, though of course none of it visible because of the snow cover."

"Of course," said Carla dryly, and Betsy laughed.

"I hope you will excuse my language," said Parker, abashed.

"Oh, I wasn't just laughing at you," said Betsy. "I was thinking of how Carla loves to talk about her favorite kind of needlework in almost exactly the same tone of voice you use talking about geology."

Carla, surprised, laughed. "It's true, it's true!" she said. "I was wondering why I liked this man. It must be because I recognize a fellow spirit. When I get interested in something, I obsess."

Jill asked, "What else have you obsessed on besides needlework?"

Carla's laugh cut off as if she'd been slapped. "What do you mean by that?"

"Nothing," said Jill, surprised. "You made a general statement that you obsess about things, and I wondered what else you had obsessed over."

Carla blinked. "Oh. Of course." She smiled. "Well, cooking; I love to cook; I have over a hundred cookbooks and a kitchen that can cook an eight-course meal for twelve—though I don't do that often; I'm a widow and my one child lives in New Zealand. And I do a lot of volunteer work for the Humane Society. I am currently on four animal welfare committees."

Betsy said, "I'm interested in animal welfare, too—I used to do wild animal rescue for the San Diego Humane Society when I lived out there. I'm going to have to check into what's needed in Hennepin County now that Excelsior's my home."

"I specialize in bird rescue when I'm in Florida," said Carla. "I've raised I don't know how many baby birds blown out of their nests by hurricanes."

"When I was nine I raised two baby robins I found in our yard after a storm," said Jill.

"I once found an orphaned baby raccoon," said Parker, and the awkward moment was quickly forgotten as the four got into a discussion of the amusing and healthy ingratitude of rescued wild animals.

8

After lunch, Jill said, "Well, back to the lounge?"
Betsy replied, "Not yet. I want to see if James can help us figure out where Sharon Kaye thought she was going to stay if Frank wouldn't let her move in with him."

Jill said, "I'm glad you're not taking your own advice about this."

"What do you mean?"

"You said you weren't going to get involved in sleuthing anymore."

"This isn't sleuthing! I mean, the police did the sleuthing and didn't find anything, so I'm going to find something that will make them try harder."

Jill could hide an emotion better than a world-class poker player. Still, Betsy narrowed her eyes at her. But Jill only nodded and said, "Okay."

"I've already told you Sharon Kaye Owen didn't have a reservation," James said a minute later, from behind the counter in the lobby.

"But did anyone change their reservation from a single to a double?" asked Betsy.

"I'll check." He checked his registration file. "Yes, Charlotte Porter changed her reservation from a single to a double about four weeks ago, and prepaid for two people."

Jill asked, "Did Charlotte tell Sharon Kaye her ex-husband was going to be here?"

James made a "How-would-I-know?" face, and Betsy said, "Charlotte didn't mention it to me when I phoned her—but she was pretty drifty from pain medication."

Jill nodded. "So it's possible Sharon Kaye didn't know Frank was going to be here."

Betsy said, "I think she did. Otherwise, she would have claimed Charlotte's room—it was paid for, after all, and Charlotte meant to share it with her. But she didn't claim it, which probably means she was hoping Frank would ask her to join him. Frank said he didn't know she was here. If that's true—" Betsy cut herself off; this was coming dangerously close to real sleuthing.

Jill asked James, "Can anyone read your check-in list to see who else is here?"

James shook his head. "If someone asks specifically, we will tell them so-and-so has checked in. But as I already said, I never saw Mrs. Owen, I had no idea she was at the lodge. Nobody asked me about her before you two did. And I'm the only one on the desk."

Betsy said, "I'm more and more sure she knew he was going to be here. In fact, I think it was his being here that made her decide to come. Because don't you think, Jill, that it's too big a coincidence that she decides to teach at a stitch-in at a time and place her ex-husband, with whom she wants to reconcile, happens to be?"

Jill asked James, "How far in advance did Frank Owen register?"

James said, "I'll have to check. But I can tell you the

Grand Marais Embroiderers Guild reserved a block of rooms back in October, and no one else had reserved a room for this weekend that far back." James turned again to his registration file. "Mr. Owen reserved his room five weeks and two days ago. I warned him about the stitch-in, but he said he didn't think they'd bother him."

Jill said, "Did he ask if Sharon Kaye was coming?"

"I don't think so. If he did, I would have said she wasn't, because I didn't have her name on the list of people coming."

Betsy said, "But that works, don't you see? Five weeks ago Frank decides to come up, and a week later Charlotte changes her reservation to a double. No, wait, if I was allergic to everything, I'd want a room of my own."

Jill said, "The room I reserved was the last of the stitch-in's block, and that was six weeks ago."

James said, "Yes, that's right. She couldn't have gotten a room of her own."

Betsy said to James, "So the lodge is full, right? Sharon Kaye had to share a room, because Jill got the last stitch-in room, and then Mr. Owen took the one room left over."

James said, "Yes, we didn't quite get the innkeeper's dream of every room but one taken."

Betsy frowned. "I should think you'd want them all taken."

"No, the rest of the dream is that a reporter for an important travel magazine has a car breakdown right outside your door and just falls in love with your place."

"So as of now you're full up?"

"No; since neither Charlotte Porter nor her roommate turned up, we've got an empty room." He smiled. "But there's no sign yet of the *New York Times* travel correspondent."

James went back to his bookkeeping and Jill said, "I

just thought of another possibility to eliminate: Call the area hospitals. She might be in one of them, too sick to let anyone know where she is."

There were a surprising number of them in the phone book. After the fourth call, Jill went away. Betsy continued through a fortune in dimes and quarters, calling hospitals and medical clinics, none of which had admitted or treated a patient named Sharon Kaye Owen.

Finished at last, she went back to her room and got a white hand towel, brought it to the lounge, and stood just inside the door. A number of the stitchers looked at her the way people will look at the scene of a car accident, and she showed them her best customer-welcoming smile until they went back to their work. Jill declared her place in the room by raising the canvas tiger in its frame and indicated an empty place across a coffee table.

Betsy found her canvas bag and brought it to the empty place. She draped the towel across her lap and got out her rose window pattern. Amazing how having a gleaming white lap made the weave so much easier to see, but she hadn't even found her place when a woman in a wheelchair rolled up to them. She was about twenty-five, a streaky blond athletic type, with the too-bright, aggressive look of a hawk in her eye.

Betsy blinked at her, surprised. She had seen the woman in the dining room and, now on this closer look, recognized her as someone she'd seen wheeling around Excelsior. She'd had no idea she was a stitcher. Certainly the woman had never come into Betsy's shop. But there on her lap was an almost-finished cross-stitch pattern of butterflies.

"Hi!" she said brightly. "I'm Sadie Cartwright." She leaned forward a little and said in a lower voice, "It's interesting you're here, because if anyone here can solve the mystery of Sharon Kaye's disappearance, it's you, correct?"

"Why do you say that?" asked Betsy.

"Because Jill Cross may be a cop, but you're the one with a nose for solving mysteries!"

"I'd disagree with you, because I see mystery I can't solve right in front of me. How come I didn't know your name, but you appear to know all about me?"

Sadie laughed. "I order my stitching supplies from the Internet, that's why I never come into your store. And the reason I know about you is that I've come to Shelly Donohue's class a few times to talk about life in a wheelchair, and I usually have lunch with her after. She loves to talk about her part-time job in Crewel World, and she's always bragging how Betsy Devonshire is a regular Miss Marple. She says you go around pretending to be an ignorant amateur, then all of a sudden someone is on his way to jail and it's all your doing. Now you're up here and we've got a mysterious disappearance, and who's the first one to sniff it out? Betsy Devonshire, the Sherlock Holmes of the needlework set!"

"I'm not Sherlock Holmes," said Betsy, "nor am I Miss Marple. I don't have any special skills as a detective, I don't like getting mixed up with crime, and I have no intention of investigating what happened to Mrs. Owen."

"See?" crowed Sadie, forgetting to speak quietly, rolling her chair back and forward in a show of pleasure. "Just like she said you do! 'Oh, I don't have any idea what you're talking about, but if you want to know who did it, just watch who I dance with tonight,' " she quoted in a high, breathless voice, though Betsy had never said such a thing in her life. "Ha! Shelly introduced me to Irene Potter, who told me you're so good you should sell your needlework store and hang out your shingle as a private eye. So don't pretend with me. I bet you'll have this little case all wrapped up before we go home tomorrow afternoon." Laughing, Sadie turned her chair in a single deft movement, and started back up the room.

"Wait!" said Betsy, but Sadie didn't.

"Durn," said Jill, "she'll tell everyone."

"I didn't know Irene bragged about me," said Betsy. "I thought she didn't like me."

"She wasn't bragging, she was dreaming out loud. She knows that if you turn private eye, you'll sell Crewel World. And you already know that above all else in this world, Irene Potter wants to own Crewel World."

"She told you that I should be a private eye?"

"She told Shelly that, and Shelly told me and probably a lot of other people—you know what a gossip Shelly is."

"Yes, I just got a reminder of that." Betsy frowned at the far end of the room, where Sadie was leaning forward to talk to a pair of women, both of whom glanced toward Betsy with wide eyes.

Jill said, "Speaking of not sleuthing, what did you find out?"

"She not in any hospital in Duluth," said Betsy. "And we're sure she's not home, and she's not with her daughter."

"She's not here, either," said Jill.

"That's because murderers don't ordinarily leave their victims strewn around."

"Sure they do," said Jill. "Especially in a hotel, because who wants to get caught staggering down a hallway with a body in his arms?"

Betsy had no reply for that. She picked up her Aida cloth, and determinedly started in. The fourth wedge forming the circle around the center medallion was quickly done, now that she could see what she was doing. She got out the spool of Kreinik metallic and cut off twelve inches of it. It felt weightless in her hand,

and though it looked like colored metal, it was thin as plastic film. Thinner. When she tried to put it through the eye of her needle, the metallic part immediately separated from the very fine brown thread it was wrapped around. Licking it didn't put it back together; she had to snip off the separated ends. On the third try she got both pieces through and began to stitch, trying to work slowly and gently so as not to snag or break the gossamer stuff.

Jill looked casually around the room, seemingly at no one in particular, then said, "Look, she's telling the whole room."

Betsy stretched, moving as if to work a kink out of her neck, and looked over her shoulder. Sadie was halfway up the room now, talking to three interested stitchers. Betsy asked Jill, "What do you think she's saying about me? Do you know her?"

"Not well. She's a good person, she won't be telling lies. She acts a little tough, that's all. Compensating, maybe. She's genuinely strong, though, runs that wheelchair up the sidewalks like it's a souped-up truck."

One of the stitchers glanced up and saw Betsy looking, touched Sadie on the shoulder, and the two looked back at Betsy, Sadie with a big white grin.

But Betsy's ear was caught by a woman nearer, saying, not quietly enough, "I hear that when there's a murder, the police always look first at the person reporting it."

Betsy felt a dash of cold anger. But she didn't want to look around to see who said it, so she went back to her stitching. In her anger, she pulled hard at the Kreinik, which instantly broke. Sighing, she turned her fabric over and used her threader to work the broken end under other stitches on the back, rethreaded the broken-off strand, and tried again to work little x's around the wedge.

But her focus remained on the talk all around her. Nan's voice rose into audibility. "I say, if Sharon is dead, she probably did something to deserve it."

And someone replied with a laugh, "If they look for motives, that would mean a lot of us are suspects!"

Betsy suddenly flashed on seeing the dead woman on the bed, reliving her own reaction of terror, sorrow, and helplessness. How dreadful to dismiss a death so callously! This was too much, she took a breath and would have risen to relieve her feelings had not Jill forestalled her by saying gently, "The air in here is getting a little close. How about we take a walk?"

Betsy glanced at Jill and saw a reflection of her own anger on that normally enigmatic face. She said in a carrying voice, "Yes, I think a walk out in the fresh air is just what I need!"

They went upstairs to change into wool slacks (gray for Betsy, navy for Jill) and cotton turtlenecks (white for Betsy, cranberry for Jill), over which they put coats, scarves, hats, and mittens. They pulled on insulated boots, went down again through the dining room to the lobby, and out the door.

The air was dry, very cold, and smelled of woodsmoke.

Betsy looked across the parking area and saw a great wall of logs and cords of fireplace wood. "Is all that for the fireplace?" she asked.

"No, they heat the lodge and its water with wood. That shed over there houses the furnace and boiler. This being March, the wood supply is nowhere near what it was back in October."

Betsy started across the parking and turnaround area. Though the sun was brilliant and the air calm, the tamped-down snow creaked under their feet, and Betsy could feel the tingle of bitter cold inside her nose and through her mittens. "This feels much colder than Excelsior. I wonder that the temperature is?"

"About ten above, I think," replied Jill. "Not too bad with no wind."

The furnace shed was about ten by twenty feet, corrugated steel painted a dull green. A metal chimney spilled fragrant smoke into the still air. Though a path had been cut through the snow to its wooden door, it had snowed after the path was dug, and instead of shoveling again, people had simply trampled the new snow down. Consequently, the path was icy and uneven, full of heel-shaped depressions, their edges worn smooth.

"Treacherous footing," Betsy noted, stepping carefully and keeping her elbows out to improve her balance.

Snow had drifted three feet deep along one side of the shed, but the ground within a foot of the wall was bare, and Betsy could feel the air grow a little warmer as she approached the door.

"Where are we going?" asked Jill behind her.

"I want to see the furnace, to see if it's big enough."

"For what?" asked Jill. "Oh," she added.

"Did the sheriff look in here?"

"Yes. I kind of followed them around once I was released from guarding Mr. Owen's door. But he was only in the shed for a couple of minutes."

Nearly to the shed, there was a thick V in the snow heaped beside the path. It looked as if someone had fallen to his knees. Other marks indicated he'd dropped what he was carrying and picked it up piecemeal. Betsy bent over the marks, expecting to see bits of garbage or wastebasket detritus, but she couldn't see anything at all.

The ground right in front of the door was covered with a sheet of plywood on which was laid a rope doormat, both of them frost-covered and marred with sooty footprints. There was no trash or litter to be seen—wait.

Betsy stooped and pried up something in the trodden snow beside the wood. It was a skein of DMC 208 cotton floss with one of its two black and gold wrappers still around it.

"I see they've already burned trash from today," said Betsy. "I wonder who threw this away? It's hardly been used. Pretty color." It was one of the colors she was using in her pattern. It didn't look dirty. She shook off fragments of ice and put it in her pocket.

The shed was empty of everything but the furnace, which took up nearly all the space. It was old and large, swathed in what looked like plaster. Its door was black cast iron, opened by lifting it clear of a stubby hook— "Ouch!" Betsy yiped, snatching her hand back—and hot to the touch. She took her mitten off and folded it in half to use as a hot pad. The inside of the furnace was half full of white-hot coals on which very pale yellow flames danced.

Betsy looked around for a poker or a stick and didn't find one. There was nothing else in the shed, not even chunks of wood. "I don't suppose there'd be anything left by now anyhow," she said, bending for a closer look. The air pouring out of the furnace was enough to singe her eyebrows.

"Not so you could just look in and see it," agreed Jill. "Close the door."

Betsy obeyed, and Jill continued. "The maintenance man comes out here pretty often to put more wood into that furnace. It's not like coal or charcoal, wood burns fast, you've got to keep feeding it or the fire goes out."

Betsy said, "So if there'd been something in there that wasn't wood, very likely he'd've seen something left of it in there when he came out to feed the fire."

Jill said, "Plus, remember the smell of woodsmoke when we approached? That isn't what a burning body smells like. He'd've noticed that. It's a very distinctive odor."

Betsy felt a prickling in her throat. "Don't tell me things like that!" she said, swallowing.

"Hey, coming in here was your idea. Make up your mind, Betsy! Let's either go on investigating, or do what I suggested in the first place: Go for a walk."

"My mind *is* made up!" snapped Betsy. "Let's walk!" But outside the shed she said, "Hold up a minute. I'm sorry. It's turned into some kind of reflex, this snooping business. I sincerely do want to stop but I'm having trouble doing that. Please be patient with me."

"Sure."

"Thanks. Now, where did you want to walk to?"

Jill led Betsy back across the parking lot then across the lawn to the lakeshore. The snow on the lawn was well over a foot deep, with a thick, crunchy top that held their weight for a second or two, then let their feet break through to their knees. But cold as the air was, the lake was not frozen, not even along the pebble-strewn shore. It was a very dark blue and stretched out to the pale blue horizon. Toward the north—well, east, actually, Betsy told herself—the land rose to form dark bluffs. Lake Superior wasn't Lake Michigan, running north and south, or the Pacific Ocean, where from San Diego one looked west; here it was a fat finger pointing southwest, and they were on the northern shore, where Minnesota formed a long, narrow arrowhead between the lake and the Canadian border.

Jill looked up and down the beach. "Here's where they put the Adirondack chairs Martha was talking about. It's like meditation to just sit and watch the lake."

Watching big water was soothing, so they did that for a minute or two. Far out, the restless surface was growing swaths of dark lavender on its deep blue. The big patterns of color had smaller, more subtle changes included in them. The sun, still well south this time of year, made golden spangles here and great, molten-brass puddles there.

Betsy's attention shifted from aesthetic to artistic. How could you capture something like that in a needlework pattern? Uneven stitch, maybe, with silks and metallics?

There was a quiet, staccato gush of the waves on the narrow beach. The eagle appeared suddenly, flying low over the surface of the water, its wings wide, its high-pitched cry a surprise in so large a bird. Betsy watched as it went up along the shore, diminished to a silhouette, then soared without effort up the split face of the dark stone bluff. The bluff was topped with a mix of pine trees standing in snow against a bright blue sky, and the eagle rose higher than their highest tops, turning around, riding a breeze. Betsy had a sudden sense of privilege, of standing in a special place.

She turned to Jill who, reading her face, laughed and said, "I see you've met Naniboujou."

"What?"

"Naniboujou, the Cree god this place is named for. This is his country. He was their god of the outdoors, though if you read his legends you realize he was also a god of joy and pranks."

"I knew there had to be an explanation for the name of this place. Tell me about him."

"Well, let's see. Oh, I know: One time, when Naniboujou was young, he saw a large flock of geese resting on the water of Gitche Gumee, which we call Lake Superior. He loved goose dinner, but he was such a large god, one goose would not make even a snack for him. And if he shot a goose with his bow and arrow, the others would fly away. So he pulled a length of bark off a white pine tree and braided a long, long twine from the fibers inside it. Then he slipped under the water, swimming up to the geese, and there he began tying their feet one to another's. Now this happened long, long ago, when Naniboujou was young and greedy, and he could not stop at nine or twelve or twenty; he had to capture the whole flock, every single one. But when he was reaching for the left foot of the last goose, he couldn't hold his breath anymore and burst through the surface to take a breath. Well, of course, the geese all flapped up into the sky. Naniboujou had hold of the end of his twine and he didn't let go, thinking he could hold them. But there were so many geese tied to that twine that instead they lifted him up into the air with them. He considered that he was a very large god, and they would soon tire and come down, but he was the one who got tired, and at last he had to let go. Down, down he fell, right into a marsh—kersplut! Up to his elbows in muck. Wet and covered with duckweed, he had to go home hungry. But to this day, geese fly in a long skein, their feet still tied together with Naniboujou's twine."

Betsy was delighted. "Is that a real story from the Cree?"

Jill nodded. "Mr. Greenfeather told it to me."

Betsy said, "That painting of him laughing must be from before he fell into the swamp and went home wet and hungry."

"Not at all—he laughs because he loves pranks, even on himself. They say if you go hunting or fishing, you should give him a pinch of tobacco or he'll run the deer off and frighten the fish away." Jill looked out over the water again. "But he isn't just a prankster, he's a god of peace, too. There was never a war fought around here, between Indian tribes or the Indians and white people."

Betsy sobered. "That makes it all the more terrible,

what's happened here now." They looked out over the water until Betsy's troubled spirit grew a little more calm, then she asked, "Do you go swimming when you come up here in summer?"

"Gosh, no," said Jill. "Lake Superior is never warm enough to swim in. It stores up cold all winter." She stepped off the snow-covered lawn onto the narrow, thickly pebbled beach. "Well, actually I suppose it might be warm enough for a short dip in September, after absorbing heat all summer. But by then the air is too chilly. Superior holds on to its summer heat so well it never freezes when winter comes again. At least this part of it doesn't. Further north cars can drive on the ice out to the islands. And of course Duluth Harbor freezes. They make a big deal of the ice finally going out in the harbor, so shipping can resume."

She stooped to pick up a stone, rub it with a mittened thumb to see if it was worth keeping, and throw it far out into the water. She threw like a man, putting her back into it, and the stone went surprisingly far. "The average life expectancy of someone falling off a boat into Lake Superior is eight minutes."

A great swath of lake began lightening into a sky blue. "Why do big bodies of water change colors like that?" asked Betsy.

"Beats me," said Jill. "But have you noticed how each one seems to have its own set of colors? The Gulf of Mexico has a light green you never see up here, and there's a shade of blue on Superior I haven't seen anywhere else."

"Yes, it's about a what, DMC 312?"

Jill laughed. "And you still think you're not a stitcher! And that's not all stitching has taught you, Miss Sharp Eyes. Come on, let's follow the shore this way." Jill walked south—well, west—okay, southwest—along the shore, past the snow-covered lawn to where naked, red-stemmed brush choked the land, to where the gravelly beach widened. The brush thinned out and Betsy realized they were coming to the mouth of a river.

The river was frozen, its ice lumpish under the snow. At its mouth, Betsy could see water flowing from under the ragged edge of ice into the lake.

Jill said, "This is the Brule, and not quite a mile from where we're standing is the Devil's Kettle Falls."

Betsy looked up the river. "Have you seen them?"

"Oh, sure. It's a nice waterfall, all set in rocks and coming down in two stages. There's a trail up along this side of the river to it, but at the end you have to go down some stairs."

"It is a big waterfall?"

"Pretty big. Each stage is maybe fifteen feet high. A lot of water comes over it, thousands of gallons a minute."

Betsy stared at Jill. "How big is the hole in this rock the water goes into?"

"About ten feet across."

"A hole that big, and thousands of gallons a minute? Parker Lundquist must be thinking of an enormous aquifer! No, he's got to be wrong, the water has to be just pouring out somewhere, if not downstream, then somewhere else."

"I assure you, it doesn't. The Brule and its waterfall is in a state park visited by thousands of people who tramp over every square foot of the place, and none of them have ever reported finding a previously unknown spring or river that water could come out in."

"Maybe it feeds a lake, and the water flows in from the bottom, so the dye they put into it was never seen on the surface."

"There are no lakes in this area. None. Well"—she turned and looked out over Superior—"there is this one humongous one. Anyway, dye floats, so someone would have seen it coming out no matter where. No, the water just disappears down this big old hole, like a drainpipe into Hades."

Betsy walked a few yards up the shore of the river to look and listen some more. A ten-foot-wide hole that had no apparent bottom . . . Upriver, she could see a bridge that took the highway over the river, but not beyond that. Nor could she hear anything. "You said there's a trail? I don't see one."

"It starts on the other side of the highway, in the park. But it's no good for cross-country skis. Too narrow, with lots of low branches and underbrush."

"Who wants to ski up it? But we could walk up it, couldn't we?"

"You saw what it was like to walk across the lawn back there. You want to do that for a mile going in— and another mile back? No, we'd have to use snowshoes, and if you think cross-country skiing is a workout, just try snowshoes."

"Is there a road we can drive up?"

"No. Do you seriously want to go up there?"

"Yes, I think I do."

"Well, we can ski up the river."

Betsy looked at the uneven surface of the river and said, "Is it safe? I thought Parker said the falls aren't frozen."

"And they probably aren't. But you can see that the river is. I've done it before, the ice is safe. It's an easy trip, not so many ups and downs as the trail. We'll get off the river before the falls, climb up the bank, and look down into the kettle."

Betsy sighed surrender. "I knew you were going to find some way to get me on those skis," she groused.

Jill laughed like Naniboujou's portrait, head back and mouth open. "All right, let's go get the skis. And tell James where we're going."

"Why does he need to know?"

"Because if we fall and hurt ourselves, we don't want to lie there until that almost-a-ranger decides to come along and finds our frozen bodies."

9

Betsy went with Jill, back to the lodge then out to her car, where they donned light, narrow skis that fastened to their boots only at the toe. Each taking a pair of poles, they started back along the lawn toward the lake's edge. It was a lot easier skimming the surface of the snow than crunching through and having to lift one's feet high to take the next step, Betsy decided.

"What's this?" she asked, stopping beside some marks in the snow. They came from the distant highway across the lawn, swooping close to the back door, down nearly to the lake before turning around and going back the way it had come in. It was the ski trail she had seen earlier, but now she noticed a difference from the trails she and Jill were leaving. The skis that made this were wider, deeper, and set well apart. And the skier had apparently dragged something behind him that fit neatly between the skis.

"Snowmobile," said Jill. "There's a constant fight going on in the legislature about whether to expand or cut back on the snowmobile trails, especially in the state parks. Meanwhile they run everywhere, in the parks, across private property, and along the shoulders of roads. Snowmobiles are noisy and fun, but dangerous when the driver is a child or drunk. People either love 'em or hate 'em, nobody's neutral."

But Betsy thought perhaps she might be neutral. She understood the desire for a wilderness experience unbroken by the stink and snarl of engines. On the other hand, a snowmobile was a fast, easy, exciting way of getting far back into the woods. One could always shut the engine off to enjoy the silence after one arrived.

They went back to the mouth of the Brule, skied alongside it for a while, then edged gingerly onto the snow-covered ice. Up here were the tracks of several skiers who had done likewise, avoiding the thin ice near the lake. By the time they were as far as the highway, they were in a head-high rock canyon. The river narrowed as they went up it, but on the other side of the bridge it was still over twenty feet across.

"This is some of the oldest rock in the world," said Jill, nodding toward the rusty brown and black bluffs on either side of them. "Older than the dinosaurs. Parker can say it's not granite, but it's as hard as granite, so it took a long time for the river to carve this deep."

"Uh-huh," said Betsy, a little breathlessly, picking herself up. Again. The surface of the river was uneven, and the drape of the snow didn't always tell the truth about what was under it.

Out of sight of the highway, the canyon deepened to over thirty feet. "The riverbed is full of big rocks," said Jill conversationally, stopping yet again so Betsy could both regain her feet and catch her breath. "The water flows over the rocks and freezes unevenly. But down underneath, it's still flowing. If you listen you can hear it."

And standing in the deep silence of a forest in winter, Betsy listened. Sure enough, there was a faint gurgle underfoot. "Are you sure the ice is thick enough to hold us?" she asked, shifting her weight back onto her skis instead of leaning so much on the points of her poles.

"Oh, yes. But if you do go through, try to grab hold of the downstream edge of the ice with your arms so you don't get swept under. The current's pretty swift here, but it's a long way down to the lake. I don't know if you could hold your breath that long."

Betsy stared at Jill, who didn't seem to be kidding. She looked around. The snow-covered surface would give no hint of a crack. Despite the evidence that others had safely come before them, Betsy wondered if maybe they should walk along the shore—except that wasn't possible. The dark canyon walls rose vertically on either side. Here and there a bush or small evergreen clung, but too few and far apart to be much aid to a person trying to climb to the top. They had to continue on the river.

"Don't worry, it's never given way to me or anyone else that I know of." Jill started off again, pushing hard on her poles. "Come on, let's keep moving."

Betsy trailed behind awkwardly, legs and arms complaining at the unaccustomed exercise. Jill went into the long, graceful movements of the experienced cross-country skier. Betsy tried to emulate her, but soon she was breathless again. This was worse than the cross country trip Jill had taken her on back in December. She realized that going upstream meant they were going up-hill. There wasn't any level place to just glide along, or any downhill place to slide.

The further they went, the steeper the incline became. As she tired, there seemed to be ever more lumps and dips where the water had apparently frozen in the act of moving over boulders. Jill seemed to find dodging among the bumps no problem, but Betsy found that between her own awkwardness and the more difficult terrain she had to stop more and more often to rest. The river was distinctly narrower here, but the slope of the canyon was less vertical, and there were more trees and bushes. In fact, just up there was an opening to a slope that was barely a slope at all, set with mature trees—and beyond it, on more steeply rising ground: What was that?

Jill, probably missing Betsy's sonorous breathing, looked around, turned, and came back. She looked where Betsy was staring. "Oh, the stairs? They built them to keep hikers from breaking branches and young trees getting down to the riverbank—The falls are just ahead and they're pretty to look at from below, too."

Betsy remembered talk about the wooden stairs, and had expected to see them. But over there, in the middle of a wilderness, was a twisting wooden staircase twenty or more landings high, much higher than the really tall trees growing near the riverbank. Almost as amazing, there were footprints in the snow that lay on the steps.

"People actually use those?" she said.

"In the summer mostly," said Jill. "If they walk the trail to see the falls, they have to come down them. They come out over there to see the foot of the falls, and then climb a steep hill beyond those trees to see the top. I guess it's lack of oxygen or something because most summertime hikers just trundle down the stairs—forgetting that the only way home is back up again. In the winter sensible people come up the river, though you can see by the footprints some people don't have good sense."

"Unbelievable," said Betsy. "Whew!" she added, feeling her knees trembling, and taking a few steps to relieve the tension in them.

Jill said, "Let's take a real rest before the final push."

She led the way to a half-fallen tree that leaned obligingly out over the water. Betsy draped herself gratefully over it for a minute, then brushed snow off and jumped up to sit on it with a heartfelt sigh.

"How much further?" she asked.

"Not far at all. If you listen, you can hear the waterfall."

Betsy cocked an ear and began to realize that not all the noise in the neighborhood was her harsh breathing. There was also the deep rush of a good-sized waterfall.

After too short a rest, Jill said, "Let's go. We don't want to start getting cold. I think we should travel along the riverbank now. The rocks along here are bigger, and the water's still excited from going over the falls, so the ice may be thinner."

The skiers who had come before them had also left the river at this point or a little beyond. Jill went to the left bank, where she took off her skis and stood them upright in the snow. Betsy followed suit, and they began to move both up and forward. It wasn't easy, the bank was steep, and her legs were still complaining about the skiing. Also, the deep snow was difficult to walk in, and what appeared to be drifts were sometimes low-growing bushes with surprising resistance in their branches. Snow leveled little hollows in the ground that ambushed their feet. Trying to keep up, Betsy brushed by spruce that sent a tumble of snow down her neck. Jill, a few yards ahead of Betsy, turned to see what the holdup was now and her feet went out from under her. She whooped in amusement as she fell. But instead of regaining her feet with her usual athletic ease, she started a half slide, half tumble backward that nearly knocked Betsy down as she came by. Betsy grabbed futilely at her, but then Jill reached and caught hold of the trunk of the snow-dumping spruce, brought herself to a halt, and stood up laughing.

"Are you all right?" called Betsy, nevertheless alarmed.

"You bet." Still chuckling, Jill dusted snow and pine needles off herself, climbed back up past Betsy, and they went on.

Soon after, Betsy felt her knees give way. She sat down in the snow. "Are we almost there?" she pleaded.

Jill did not answer. She was up and ahead of Betsy, looking downward, motionless. Betsy staggered to her feet to climb that last distance, then she, too, stood and stared.

The falls were even more impressive than Betsy expected, broader and thicker, set among huge boulders. The water was mostly white, and it split into two streams as it poured down the first step, divided by a thrusting thumb of rock. At the base, half the water swirled forward to cascade down again; the other half poured into an immense black rock split open on its flat top. The rock with its opening was half hidden under a thick coating of ice.

But the water was not flowing smoothly into the opening, as she expected. Instead the hole was throwing water outward and back up into the face of the waterfall, spurting like a full bottle held under a running faucet. Then even as they looked, the spurting stopped and water poured smoothly into the rock—only to suddenly start fountaining upward again, splashing onto the trees and rocks on the nearer shore. Everything within reach of the spatter was thickly coated with ice, the tree branches hanging heavy all around.

Betsy said, "Gosh, that's even more amazing than what you described!"

Jill said, "It's not supposed to be acting like this. Normally, the water just pours into that opening and vanishes. I've never seen it jump up and spill over like that." Jill started moving forward again. "Maybe a big rock broke loose and went in there, partly blocking it up somehow."

Betsy said, "No, no, Jill! Stop!"

"What's wrong?" Jill asked, pausing to look around.

"We're not the first ones here," Betsy said, pointing to numerous footprints near the falls, some of them ice-coated, too.

"Well, I told you, people come back here all the time."

"No, you don't understand. I don't think it's a rock blocking the inside of that kettle. Let's not go any nearer and spoil the footprints. Let's go report this right away."

10

The trip back down the river was difficult. Betsy was frightened, tired, and in a hurry, an inefficient combination that slowed progress and produced lots of tumbles.

"Go on, go ahead, tell them!" gasped Betsy at last, no longer struggling to rise.

"No, no, we're staying together," said Jill, coming back to pull Betsy to her feet by one arm.

After what seemed hours of effort, they arrived back at the lodge, unfastened their skis, and knocked the worst of the snow off themselves before hurrying in.

James was not in the lobby. Leaning on the counter to peel off her coat, Betsy said to Jill, "Will you call Sheriff Goodman? I'm too tired to make sense. Tell him to hurry."

She went into the dining room to drape her coat, hat, and mittens over the back of a chair and sit on one of the couches in front of the fire. She held out numb fingers to the flames.

He just has to believe us now, she thought. *How dreadful to put her in that kettle thing! Whoever did that thought she'd vanish forever, like a dead bug washed down the drain. Instead she's stuck inside the rock somehow, clogging it. And the water is beating down on her . . . They must come, someone has to get her out of there. He just has to believe Jill.* After a while there was the sound of china on china, and she looked up to see Frank Owen standing in front of her with a steaming cup on a saucer. As he bent to present it to her, the scent was of cocoa, not coffee.

"You looked like you could use this," he said.

"Oh . . ." Betsy's words stuck in her throat. "Th— thank you," she managed, and took it from him.

He sat down across from her. "You look cold. Did you stay out too long?" he asked.

"No," she said. "I mean, yes, I suppose so." She realized she was trembling, which he had taken for shivering. Though she was probably shivering, too. Here perhaps was the person who had put Sharon in that place, yet he was showing a casual compassion to the person who had found her. Or was he? Not very long ago, someone else tried to give her some arsenic-flavored nourishment. She took a tiny sip of the hot cocoa and said, "Ow, it's too hot."

"Sorry!" he said, and took the drink from her. "I didn't realize," he apologized.

"That's all right. Where did you get it? There's only coffee out, I thought."

"I asked the kitchen staff. You were looking very miserable, and I know how bad it can be to get really chilled. They always take good care of their guests here at Naniboujou." He pinched the cup between thumb and forefinger, testing its temperature. "I don't think it's all that hot, it's just that you're so cold. Come on, try it again. You need something to warm your inside."

"No, thank you," she said. "I—I'm not really cold."

"No? Then what's the matter?"

"I think we did too much. I'm . . . tired."

He sat back. "Where all did you go?"

He was uncomfortable asking that casual question, Betsy could tell. From their first meeting she realized he was probably like Jill, a careful guardian of his real thoughts and feelings, and therefore unwilling to pry into another's. But apparently genuine concern overrode his reticence.

Or a need to know.

Watching him closely, she said, "We went out to see the woodpile—I don't think I've ever seen so much firewood in one place before."

"Yes, they buy logs all summer, cut and split it themselves to the right size. Is that all you did? Walk around the woodpile?"

"No, then we walked along the shore, where we saw an eagle flying."

"Oh, that's The Old Codger. He's kind of a fixture around here. He doesn't fly south but stays here year-round. His favorite perch is on top of that broken birch down near the beach."

"Yes, I saw him land on it yesterday. He kind of vanishes into it, it's easy not to realize he's there. The Old Codger—has he been around for years, then?"

"Actually no. James says he turned up here three summers ago. Some guest took a photograph of him that he sold to a calendar company. It was labeled THE OLD CODGER. How far did you walk along the shore?"

Betsy said, watching for a reaction, "Not far, but then we skied up the river to the Devil's Kettle."

"Ah, that's why you're tired. Is it frozen over? A frozen waterfall is attractive, though attractiveness isn't the attraction of the Devil's Kettle." He smiled under the thick mustache. "If you know what I mean."

Either the man had nerves of steel or he knew nothing. Betsy replied, "Yes, it's the fact that half the water goes down to no one knows where. And no, it isn't frozen over."

"Any theories as to where the water goes?" he asked, again holding out the cocoa. "Are you sure you don't want this? I think it's cooled down enough to drink now."

"All right. Thank you." Betsy took it. "There's a geology grad student here studying it. He thinks there's a big, slow-moving aquifer deep underground, and that someday a fisherman will be amazed to see dye that was poured into the waterfall years ago at long last coming out into the lake."

"I'd like to be the person who sees that," said Frank, tickled at the idea. "But that aquifer must be down really deep; I understand we're sitting on top of a thousand feet of solid granite left by ancient volcanoes."

Betsy didn't want to get into a discussion of the difference between mafic rock and granite. She blew on the surface of the cocoa then took a cautious sip. It was rich and sweet, not at all too hot. "Well, the alternative theory is that the water goes down to hell, and I think I'd sooner believe in a deep aquifer than that hell is only a thousand feet down from here."

"If it were, you'd think the winters up here would be milder," he said, surprising Betsy into a chuckle.

He asked, "So if it's not because you're cold, and you weren't disappointed at the waterfall, what is it that's got you sitting here looking like a funeral?"

Betsy was at first struck speechless at this close brush with the truth, but then got angry—was he playing with her?—so she asked bluntly, "Mr. Owen, where is your wife?"

"Ex-wife," he corrected gently. "And I told you, I have no idea."

"Why did you divorce her? Because she was sick all the time?"

"I didn't divorce her, she divorced me. Not that I wasn't thinking about it. She wasn't one of those women who turn sweet in adversity."

"Why did she divorce you?"

"She said she found someone who was better at meeting her needs. His name was Eric Handel—"

"Not Eddie?" interrupted Betsy.

"No, Eric. Why?"

"Because when I talked to her, she said something about going to get Eddie. Or meet Eddie." It had been "get Eddie," hadn't it? That sounded more like a staff member than a boyfriend.

Frank was talking. ". . . it's possible the man presently meeting her needs is named Eddie. Eric was a long time ago, and they only stayed married a year."

"Was there someone else after Eric?"

"Oh, yes, several. You want names? Let's see if I can remember them all. She left Eric to come back to me, but she only stayed three months because I'd quit teaching chemistry to work in a chemistry lab, and I couldn't get clean enough for her. After that there was a fellow named . . . Jack, I think. Jack Mallow? Merrow? Merrill? He lived in San Francisco. The kids really liked him, they spent a summer out there with him and Sharon. I thought that one would last, but he didn't. Then there was Max, but after that . . . my memory fails me. There was another one or maybe two after Max, but I don't remember their names. One may have been an Eddie. But the only one she married was Eric."

"Is she seeing anyone now?"

"The last I heard, someone named Tony. She's pretty serious about him, though she's generally serious, and that can change at anytime." He cocked his head sideways at Betsy. "Maybe she's moved on to this Eddie—

dammit, now you've got me believing you saw her. No, no, there's no Eddie."

"Are Sharon and Tony living together?"

"As I understand it, she would have moved in with him, but his condo association allows pets. He hasn't got one, of course, but other condo owners do, and just walking down a hallway where a dog has been could put Sharon in the hospital."

"Her allergies are that serious?"

"Oh, I'm afraid so. Used to be, we did a lot of challenging things, but now just walking outdoors in the spring is dangerous for Sharon. She built a house specially designed for the hyper-allergic, two kinds of air filters, sealed walls and floors, everything washed only with water, baking soda, and vinegar."

"What about your children? Do they have allergies, too?"

"No, thank God. Elizabeth and Douglas are both out of school, they both have jobs, and there's never been any sign of even hay fever."

Was he talking this openly to convince her of his innocence? Or because he still halfway believed her and was trying to talk himself out of it?

Betsy asked, "That house Sharon built. That must have cost you something."

He shrugged. "Not me, it was built with her money. She can afford to build whatever kind of house she wants. She could build one like it on every continent if she wanted to."

"Oh, I didn't realize—"

"Sharon's grandmother invented a couple of gadgets, one of which still turns up on every washing machine made. That started the family fortune, but it really took off when Sharon's father proved himself brilliant in surgical instruments and real estate. But Sharon and I signed a prenup—which was fine, I make a sufficient living, especially since I only have to support myself. Because she set up a trust fund for each of our children that has fed, housed, entertained, and educated them with no strain. When they turn thirty they'll be able to access the principal and they'll become very wealthy, too. But the rest of the money, and there's still a whole lot of it, is all hers."

"Who gets it when she dies?"

"I don't know. Not me."

Betsy said, "It seems kind of sad. She could buy anything, go anywhere, but she became allergic to everything she used to love."

"It is sad. And Sharon's angry about it, which is why she's often bad company."

"Was bad company, Mr. Owen. Sharon's dead."

He bristled, a little. "Why are you so sure she's dead?"

"Because when we skied up to the Devil's Kettle, it was acting very strange, as if someone had put something inside it, something big enough to partly plug it. I'm afraid that's where Sharon's body went when it was taken out of your room."

He stared at her. "The hell you say."

"Jill's calling the sheriff now."

"Did you see her inside the kettle?"

"No, but Sharon was here and then nobody could find her, and now the Devil's Kettle is plugged with something."

He stood. "And you think—? My God, why? It could be a chunk of ice, a tree limb, even a dead raccoon!"

"Jill says she's never heard of the falls being plugged up before."

"And so you leap to the conclusion it's my dead ex-wife? How did you convince this Jill person that you're right?"

"She's a friend. And she's a cop."

"What, a captain of detectives?"

"Well . . . she's a patrol officer—"

"In some dinky town somewhere south of here. So you got her to do your dirty work, call the sheriff for you, even though nobody but you thinks Sharon is dead in the first place. Is this how you do that famous detecting, going around to different places, finding meaningless 'clues' and scaring folks?"

Betsy wondered who told him she was an amateur sleuth. "I am not scaring people needlessly, Mr. Owen," she said. "I have investigated very real crimes, and though I dislike getting involved in yet another one, it seems I have no choice until I can convince the proper authorities to take appropriate action."

"And if the sheriff refuses to take action? Then what, you call the local TV station?"

"I'll do whatever I have to—"

"If you get this story into the papers or on television, I'll encourage James and Ramona to take legal action against you!"

"Why?"

"Because you would presume to damage the reputation of their lodge, thereby hurting them and their loyal employees and their faithful customers—for no good reason!" He cut himself off with an angry gesture, turned on his heel, and walked away.

Betsy, looking after him, thought, *What if he's right?* and then, *But what if I'm right?*

The cocoa was cold. She carried the cup to the sideboard outside the kitchen and put it down next to the nearly empty and acrid-smelling coffeepot. She walked up to the lobby, saw Jill just hanging up the phone, and waited for her.

"That took a long time. What did he say?"

"It was a hard sell. I don't think he believed the falls are acting like I described. He says he's never heard of the Devil's Kettle acting that way, so I said maybe he'd better have a look. Was that Frank Owen stomping through here just ahead of you?"

"Yes, he's angry with us for hurting the reputation of the Naniboujou Lodge and its loyal employees and customers by saying someone died in one of their rooms. Jill, what if I'm wrong?"

"I don't think you are. Sharon's car is here, she had an important role to play here, she was seen here, and she doesn't seem to be anywhere else. I've listened to a lot of sadly mistaken stories, and your story doesn't sound like one of them."

They walked back to the fire, which had burned down to a few weak flames among black and broken pieces of log. Betsy selected a birch log from the little stack in the holder and put it on the coals. The firebox was hot, flames immediately leaped up to crackle eagerly at the white, paperlike bark of the log. She added another log and they sat down to watch the progress of the burning in silence, each lost in her own thoughts.

So it was a while before they realized someone was standing near, waiting patiently to be noticed.

Betsy looked up and saw a tall, extremely attractive woman with dark red hair and a scatter of freckles across a queenly nose. "Hi, I'm Liddy Owen," she said in a low, pleasant voice. When Betsy didn't at once recognize the name, she added, "You called me to ask where my mother was."

"Oh, of course!" said Betsy, standing. She asked eagerly, "Did your mother get in touch with you?"

"No," said Liddy, adding, when Betsy's face fell, "and I take it you haven't found where she went, either."

Betsy hesitated but Jill said, "No. I assume you're here because you're worried about her?"

Liddy looked inquiringly at Jill and Betsy said, "Ms.

Owen, this is Jill Cross, a friend of mine from Excelsior, where we both live."

"How do you do?" said Liddy, adding to them both, "Mama usually calls me when she's broken an engagement, once she thinks about it, in case someone else calls me looking for her. But she hasn't yet. I was at work all day Friday and at home until a couple of hours ago, so she could have gotten in touch if she wanted to." Liddy pulled off her right glove to begin unbuttoning her black woolen coat. "And I can't locate her." Under the coat she wore a finely knit cream dress embroidered with thistles around the neck. She let the coat slip off her arms and Betsy saw she had the slender figure it took to do the dress justice. She looked around the big room and said, "I haven't been up here since I was twelve, but it's just as amazing as I remember." She turned to look up at the laughing head of Naniboujou high on the far wall, surrounded by the brilliant colors of a sunrise. "I just love that painting. So happy—just like we were when we used to come up here, back when I was a little girl."

"Jill says that Naniboujou is a god of peace, the outdoors, and pranks. I should think that such a god might make a perfect summer realm for a child."

Liddy's big gray eyes searched Betsy's. "What a lovely thought! And you're right, we had such fun back before—" She turned and said, "Is there coffee?"

Jill said, "Only what's left over from lunch. It's probably pretty rank by now."

"Well, then, let's not have any. But can we sit awhile? I want to talk to you."

"Of course." All three sat down.

But Liddy apparently couldn't think how to start, so Betsy asked, "Are the other faces also Cree gods?"

"So I was told," said Liddy, looking at the wall over the French windows. "I understand one of the two at this end of the room is the god of Lake Superior." Her eyes moved over the gods painted on either side of the fireplace. "And another is the Cree god of death." Her fingers, clasped in her lap, tightened. "I hope Mama's all right."

"I hope she is, too," said Betsy.

Liddy made a wry face, one corner of her mouth pulled back, one eyebrow lifted. "Mama has never been very reliable, and I wouldn't have come, but she really did seem eager to be here, and when I found out she wasn't, I got worried."

"Could she have gone to Chicago to be with her boyfriend?" said Betsy.

"No. After we talked, I called down there to ask. But he hasn't heard from her since Thursday. Tony Campanelli is very nice, very reliable. He's younger than Mama, but Mama doesn't look her age. And she's good with Tony's children. He shares custody of his little boy and girl. They adore her, of course, just like Doogie and I did when we were their age." But she waved that away as irrelevant. "I saw Mama's car in the parking lot; I assume you did too?"

"Yes." Betsy nodded. "The sheriff was here a while ago—" She looked at Jill. "Did they search her car?"

"Yes, but they wouldn't let me come near. They didn't take anything away; her luggage is still in it. Who's Doogie?"

"My brother, Douglas."

Betsy asked, "Where is he? Is it possible your mother is with him?"

"No, I called him, too. But she wouldn't have gone to stay with him. Doogie is playing forest ranger this year, and he's got some incredibly grubby cabin outside Grand Marais, where the kitchen is a hot plate and the toilet is at the end of a path. Mama likes her comforts. She considered staying here the moral equivalent of camping." She looked around the beautiful room and smiled. "And that was before she got all those terrible allergies. I'm so glad Doogie and I didn't inherit them."

"Yes, if you're allergic to a lot of things, you couldn't be a forest ranger." Betsy smiled.

"Oh, he's not a ranger, he's kind of an apprentice. He doesn't even get to wear a uniform. He does things at the station like sweeping up and answering the phone." She shrugged and did a brief reprise of the wry face again. "But he says he likes it, he may even go back to college in the fall to study forestry."

"Does he work at the ranger station across the road?" asked Jill.

"No, in Grand Marais. That station in the Judge Magney Park isn't open in the winter. At least it wasn't when we used to come up here. God, those were happy times!" She said that devoutly, then realized she'd already said something like it, and gestured as if to erase the strong feeling in her words. "But that was a long time ago, it's old history, not important. What's important is, where on earth could Mama have gone?"

"You're from Duluth, is that right, Ms. Owen?" asked Jill.

"Yes, that's right. Call me Liddy. I probably shouldn't have come up, but it's not that long a drive, and I couldn't just sit at home waiting. You know how it is."

"I'm sorry you're being worried like this," said Betsy.

"Not your fault," said Liddy. "She probably got a call from friends going to sail around the British Virgin Islands and invited herself along for an impromptu vacation." She shook her head ruefully and asked, "Is my father still here?"

"Yes," said Betsy. "I was just talking with him before you came." She wished she hadn't said that; she could see Liddy was going to ask about that, and she didn't want to tell Liddy about her conversation about the waterfall.

She looked away and saw someone standing in the doorway to the dining room, wearing a dull orange goosedown jacket and gray denim trousers. He was a young man, tall and thin, with brown hair and a redhead's freckled complexion. His nose was slender and prominent, his mouth sensitive, his pose somehow defensive. Betsy had the curious feeling she'd seen him before.

Liddy called, "Doogie!" and stood. Of course, he looked very like her. He started for her, but Liddy gestured at him to wait, said "Excuse me" to Jill and Betsy, and hurried to meet him. She led him behind the long counter at the far end of the room and began an intense discussion.

Betsy asked, "How long do you think it will be before we hear if they found her at the falls?"

"I don't know, but it won't be right away. So let's go into the lounge."

They barely noticed the lifted heads or murmured remarks this time, so focused were their thoughts on what dreadful thing Sheriff Goodman might find in the Devil's Kettle.

Betsy got her Rose Window project out. The sun was low enough in the sky to make a strong, slanting light on the white towel she draped across her lap. But the pattern was full of pitfalls. Betsy finished another wedge in light olive and antique pink. The first wedge had been worked in horizontal and vertical stitches, the second in diagonal, then the third like the first and the fourth like the second. It seemed that just as she got used to thinking horizontally, she had to think diagonally. Betsy grumbled under her breath at the heedless cruelty of designers who made such unnecessary complications.

And each must be surrounded by the nasty, delicate

Kreinik, slowly, carefully, accompanied by more grumbling.

But held at arm's length, Betsy's grumble melted into a pleased smile, as she saw how attractive the pattern was, its subtle complexities only adding to its beauty. Only, it looked a little off balance. Perhaps because the circle wasn't finished?

"Officer Jill Cross?" called a man's rough voice. Betsy looked around. Standing in the doorway was Sheriff Goodman in his fur-collared coat. His matching hat had earflaps and a gold badge pinned to it. He lifted his chin at them, his face full of grim news.

"Come with me," muttered Jill, but Betsy was already putting her needlework into her bag.

The two hurried toward Goodman, who turned and walked away, leaving them to follow him into the center of the dining room, where a deputy waited. Doogie and Liddy were gone.

"What have you found?" Jill asked the sheriff.

"There was the body of a woman inside that hole in the rock," said Goodman. "It was a hell of a fight to get it out, we've got a deputy with a broken arm and a ranger with a wrenched back."

"I'm sorry to hear that," said Jill, her voice shocked and sincere.

"Is it Sharon Kaye Owen?" asked Betsy, ruthless in her need to know.

"It could be. The body is a blonde, real skinny, wearing a blue and white sweater under a dark blue coat. The ME thinks it wasn't in there more than a day. But of course we need someone to give us a positive ID. Is Mr. Owen still here?"

"Yes, and Sharon's son and daughter are here, too," said Betsy.

Goodman's eyebrows lifted. "They are? When did they arrive?"

"A couple of hours ago."

"They're possibly up in their father's room," offered Jill. "They're adults."

"What are their names?" asked Goodman.

"Liddy and Doogie Owen," said Betsy.

" 'Liddy and Doogie'?"

"Nicknames for Elizabeth and Douglas," said Jill.

The sheriff looked at his deputy, a short, heavyset man who looked part Indian, and jerked his head toward the lobby. "Room at the top of the stairs. I want all three." The deputy departed unhurriedly.

"Are you going to arrest them all?" asked Betsy.

Goodman looked pained. "For what? Ma'am, we don't know that she was murdered. There were a lot of footprints in the area, some leading right across the ice to that waterfall; it's possible she went to see it up close, slipped, and fell in."

Betsy wanted to shout at him that Sharon Owen couldn't have gone to see the falls, she was taken up there dead, she'd died in an upstairs bedroom rented by her ex-husband. But as she drew an angry breath, Jill caught her eye and shook her head very slightly, and Betsy bit her tongue.

"Hello?" said Liddy's voice, and they looked around to see Liddy and Doogie approaching, their father behind them with the deputy bringing up the rear.

The sheriff immediately removed his furry hat, and his face went solemn.

"Oh, my God," Liddy said, the question she was about to ask dying on her lips. Her brother suddenly looked scared, and his mouth opened, but Liddy spoke first. "What is it?" she said. "Tell us what's happened."

"Are you Sharon Owen's daughter?"

"Yes, I'm Elizabeth Owen, and this is my father, Frank Owen, and my brother, Douglas. Please—"

"We found the body of a woman under the Devil's

Kettle Falls up the Brule River. I'm very sorry to say it's possibly your mother. I'm going to ask you, Mr. Owen, to take a look at it, see if you can identify it." He was addressing Doogie, not Frank.

"Oh, no, no," said Doogie, his scared look becoming more pronounced, "I can't do that, please don't ask me to go look at her. My dad here, can't he go?"

"You are the immediate family, sir. Unless—How old are you?"

"Twenty-one." Just admitting to being of age seemed to put some backbone into the young man.

"You see," said the sheriff, "since your father and mother are divorced, he's not really next of kin."

"Oh. Well, I suppose—I mean, of course, I . . . understand. Where is . . . where is the body?"

"In Grand Marais. If you'll come with me?"

"Shall I come, too?" asked Liddy.

"No, ma'am, I don't think you'll want to see this."

"Perhaps I ought to—" began Frank.

"No sir, there's no need for you to come." His tone indicated dismissal.

"Very well." Frank touched Doogie on the arm. "We'll be waiting right here for you, son."

"Yessir." Doogie turned to Liddy. "I'll be back as soon as I can. And it'll be all right. I mean, maybe it's not her."

"That's true," said Liddy, grasping at straws. "Now you listen to the sheriff, don't do—don't make any decisions without talking to me first, understand? And Dad, too, of course."

"Yes, yes, all right," said Doogie. To the sheriff, "Let's go."

Liddy and Frank watched them leave, Frank with concern, Liddy with a painful intensity. When Liddy turned back, it was awkwardly, and her face was white.

Frank said, "Here, what's the matter?"

Jill said, pulling out a chair, "She needs to sit down. Can I get you something, Liddy? A glass of water?"

"Yes, water, thank you." Liddy put her long fingers on the table, palms hanging off the edge, and bowed her head, eyes closed.

"Now, hon, where's my brave little soldier?" Frank murmured, coming to stand behind her and put his hands on her shoulders. Without lifting her head she reached up to touch one of his hands, and her mouth firmed into a straight line.

Betsy sat down across from Liddy and said, "I'm so sorry."

She looked at her. "You think it's my mother they found, don't you?"

"Yes, I'm afraid I do."

"Why?" When Betsy didn't reply at once, Liddy demanded, "What do you know you're not telling me?" She looked at her father. "What do you know?"

Jill put a glass of water in front of Liddy and said to her, and Betsy, "Let's not borrow trouble, all right?"

And Liddy suddenly pulled herself together, shoulders squaring, chin lifting, displaying a stronger version of the backbone her brother had also found. "Yes, you're right. I'm sorry." She lifted the glass and took several small sips.

Betsy looked toward the row of French doors overlooking the parking lot, her eye caught by movement, and they all watched as Sheriff Goodman and his deputy put Doogie into the patrol car's backseat. It wasn't until the car's headlights came on that Betsy realized the swift purple twilight of winter had fallen.

Too awful how the world goes right on, thought Betsy, remembering how it continued after her sister was buried. Here, too, the sun had gone down. The delicious smell of roast beef had grown strong without her noticing. Soon the stitchers would be coming in to eat and drink and talk about silk and overdyed floss, and how seductive linen was to stitch on. Betsy felt cold and stiff, and wished she were home.

How much worse this must be for Liddy!

They stayed at the table they were sitting at as the stitchers came in. The waitress took Liddy's name and advised the kitchen they'd need an extra meal. The beef was prime rib, tender and medium rare, just the way Betsy liked it. But she couldn't do it justice, and Liddy ate only a few bites. Jill and Frank, on the other hand, conscientiously cleaned their plates, and kept the conversation firmly on cross-country skiing.

They had nearly finished dessert when Doogie came back. He looked badly shaken. "It's her," he said, pulling a chair away from a nearby table and sitting down hard.

"Oh, my God!" said Liddy. "Oh, no, oh, no!"

"Oh, yes," said Doogie flatly. "What's more, they asked some damn hard questions about where I was on Friday. I don't know why they talked to me like that. It's perfectly clear to anyone with a brain that she was glad to be visiting a place she loved, that because it was winter there were no allergens to keep her from taking a hike to the falls. They even agreed I could be right, that she got here and went for a hike in Judge Magney Park, and walked right to the edge of the falls from up on top, where the ice broke and she fell in. They said the opening in the top of the rock narrows inside, so she stopped it up instead of going on down." He locked eyes with Liddy and said, "It was horrible, having to see her like that. I couldn't even tell it was her at first, because she was so beat up from being inside the Devil's Kettle. Our mama was so beautiful, but this person I saw was all crooked and—"

Liddy made a faint sound of protest, swayed, and fell out of her chair.

"For God's sake, Douglas!" barked Frank, moving swiftly to kneel beside her. Doogie rose, looking stern rather than apologetic. Jill whipped around to kneel on the other side.

James appeared as if out of nowhere. "What's the problem?" he asked. "Shall I call an ambulance?"

"She fainted, that's all," said Doogie with a curious indifference. James backed off but hovered at a distance.

Jill was checking her for injuries, murmuring in a soothing voice. Frank lifted her limp hand to rub it gently while Doogie and Betsy watched.

At last Liddy muttered something and Frank lifted her back into her chair. He patted and stroked her hand some more. "Are you all right now, soldier?" he asked.

"Yes, yes, 'm all right," she said, her voice tired and cross, pulling her hand free. "Sorry, I'm sorry, making a spectacle of myself. Oh, Mama, Mama!" Frank knelt to offer a shoulder, and she wept on it.

James, satisfied the emergency was over, went away.

After a bit, Doogie said, "Take it easy, Liddy, take it easy." He gave a hard look at the the people at the nearby tables, who turned away, embarrassed.

"Is there anything we can do?" asked Betsy when Liddy's weeping slowed nearly to a halt.

"Oh, I think you've done enough," said Frank.

"What—what do you mean?" asked Liddy, lifting her head to look wildly at her brother, who shrugged, then back at her father.

"I'm not talking about your brother, but these two. Didn't they tell you? That one"—he pointed at Betsy—"says she saw your mother dead on my bed yesterday afternoon." His voice swelled with anger. "She and her friend here call the sheriff out and he searches my room, searches the whole damn lodge. Can't find hide nor hair of her, of course. Then she and her friend go on a hike up the Brule and come back saying they saw the waterfall acting strange and they get the sheriff and his deputies out there, and they find Sharon's body inside the Devil's Kettle.

"Now the sheriff is looking slantwise at us because of this one's story, but you two weren't even here on Friday, and I haven't seen Sharon in months! What's more, no one else saw Sharon here at Naniboujou. I told the sheriff that when he was here the first time, and I told the deputy when he came up to my room. When he says what do I think, I said to him what I say to you: Look at the ones who are telling all these strange stories, the ones who see Sharon when nobody else does, the ones who told the sheriff where to find Sharon's body. Look at these two!"

11

Frank Owen's voice had been getting louder and louder, and more and more attention was being paid to him. By the end of his speech the whole room was looking their way. Without being aware of the attention, or not caring, Frank left the room.

The diners broke into murmurs. Liddy, casting angry looks at Jill, then Betsy, stood and hurried out after her father, Doogie close behind. Betsy heard Doogie murmur, "Isn't Dad brilliant?" to his sister's back.

A waitress, bearing down on Betsy's table with a fresh dinner, stared after Doogie, then shrugged and headed back for the kitchen.

Betsy turned her face to her plate to avoid her eyes being caught by anyone sitting nearby.

"Heck!" muttered Jill, the sincerity in her voice lending weight to the mildness of the epithet.

"What are we going to do?"

"Nothing!" said Jill, and raised her own voice. "You told me, you told the staff, you told the sheriff she was dead, and no one believed you. Now she turns up dead. All that means is you were right. The fact that the body was moved from where you saw it indicates foul play. Sharon Kaye told you she was here to see Frank, to try to get their relationship back on track. It was his room you saw the body in, but someone took it away. You had obviously never been to the Devil's Kettle before I took you there this afternoon, at which point Sharon's body had been inside it for hours." Betsy had looked at Jill when she started speaking and Jill never broke eye contact, but she was addressing the room. "The police don't suspect you. Why should they? You're not lying or hiding facts, you're the one reporting what you find. They're suspicious of the obvious person, the person who knew Sharon, the person Sharon was coming to see, the person in whose room she died!"

The room filled again with murmurs. Jill took a bite of apple crumble and said, much more quietly, "That'll fix 'em."

And indeed it did. Before leaving the dining room, perhaps half of the stitchers came by the table, casual and friendly (as if they hadn't made imputative remarks in the lounge earlier, or listened minutes ago with growing belief to Frank Owen's accusations).

Nan wanted to know if Jill had ever known another murderer who tried to get rid of a body in some strange way, and Linda Savareid remarked that of course it would have taken a strong man to carry a dead body through all that snow up to the Devil's Kettle.

Which was something that hadn't occurred to Betsy. There had been ski trails on the river and footprints on those remarkable wooden stairs. And all around the falls. Jill said it would be a very difficult walk up the snow along the river without snowshoes. How much more difficult while carrying a dead body. Who but someone in fine physical condition could do that, much less venture to climb that steep bank or come down those many icy steps?

Isabel came by to say, "I think this whole thing is so sad. Frank was disappointed and impatient with Sharon over her illness, but I will admit, Sharon treated Frank shamefully."

"Frank was as understanding and patient with Sharon as it is possible to get!" muttered Carla to Isabel as she brushed by her. She did not look at Jill or Betsy.

The last person to stop by was Sadie Cartwright, rolling up in her wheelchair. "Now that they've found the body just where you said it was, we'll see some action, right? Who do you think moved it? Not Frank, he's too obvious. It's always the least obvious one, isn't it? I think it's Doogie. Who would suspect a person with a silly name like that?"

And with another of her loud laughs, she whirled away.

Betsy said, "Gosh, she's annoying!" She turned back to Jill. "I wonder what time Carla checked in on Friday?"

"That may not matter," Jill pointed out. "I didn't need a key to open the back door to our wing, and I wouldn't need one to get into the other wing, either. Anyone who has been here before might know that." Jill sat back in her chair and looked hard at Betsy. "Decision time, girl."

"What do you mean?"

"I mean, when the autopsy shows Sharon Kaye Owen wasn't drowned, they are going to arrest Frank Owen, if only for attempting to hide a death. If that's okay with you, fine. On the other hand, if you don't think Frank is guilty of any crime, then you have to decide whether or not you're going to try to get to the bottom of this mess. Whatever you decide, I'll be with you. But this speculating and prying while claiming you don't want to damage your psyche with another investigation is getting old."

Betsy said angrily, "I am not—Well, so what if I try to figure out what happened? Everyone in this room was talking about it, you heard them!"

"They're going back to the lounge to stitch. What are you going to do?"

Betsy fell silent. What she had planned to do was go ask James if he could tell her who was checked in by 3 P.M. on Friday.

Jill said, "Face it, you have the biggest curiosity bump in Excelsior, which makes you probably the nosiest person in the state—if not the entire upper Midwest. Plus, you have a gift for investigation. I know that combination has brought you all kinds of grief, but on the other hand, there are two murderers and one would-be murderer whose names would be unknown if it wasn't for that gift. Only you know if that's a fair exchange. But the question has to be answered, you can't keep whipsawing yourself like this."

Betsy sighed. Jill waited her out. At last Betsy said, "I appreciate your unwavering support of my wavering. I really, really don't want to get involved in murder anymore. The quiet life has never looked so attractive to me. On the other hand, I had a nice talk with Frank Owen earlier today, and I liked him. It's not just that he seemed nice—because he wasn't when he thought I might hurt some innocent people—his reactions to my questions were of a crystalline innocence I found convincing. I don't think he's guilty of murder."

Jill said, "And you're going to report all this to the sheriff, and let him investigate?"

"Yes. So okay, he can ask James about check-in times."

"So it's back to the lounge, right?"

"Yes, let's go see if Carla is in there. I'm wondering

if her bad-mouthing Sharon has less to do with a dislike
of Sharon than a liking for Frank."

Jill coughed, fist to mouth, and followed Betsy to the
lounge. Carla was not there.

Jill said, "She'll probably be here in a minute. Meanwhile, Ginni Berringer promised to show me a project
she's working in Schwalm embroidery. I know you used
to do embroidery, so let's both go see it."

Ginni was a plump woman with dark eyes and dark
hair pulled back into a little bun. The embroidery was
done in white coton Broder on 32-count white linen,
hearts and tulips in a design that made Betsy think of
rosemaling, or the kind of artwork produced by the
Pennsylvania Dutch. Ginni was an advanced embroi-
derer, Betsy used to embroider, so in another minute the
pair were talking about coral knots, chain stitch, and
buttonhole scallops. "I've pulled every fourth thread inside the heart," Ginni said, "and I'm about to start the
eyelet filling."

"Very nice," said Betsy.

"I wouldn't want to try that," said Jill, who had never
done embroidery. "But it's very handsome." She went
off to do more work on her tiger.

In another minute Betsy said, "I think I'll quit both-
ering you with questions and join her."

Betsy got her canvas bag and pulled out the rose window pattern. Slowly and carefully, with only two errors
found immediately and corrected, she finished the last
wedge. She clipped a short length of the Kreinik, consulted the pattern, looked at the wedge—and saw she
had started it a stitch further over than the pattern called
for. Growling softly, she frogged—rip it, rip it, rip it—
the error out and started working it again. But after a
dozen stitches she saw that while she had corrected its
placement in relation to the previous wedge, now it
didn't sit correctly in relation to the inner medallion. Or

the first wedge, which was next to it. She looked back at the previous wedge, and saw it, too, didn't sit where it should in relation to the center.

Jill heard her groan of dismay and asked, "What's wrong?"

"I have messed up big time. These last two wedges are wrong. It would break my heart to frog them. I know people find a way to work around an error, but I can't see how to do that here. Can you?"

Jill shook her head. "I'm sorry. Counted cross stitch broke my heart years ago and I gave it up. Maybe you should talk to Nan or Sadie or someone else here who does counted."

But Betsy couldn't face the other questions that would come if she initiated a conversation.

"I'll ask them tomorrow. It's getting late, I think I'll just go up to bed."

She wasn't all that sleepy, just tired and discouraged. She brushed her teeth and discontentedly got into her pajamas. As she crawled between the sheets, she wondered if she should take some aspirin against the muscle soreness she would probably wake up with because of that strenuous trek up and back down the frozen Brule, but the thought was only half formed before she slid off a dark cliff into slumber.

Soon she was in a canoe floating down a fast-moving river. It was summertime. The banks were level, scattered with trees and flowers. But the water was a little rough, complicating her efforts to work on a counted cross-stitch pattern of a big barking basset hound.

Suddenly a roar ahead indicated she was coming to a waterfall, and she knew it was the Devil's Kettle. Unless she paddled for shore, she would dive, canoe and all, into that hollow black rock and never be seen again. She began stitching faster, because she could not put down the stitchery until it was finished. The water grew

rougher, the canoe bouncing over the rapids, and it became difficult to get the needle through the right place
from underneath. Fumbling with it, the needle slipped
out of her fingers and came off the thread to fall into
the bottom of the canoe. Somebody on the shore shouted
at her to hurry, the water was cold. She bent over to
look for the needle among the leaves and pine needles
that covered the ribs on the bottom of the canoe, and
noticed she was barefoot. The roar got louder, but bending over was all right, because she didn't want to watch
the falls come closer and closer. As the person on shore
shouted at her to stop, she felt the canoe tip over the
falls, and woke with a start. She was alone in bed.

There was a conversation in distressed voices going
on out in the hall. "I'm all right, please stop fussing!"
someone was saying.

Betsy climbed out of bed and reached for her robe,
holding it around her shoulders with one hand while she
hurried to the door and opened it.

Jill was out there, wrapped in her thick terry robe,
with auburn-haired Liddy in a lush, cream-colored,
ankle-length silk nightgown trimmed in ecru lace, sun
tanned Carla in a pale green chiffon peignoir, and plump
Isabel in a pink flannel nightgown stitched with her in-
itials in elaborate script. Liddy was barefoot, tousled, her
eyes wide and confused, tears streaking her cheeks.

"What's going on?" asked Betsy.

"Sleepwalking," said Jill.

"I'm fine, I'm awake now," said Liddy.

"She's staying in my room, and I heard her open the
door on her way out," said Isabel. "I got up and called
her name, then realized she was sleepwalking. They say
not to wake them, but I followed because I was afraid
she might fall down the stairs."

Carla said, "Isabel knocked on my door as they went
by, and I came out, and I told her she should take Liddy

gently by the hand and lead her back to bed."

Isabel continued. "But I didn't want to because what if she woke up, and just then your door opened and it was Jill. She said it's okay to wake sleepwalkers, if you do it gently. But by then Liddy was halfway down the stairs. I still thought we shouldn't touch her, but Jill insisted, so we let her go get her, and sure enough, as soon as she took her by the arm, Liddy woke up and started crying."

Jill said, "She's scared, that's all."

Liddy, who wasn't crying now, said, "I'm telling you, I'm all right."

Isabel said, "I told her, 'Hurry, let's get her back to bed before she catches her death of cold.' I mean look at her, barefoot on a night like this! But see how she's crying. I don't know if Jill did the right thing."

Jill said, "If we'd left her alone, she might have gone outside."

"I wouldn't have done that!" exclaimed Liddy. When she saw them looking at her, she went on, shamefaced. "I don't know what made me walk in my sleep. I haven't done that since I was a child. I'm sure I won't do it again."

"What were you dreaming about, do you remember?" asked Betsy.

"No. Actually, I don't think I was dreaming," said Liddy. She wiped her cheeks with the backs of her hands and sniffed hard. "I'm sorry for creating such a disturbance—again. It seems to be what I do up here, fall out of my chair, walk in my sleep, scare people."

"We're not in the least afraid, we all know you're upset about your mother," said Isabel, taking her by an elbow and leading her away. "Good night," she said firmly over her shoulder, a hint to the others to return to their rooms.

"Well!" said Betsy a few minutes later, climbing back

into bed. "What do you think about that?"

"I think Isabel's right. Liddy is upset about her mother. It's sad when a parent dies, and Sharon died in an awful way. Liddy came up here because she was worried about her, remember. I wonder if it's true she wasn't dreaming? She was rubbing her fingers as if they were cold."

"I was having a bad one," said Betsy. "I dreamed that I was about to go over the falls in a canoe." She began squirming around and pulling at her too-big pajama bottoms to smooth away a fold. "Maybe you should go order her not to sleepwalk, like you told me not to have any more nightmares last night. It worked, you know."

Jill sighed, but gently, and said in a firm voice, "No more bad dreams. That's an order."

"Yes, ma'am," said Betsy, composing her mind to obedience.

And again, it worked.

"You should bottle that voice," Betsy said the next morning at the breakfast table. "Or, anyway, sell recordings of it."

Jill protested, "You are the one in control of your own head. Just listen when you order yourself not to have any more bad dreams. You don't need me to do that."

Betsy took her first bite of Wake Up Huevos—eggs scrambled with tomatoes, jalapenos, cilantro, scallions, and a hint of garlic, served over tortilla strips and topped with sour cream, grated cheddar, and salsa—and focused intently on that. "Wow," she murmured, and took a second bite to confirm it was as good as it had seemed. "Forget the cattle drive, let's come up here again in September," she said.

Off and on, Jill and Betsy talked about going on a late-summer cattle drive offered by a dude ranch. Jill said, "Speaking of that, I found a new place, not a dude ranch, that allows people who can ride to come along.

It costs a thousand dollars for two weeks. They supply the horses, but you have to be able to ride and work cattle."

Betsy hadn't been on a horse since she started getting plump—or had she started getting plump when she gave up riding? Now she was wealthy enough to afford a health club membership and lose that weight, get back in shape. She put down her fork, immediately determined to at least not put on another pound.

Because she could just see herself rounding up strays while dust kicked up, and the cattle bawled, and the cowboys whistled at the herd to keep it moving. And maybe a cow with a sore back would need to be cut out to have it doctored. Savvy cow ponies did all the work of cutting a steer out of the herd; all a rider did was aim him at a cow and hang on.

Betsy had attended a horse show at which there was a cutting contest. A horse had to separate a steer from a small herd and keep it from returning. Betsy remembered how badly the cow had wanted to rejoin its fellows, and how that horse had jumped and dodged so nimbly it was a wonder the skilled rider wasn't flung off. She said, "Do you know someplace I can get some riding lessons? Now I think about it, I'm kind of rusty."

Jill said thickly, around a sticky pecan muffin, "I'll check into that. Have you ever ridden a quarter horse?"

"No, but I rode a mustang for a couple of years."

That began an animated discussion about horses. Betsy picked unconsciously at her *huevos* while they talked until she suddenly realized she was looking down at a clean plate. The food here was simply too good to resist.

They were having a final cup of coffee when Sheriff Goodman sat down at their table as abruptly as if he'd been teleported into the chair. "Where's Elizabeth Owen?" he asked without preamble.

Betsy and Jill both craned their necks, looking around. "I don't see her," Betsy said at last.

"Liddy had a bad night last night," said Jill. "I guess she's sleeping in this morning."

"She's staying here, then?"

"She was in Isabel's room last night," said Betsy. "I don't know about Doogie." She looked at the lawman. "You've got news?"

"Sharon Kaye Owen was dead before she was put in that hole in the rock. From the look of her lungs, the Cook County medical examiner thinks she was suffering a severe, possibly lethal, allergic reaction. He's asking the Mayo Clinic down at Rochester to do fancier tests than he can. But you see how that makes it more likely that what you told me about seeing her body in Mr. Owen's room Friday afternoon is true. You're sure it was Mr. Owen's room?"

"It was on the second floor, a room painted green, with a fireplace, and whose door is at an angle to the corridor. There is no other room on the second floor of the lodge with a fireplace except ours, and our room is paneled in knotty pine."

"You're sure you went up to the second floor?"

"Absolutely."

"But Mr. Owen wasn't in there when you went in?"

"No. I tried to use my key and it didn't work, but when I tried the door, it was unlocked."

Jill said, "It has occurred to us that it was very foolish of Mr. Owen to leave the body in an unlocked room, but the door wasn't locked when the two of us went to talk with him later, and it was unlocked when your crew arrived to search the room. He apparently doesn't lock his door when he stays here."

Goodman shrugged. "Hardly anyone locks their doors at the lodge." He looked around the room. "Have you seen Frank Owen this morning?"

"Wait a minute," said Betsy. "Are you going to arrest him?"

"No, I'm going to have a little talk with him." He looked around the room. "Is he here?"

Jill said, "He's over there," and nodded toward the big stone fireplace.

Betsy looked in that direction and saw him at one of the larger tables, where the geologist Parker Lundquist sat with Anna, Isabel, Carla, and three other women. When the sheriff stood, Owen glanced over, and his face became still. The others at the table looked where he was looking, and they, too, became still. It was like an infection, that stillness. By the time the sheriff reached the table, no one else in the room was moving or talking.

Goodman bent over and spoke very quietly to Frank, who nodded gravely and stood. "I'll see you later," he said, or something like it, to the others at his table, and they nodded confusedly at him, not sure whether to believe him, pretend they believed him, or openly doubt him.

As Goodman escorted Owen from the room, a wave of whispers followed behind them, which broke into speech the instant they reached the lobby.

"Did you see that?" seemed to be the gist. A few dared the scorn of their fellows by adding, "I knew it, I just knew it."

There was a high-pitched cry of rage from the lobby. Jill was on her way toward the sound before Betsy could stand, but she hurried to catch up.

In the lobby were Liddy and Doogie, a single suitcase between them. Liddy was in a hysterical rage, shouting at the sheriff, "He's done nothing, nothing! You can't take him! I'll have you fired if you don't let go of him!"

"Ma'am, ma'am," the sheriff kept saying, stepping back with one hand on Frank's arm, the other reaching to ward her off, "he's not under arrest. We just want to talk to him."

Doogie moved to stand between Liddy and the lawman, facing her. "Listen to me, soldier," he said very firmly. "You are behaving like a little girl, and we can't have that. This is a serious situation, and you need to pull yourself together."

"He's right, Liddy," said Frank, and to the sheriff, "May we go upstairs and get my coat and hat?"

"Yessir, no problem."

"But, Daddy, Daddy!" cried Liddy. "You can't leave me! Make them let you go, I want you to come home with me!"

"I can't do that right now, soldier. But I won't be long. You stay here until I get back."

"I can't! I can't!"

"Of course you can," he said. "I expect you to calm down right now."

And amazingly, she took a shuddering breath and fell silent.

"Here—" He pulled his room key from his pocket and gave it to the sheriff. "Let's go up."

Liddy, her eyes two blue wounds, stared after him. "I'll be brave," she whispered. "But I want to go home."

"We're not going home until we find out what's going to happen," said Doogie. "Dad might need us, and we both had better be on the spot, ready to do whatever needs doing." Liddy nodded, then closed her eyes and put her face on her brother's chest. After a moment, Doogie put a stiff arm around her and stood firm. This controlled young man was a striking change from the scared boy of yesterday.

Betsy caught a movement from the corner of her eye and turned to see Carla come into the lobby. "What's going on out here?" she demanded.

"The sheriff is taking my father away!" cried Liddy.

This confused Carla, as obviously the sheriff was following Frank upstairs.

Doogie said, "They're going to get his coat, then he's taking him into Grand Marais."

"I can't bear it, I can't bear it!" Liddy wept.

Carla stepped around Doogie to take Liddy from behind, saying gently, "Come up to my room, both of you."

"No," said Doogie. "The two of us are going up to Dad's room as soon as they leave."

"Please, will you come with us?" said Liddy, surprising Doogie.

Before he could object, Carla said, "Of course, baby, of course."

Betsy said, "If you don't mind, I would like—"

"Not now," said Carla. "Not now." Her voice continued, sweet and gentle, and already Liddy's anguished sobs were lessening as they vanished up the stairs, Doogie following close behind.

In another minute, Frank came back down with Sheriff Goodman, and they went out to the parking lot without either of them so much as nodding at Jill or Betsy. Through the window set into the door, they watched as the sheriff led Frank by the elbow to his patrol car and put him into the back seat. Beyond them, the lodge maintenance man came out of the furnace shed brushing bits of bark off his front. He halted and stared at the scene in front of him.

Jill said quietly, "Poor fellow—but no wonder Liddy likes Carla. When you're brokenhearted, you naturally prefer 'baby' to 'soldier.' "

Betsy started to reply, but turned it to a wordless exclamation, and ran out the door to the parking lot. Jill started to follow, but stopped on the little front deck to watch as Betsy, slipping and shouting and waving her arms, ran up the lane after the patrol car. Its brake lights came on, and Betsy, huddled against the cold, bent to speak to the sheriff. Then she went around to climb in the back, and the car's backup lights came on.

When the car stopped beside the door, Betsy climbed out and rushed in. "Where is it?" she said.

"What?" asked Jill.

"That floss I found out by the shed. Where is it?"

"How should I know? Last I saw it, you were putting it in your coat pocket."

Betsy fled into the dining room.

"I'll wait here," the sheriff said, and Jill stared at him uncomprehendingly.

12

Betsy dodged among the tables as she dashed across the dining room, through the door, up the stairs, and into her room. She was back a minute later to hand the floss to the sheriff. "See if—it's pure cotton—or not," she gasped, all out of breath.

"Why, what's this about?"

"Murder. If this floss is—something other than pure cotton—If it's got peanut oil, pollen—dust, cat hair—wheat flour, dried milk—anything Mrs. Owen—was allergic to—this—this could be—murder weapon."

Goodman looked at the slim lavender skein. "Where did you get this?"

"Out by the furnace shed. Dropped."

"And you probably didn't pick it up with tweezers or keep it in a plastic bag."

Betsy waved a finger at him. "You—there first—didn't find it at all." Jill cleared her throat, and Betsy flinched and then said more humbly, "No, I put it in my coat pocket."

"Uh-huh."

But Goodman put it in his shirt pocket, buttoned the flap down, and went away.

Betsy went into the dining room and sat wearily on the Victorian round couch with the pillar growing out of its center.

"All right, tell me what that was about," Jill said.

"I remember that Sharon Kaye put the end of her floss in her mouth to wet it before threading her needle. Stitchers who do that, do that habitually. Someone who knew Sharon was a floss licker might think to switch flosses, put something she was allergic to in place of her cotton floss, or dip the floss into something she was allergic to. Or spray the floss with something. But then the evidence had to be destroyed. Remember that place in the snow by the furnace shed, where it looked like someone fell?"

Jill nodded.

"Okay, that was him. Or her. The idea was to get rid of the body and everything of Sharon Kaye's he could get hold of, any proof she had been here at all. He, or she, was in a hurry. He was carrying everything, including her project bag, out to the furnace, and he slipped and fell, and in his haste to pick everything up, he missed one little something. I think it's a very important thing."

"The lavender floss."

"Yes, I remember she was using lavender floss. And though I very cleverly found it, I didn't realize its significance and much less cleverly put it in my pocket and forgot all about it. I hope they don't delay the test, or have to send it away to get it tested."

"I can't imagine the lab test for fibers is all that elaborate. We'll probably know fairly soon."

"But that's not all. There is no Eddie. What she said was, 'I have to go get my EpiPen.' "

"Are you sure? Wait a second, why did she have to leave to get it? People who need them have them at hand. Why wasn't it right there with her?"

"Because it was in her purse, and she didn't have her purse with her. All she had was her canvas sewing bag. "Maybe she went right up, as soon as she arrived. If Frank was out, she couldn't ask him if she could stay, so she didn't bring her luggage up to his room."

"So why didn't she bring the coat and purse down again?"

"Maybe she was pretty sure she could convince him to take her in. Or she did bring them down and left them—where?"

"In the ladies' room," said Jill. "There's a coat rack in there."

"Then her murderer is a woman," said Betsy. "Because she went in there to retrieve them and bring them up to Frank's room, where I saw them."

"That all fits. But why was her car still here, then? If the murderer had her purse, he had her keys."

Betsy blinked at Jill and felt the confident structure she'd been building sway dangerously.

From the other side of the counter came the sound of someone rapping on a table. Isabel's voice said, "Good morning, everyone!" with no trace of her usual good humor. Jill and Betsy stood to watch.

Isabel was standing in front of the fireplace, hands raised to command attention. She continued. "I'm sorry to be the bearer of bad news for those of you who haven't already heard—though I suspect that's very few of you. Sharon Kaye Owen of Escapade Design was found dead in Judge Magney State Park yesterday. And as you just saw, Cook County Sheriff Goodman took her ex-husband away for questioning. This is very sad and distressing for those of us who knew Sharon Kaye and Frank. Sharon was so vibrant, and Frank always seemed so very pleasant." She paused and showed her own distress by intertwining her fingers and squeezing them into painful configurations. After a few moments she said, "I am going to call for a vote. The stitch-in is going to end at three this afternoon in any case. Should we call a halt to it now, and quietly go home? Or should we continue? I'll ask for a show of hands. Everyone who thinks we should go home now, raise your hands."

Three women immediately raised their hands, saw they were a minority, and yanked them back down again. One shook her head to show she'd changed her mind.

Sadie, wheeling forward, raised her hand, but it was for permission to speak. "I didn't know Sharon Kaye or her husband, so maybe it's not right for me to have an opinion. But I came up here to meet some stitchers, learn new techniques, and—and just be around people who share my passion for needlework. I don't want to go home till I have to."

Anna, who had been one of the trio to raise her hand to vote to go home, stood. She looked wretched, and her voice was uneven as she said, "I want retract my vote to end the stitch-in. I think Sadie's right, I think we should stay. Some of us have fond memories of Sharon, and perhaps we can share them."

Betsy turned to Jill, but saw she was already thinking the same thing Betsy was: Anna had displayed no fondness for Sharon yesterday. Jill murmured, "The workings of conscience in the presence of death is a mysterious thing."

"I agree with Anna," said Nan, who looked equally distressed, and several others nodded and raised their hands as if to vote in favor of sharing fond memories.

"Very well," said Isabel, not sounding happy about it, "the stitch-in will continue. Let us adjourn to the lounge."

Jill and Betsy sat down again.

Betsy said, "Every time I think I understand what happened, there's always this odd piece sticking out. I probably ran after the sheriff for nothing, too. That floss will turn out to be totally innocent."

"Then how did it get out by the furnace?"

"It could have fallen out of someone's pocket. I doubt we're the only ones who have gone for walks."

Jill said, "All right, the floss is innocent. What does that mean? Sharon's death was an accident?"

Betsy thought a minute, frowning. "Suppose she did go see Frank, and he induced the allergic reaction accidentally. He said he was pleased to have things around that she was allergic to, like pizza and peanut butter; maybe she walked in on him enjoying a peanut butter sandwich."

"Then all she had to do was walk out again, probably. But all right, suppose. She walks in, turns blue, collapses. If it was an innocent accident, why not just report it? In fact, suppose the reason you walked in and she was in there all alone was that he was downstairs trying to find someone to report it to. That would explain why he wasn't there when you walked in."

"But he didn't report it, or someone would have said something. And he told us he never saw her. So if he didn't go to report it, where did he go? No, if he was there when it happened, and he went out, it was to prepare to take her away. You know, go unlock his car."

Jill said, "Maybe he was in the bathroom when you came in, and didn't want to answer embarrassing questions. But we haven't answered two basic questions: If Frank isn't responsible for Sharon's death, what was she doing dead in his room? And why was she taken away?"

"You think they're going to arrest him?"

"I think they're going to hold him for twenty-four hours."

"I wish—" said Betsy, then cut herself off.

"You wish what?"

"Nothing." Betsy's smile was a little sour. What she wished was that Sheriff Goodman appeared a little more confidence-inspiring, but she didn't want to bad-mouth one law enforcement officer in front of another.

Jill said, "How about this: Frank deliberately had something in his room that would induce an allergic re-action, knowing Sharon was going to come and see him."

Betsy thought a moment. "And he could claim he didn't know she was going to walk in on him. But that puts us right back to your basic question: Why, if he was setting up an accident, ruin it by taking the body away?"

"Frank didn't do that, someone else did. Frank in-duces the reaction, somebody else sees the body and moves it."

"But who? Neither Liddy nor Doogie was here to do that."

"I bet Carla was. You said you think she's in love with Frank. Okay, maybe he's in love with her, too. Maybe he came up here to see Carla as well as get a little skiing in. But here comes Sharon Kaye, as usual, to spoil things. So Frank decides to murder her. He sets it up to look like an accident, but before he can finish things, Carla pops in for a little kissy-face, sees Sharon Kaye on the bed, and thinks, 'I must protect my man.' "

Betsy said, "I don't think Carla's capable of carrying a dead body up that trail."

"You'd be surprised what a person who is really scared can do."

"Well—maybe." But Betsy thought about those many flights of icy wooden stairs.

"All right, suppose you're right, someone doctored the

floss. I vote for Liddy; she probably knows Sharon's needleworking habits better than anyone."

"Except Carla," said Betsy.

"But if Carla messed with the floss, then who—Oh, I see! Sharon Kaye staggers up the stairs into Frank's room, and he's the one who panics and hides the body!"

Betsy nodded. "That sounds more like it."

Jill said, "Still, I wish we could have gotten to Liddy before Carla took her away. She's gone all to pieces since they found Sharon's body, just about like you'd expect if she's the one responsible for this mess. If we talk to her, she'll probably confess, if she's guilty."

Betsy said, "She couldn't have done it. Sharon disappeared on Friday during working hours, and Liddy said she was at work all day. That's too easy to check, so I doubt Liddy would lie about that."

"Murderers as rattled as Liddy is tell stupid lies. She's acting very hinky."

" 'Hinky'?"

"It means suspiciously, in a criminal sense. Backing into a doorway when a squad car comes by is hinky."

"I see," said Betsy. "Motive?"

Jill said, "Money, probably. But also, from what we've been hearing, Sharon was a beautiful, charming, self-centered woman with a jealous, controlling streak. Probably Liddy has a lot of mixed feelings because her mother kept coming back and then abandoning her again. If it turns out the floss was exchanged or doctored, we'll get the sheriff to check her alibi. Because I think she's our best candidate for this."

"Doogie has the same motives as Liddy, money and abandonment."

Jill said, "But he's really risen to this terrible occasion. Before, he was an awful wuss. Anyhow, he was at work, too. Sweeping up the ranger station in Grand Marais."

"Maybe we should suggest the sheriff check his alibi, too. Did you see how Carla is suddenly acting like the surrogate mommy to those two? Her concern seems real. And they like it, especially Liddy."

Jill nodded. "Yeah, but I'll bet you a dollar she's got no alibi at all. Love can also be a powerful motive."

"All right, it would be hers. Along with anger that Sharon Kaye was trying to come between her and her man. Still . . . I wish I knew who gets Sharon Kaye's money. There's a whole lot of it. Frank doesn't get any, thanks to a prenuptial agreement he signed. He told me he doesn't know where the rest goes. The obvious answer is, to the children. Liddy and Doogie had large trust funds set up when they were born, and they can't access the principal till they're thirty. They're living comfortably off the income from the trusts, but I wonder if one or both of them uses drugs, or is a gambler."

Betsy looked up the stairs. She was sure that with Carla as a gatekeeper, they were not going to be able to question either of the Owen siblings until Carla chose the time. In the controlling arena, Carla shone as brightly as Sharon.

James walked into the dining room and stopped, looking around. He saw Jill and Betsy and said, "There you are, Ms. Devonshire. I'm very sorry, but that young man is on the phone again. Mr. DuLac?"

"Oh, help." Betsy sighed. "All right, where?"

"In the office, like before. I left the door open for you." He headed off in the direction of the kitchen.

"I'll be in the lounge," said Jill.

Betsy picked up the heavy black telephone receiver in the office and said, "Okay, Godwin, what is it now?"

"A man just walked in here with a letter for you. Instead of a stamp, it has 'By Hand' typed in the corner, and he made me sign for it. The return address is 'Touhy and Howe, Attorneys, in the IDS Center, Minneapolis.'

Betsy, do you know who they are?" He said that as if
he knew, but wasn't sure Betsy would.

"Sure, Mr. Touhy is one of Joe Mickels' lawyers."

"I *knew* he would try something, I just *knew* it!
There's probably a *summons* in here! He's taking you
to *court*!"

"No, a summons has to go to the actual person, and
it's never in an envelope. This probably has something
to do with the sale of the building."

"Oh, then this is about the *water leak*! He thinks he's
found a way to make *you* pay for it, I bet! But he can't
do that, can he? I mean, the building *still* belongs to
him, right?" Godwin in a panic put up italics like a por-
cupine erects its bristles.

"Calm down, Goddy! If you want to know what it's
about, open the envelope."

"Can I? Is that legal?"

"Why not? You signed for it, didn't you? So you have
legal custody. It's addressed to me, so I can give you
permission. For heaven's sake, open it and see what kind
of headache it contains."

The letter was a formal notification of a meeting two
weeks hence in the office of Mr. Langston Touhy, Es-
quire, in the IDS Tower in Minneapolis, at which time
and place papers concluding the sale of the building in
which Betsy's apartment and shop were contained would
be signed.

"Oh," said Godwin, considerably let down. "Well,
why'd he send something this ordinary by courier?"

"Because he agreed to give me two weeks' notice of
this signing, and the date is exactly fifteen days from
today. I think you're right: He's trying to conclude the
sale quickly now, in case there's more water damage that
hasn't shown up yet."

"It's today's date on this thing. Getting an attorney to

work on a Sunday isn't exactly cheap," Godwin pointed out.

"How much was the estimate for the water damage?" asked Betsy.

"Oh, my God, Betsy, wait till I *tell* you! The water is coming from the roof, it's been spilling down an opening in the side wall for days, running between the floor of your apartment and the ceiling of the shop, and pooling right in the center, where it finally soaked through! I asked for a ballpark figure on what it's going to cost to fix it, and he said *nine thousand*! I told them to put a temporary patch on the roof, which all by itself will cost about five hundred but that's only *temporary*! And that doesn't include the cost to repair the ceiling or replace the damaged goods!"

"And how often are ballpark estimates way under the actual cost?" asked Betsy, and answered herself: "Often. It's going to cost much more than nine thousand before we're through. What Joe will do is offer to deduct nine thousand from the price of the building. That's why the rush, he wants the deal done before we find out we need a whole new roof. I guess the bloom is off the rose."

"What does that mean?"

"In the face of spending real money, any chance at romance is dead, dead, dead."

"That evil, *sneaky* old man!" said Godwin, at length and not exactly in those words.

A few minutes later, Betsy hung up with a sigh. Maybe she shouldn't have gone away. What with troubles she wasn't allowed to leave behind in Excelsior and a mystery up here, she wasn't getting much of a rest.

She left the office, checking the door after she pulled it closed to make sure it locked. It was a fine old door, to judge by the solid thickness of the wood, but ill-fitted to the frame. At the hinge end she could fit the toe of her shoe under it.

Betsy stood a moment, frowning at the door, then went off on a search for James.

She found him in the kitchen, checking the blend of lettuces in a very large salad bowl. "Did you find an EpiPen on your desk yesterday?" she asked.

"EpiPen? Oh, that plastic thing for allergic reactions. Yes, I did. I wondered where it came from. Is it yours?"

"No. I found it on the floor of your office and left it on the desk. Are you sure it doesn't belong to an employee or someone who has access to that little office?"

"Yes, I'm sure. Anyone needing help as serious as that pen offers would be sure to warn us all about it." He shrugged. "Plus I asked."

"Then I think I know who it belongs to. May I have it back?"

"Of course. Come with me."

The device had been put in a drawer behind the lobby counter. Betsy took it and asked, "So long as you're back there, can you tell me when Carla Prakesh checked in?"

"All right." He checked his log and said, "She missed dinner on Friday, she didn't drive up to our door till almost nine. I remember because she asked for help unloading her car."

"Thanks." Betsy went into the dining room and sat on the circular couch with the pillar to take another look at the EpiPen. If Sharon hadn't dropped it, might it have saved her life? She held it up and jiggled it gently. The liquid inside was thin as water. The plastic was heavy, and formed a blunt point at the needle end. She gripped the safety cap and tried it. It would not move. She tried harder, but it was stuck fast.

Perhaps it had jammed when Sharon dropped it. She held it closer to her eyes. Was that something—? A thin trail of some clear substance ran around the cap. She prodded it with a fingernail, but it was as hard as plastic.

No wonder it wouldn't turn, the cap was sealed to the body of the pen.

She had seen this same thin, unyielding seal before, on a favorite mug she had dropped, broken, and repaired. Impermeable, unbreakable, permanent. Superglue.

She had a sudden, sharp vision of Sharon, eyes red and tearing, skin flaming and itching, as she frantically twisted the cap, trying to get it off. As her throat began to swell shut, the one thing that could fend off death would not open for her use. Realizing that, she either dropped it as useless, or threw it down in frustration— and it had rolled under the door.

Where the person who had sabotaged it could not retrieve it, as he had retrieved the betraying canvas bag of stitchery and burned it.

Betsy put the EpiPen in her skirt pocket and went to the lounge. Jill had a group of five or six stitchers sitting or standing around her, watching as she stitched something on a piece of scrap canvas, talking quietly as she did so. "You can see how the arrowhead shape of the Amadeus stitch is formed," she was saying as Betsy approached. It appeared that the group was getting its surprise teacher after all—though it was likely Jill was as surprised as any of them.

Ingrid, sitting near Jill but working on her own project, looked up as Betsy came in, and her face filled with compassion. "More badt news?"

"Yes, I'm afraid so. Jill, may I see you alone for a minute?"

"Sure." Jill handed the canvas to Linda Savareid, seated beside her, and said, "Now I've got the second one started, you finish it and start another beside it. The rest of you watch, and kibitz to your hearts' content." She followed Betsy through the dining room, where

James was supervising the lunch setup, and into the lobby, which was empty.

"Look at this," Betsy said, pulling the EpiPen out of her pocket.

Jill took it, read its printed instructions, noted that it was fully charged, and said, "Where did you find this?"

"Under the desk in the office, when I took that first call from Godwin. I thought it belonged to someone who worked here, so I left it on the desk. But it doesn't. James put it behind the check-in counter, waiting for a guest to ask about it, and no one has. It must be Sharon Kaye's. Look at it, the cap has been glued on."

Jill twisted the cap, gently then harder. Then she, too, pried at the thin line of glue around the cap. "Very nasty. How did it get into the office?"

"My guess is, it rolled under the gap in the door."

Jill walked to the office door, tried it, and found it locked, then fit the device to the space under it. Toward the hinge end, there was ample room.

Betsy said, "This is murder, Jill. Someone sabotaged her EpiPen, got her a long way from medical help, and triggered an allergic reaction somehow."

"Who?" asked Jill.

"I don't know. Someone who had access to her purse or whatever she kept her EpiPen in. And probably not too long before she came up here, in case she was in the habit of checking the thing. I checked on when Carla got here, and it was late Friday night. And I bet if you check, she'll have a solid alibi for the afternoon."

"Well, that eliminates her."

"Actually, it doesn't. If you think about it, that puts her on the list. It wasn't a case of getting Sharon Kaye up here and then triggering the attack. The attack was arranged somewhere else, then she was sent up here. I'm sure that when they test that floss, they'll find it exchanged or coated with something. This was set up by someone who wanted to be at a distance when Sharon Kaye had that allergic attack. So when they heard the news they could murmur sadly, 'How awful, how tragic,' and maybe produce a tear." Her mouth tightened. "How wicked."

Jill said, "So your original theory is right. The person who took the body away is the one sitting down with the sheriff right now. He came back to his room and found her and panicked. We've got two crimes, two different perps."

Betsy nodded. "Yes, I think that must be it. And as for the car, I think he missed his chance to move it. People were arriving, maybe he thought it had already been seen, or was afraid he'd be seen driving it away."

Jill said, "You should call Sheriff Goodman right now and tell him about the EpiPen."

"All right." But as Betsy got out her wallet to dig for change, she heard footsteps on the stairs and looked up to see Doogie coming down.

"Ah, nuts, I might've known I'd run right into you two," he said, half annoyed, half amused. "But I told Liddy that if I saw you I'd ask, so maybe you can tell me when they are going to release my father."

Betsy replied, "I have no way of telling that. I'm not connected with any law enforcement agency."

"How about your friend, the cop?"

Jill said, "I have no connection with local law enforcement."

Betsy said, twiddling her left eyebrow significantly, "Jill, why don't you call the sheriff and ask him? I think he'll be willing to talk to you, as a fellow law enforcement person. Ask him if and when he's going to release Frank. Meanwhile, I want to talk with Douglas." Betsy could not bring herself to call a murder suspect Doogie.

Faced with this offer of quid pro quo, Douglas could only nod. "Come up to our room, okay?" He looked into the dining room and led the way back up the stairs.

He gave two brisk knocks on the angled door to his father's room even as he turned the knob. Apparently his whole family wasn't big on locks.

Betsy followed him in. Liddy was lying on her stomach on the bed, propped up on elbows. Carla was sitting in a little upholstered chair by the fireplace, in which a small fire burned.

Douglas said, obviously in response to a request he go down and check, "They're still setting up lunch, so we'll have to wait awhile longer."

Liddy sighed and lay completely down.

"Well, it's your own fault," Douglas said. "You should have eaten last night, or come down this morning for breakfast."

Carla said, "Doogie, have a little sympathy for your sister."

"How little can I have?" Douglas made an amused wincing face and said, "Sorry. Oh, by the way, Ms. Devonshire here has asked her friend to find out Dad's status, so in return I said she could talk to us a little bit."

Carla stood. "I won't agree to that."

"Fine," said Douglas. "Why don't you go watch them setting up in the dining room and let us know when lunch is ready?" He walked to the door and opened it for her.

Carla sniffed and walked out.

13

Douglas went to the chair she'd vacated and gestured for Betsy to sit on the straight-backed chair near the door. She obeyed.

Liddy said, "We heard you're some kind of private eye."

"Oh, no. My friend Jill Cross is a police officer—a patrol officer, not an investigator. I don't have any official status at all. Except in my needlework shop, and even there one of my employees is the person to ask for real help." Betsy crossed her legs and leaned back with what she hoped was casual grace. "Do you do needlework, Liddy?" she asked.

Liddy eyed her suspiciously, but the question was innocuous, and Betsy kept her expression light. The young woman had changed into jeans and a cotton sweater, and she looked very young. She rolled over and up to sit cross-legged on the bed, hands on her knees. There were dark shadows under her red-rimmed eyes. "Yes, Mama taught me to crochet and do needlepoint when I was nine

or ten, and then I counted cross-stitch when she started
doing that several years later. After the divorce, actually.
It was in San Francisco; we spent a whole summer out
there, remember, Doogie? I love San Francisco, it's so
beautiful and sophisticated. And we both liked Jack a
whole lot. I hadn't been there before, and so I thought
anyplace in California was warm and sunny and I
packed swimsuits and shorts, but San Francisco is chilly
and I hardly got to wear them at all. Instead, we shopped
for new clothes for me and rode cable cars and explored
Chinatown and Fisherman's Wharf, and when we went
home at the end of a day, Mama taught me to do
counted. I guess I was her first student."

"I've heard from several people that she was very patient with her students. Was she as patient with you?"

Liddy relaxed further, pleased to talk about her
mother. "Oh yes. Very. Well, at first. It was all so wonderful in San Francisco until she and Jack started to
fight. Things got very tense the last couple of weeks."
Liddy frowned. "I wish she could have stayed with Jack.
She would have been happy, and then so would we. But
Mama was very fickle."

Douglas cleared his throat. She gave him a "What-
did-I-say?" look and deliberately continued to Betsy, "I
loved my mother." She had to stop and swallow before
she could continue, in a higher, more wavery voice. "But
my mother could be very difficult. I used to think she
was indifferent to our needs. Now I think it was because
of the allergies. She had to concentrate on not getting
sick, on staying away from things that made her sick,
and that took all her attention. Even so, there were times
when she came home and was wonderful to us. But she
always went away again." She folded her lips inward,
and fell silent.

Betsy said, "Did the allergies start before she divorced
your father?"

"Oh, yes." Liddy nodded. "We were eight and nine when it started. That's the same age Tony's children are now."

"Tony was her current boyfriend."

Douglas said, "But our parents were younger than Tony when we were that age. So it wasn't the same."

"No," said Liddy, "and it's not the same. They won't—" She put her hand over her mouth, and tears flowed over the fingers. In a moment they stopped and she said in a much firmer voice, "Nobody could possibly think my father murdered my mother!"

"Of course not, Liddy," said Douglas. "Once they talk to Dad, they'll see he couldn't possibly have anything to do with any of this and turn him loose." He looked at Betsy. "You don't think he's a murderer, do you?"

"No, I don't," replied Betsy, almost truthfully. "What's more, the sheriff didn't say a word to indicate he thought Sharon was murdered." Unless Jill was talking to him this minute. Which was extremely likely. "In fact, the sheriff told me your mother suffered a severe allergic attack before she died. Perhaps she was seeking a private place to use her EpiPen and went to your father's room. I saw her there, dead. She did have an EpiPen with her, of course."

"Liddy, don't talk to her about this!" ordered Douglas.

"Yes," said Liddy, ignoring him. "She had several, and never went anywhere without them. It saved her life once that I know of."

"So let's say she was having an attack. She would need to use the pen and then lie down, wouldn't she?"

"No, what she would need is to go to a hospital," said Douglas, not quite so belligerently.

"She would need to be driven to an emergency room," agreed Liddy. "The EpiPen only keeps her alive long enough to get to one, it doesn't stop the anaphylaxis."

Betsy nodded. "And if she had an attack here, then

possibly there was no one in the lobby to ask for help
to get to a hospital. The front desk isn't always manned,
I've noticed. But she knew your father was here, she
said to me that she came here to talk to him, to be rec-
onciled with him. So let's suppose she went upstairs and
knocked, and when there was no answer, she tried his
door. It opened and she went in. She must have been
very sick—climbing stairs has to be hard on someone
having trouble breathing. So she used the pen and lay
down to wait for it to go to work. But if you're right,
the pen wasn't enough, she needed more drastic aid."

"Why didn't she use the phone?" asked Liddy.

"Because there aren't any phones in the rooms, didn't
you know that?"

She looked around. "No, I didn't notice that. How
odd. Weren't there phones when we came here years
ago, Doogie?"

"I think so. I don't remember," he said.

Betsy took the reins of the narrative back. "There is
a pay phone in the lobby, but it's off in a dim corner.
Maybe she didn't notice it when she went into the lobby
from the lounge. So she went up to your father's room,
but he wasn't there. She didn't have the strength to go
back downstairs. So she lay down on the bed and died.
When I saw her, her lips were blue, and I thought she
might have been smothered, you know, as if with a pillow."

Douglas made a sound of shock or distress but when
Betsy looked at him, he looked away with a gesture for
her to continue.

"When I found her, I was scared and ran to tell someone. If in the meantime your father came back and found
her dead, he may have panicked. He had told people he
would never take her back, and if he said it angrily, they
might think he had something to do with her death. So

he decided to get rid of the body. Do you know if they had quarreled recently?"

Douglas said, "I don't know. But what you said . . . that sounds plausible. They were always quarreling—"

"But not recently!" cried Liddy. "You know Dad hasn't talked to Mama in weeks, he hasn't seen her in months, so why would he panic? He hasn't got anything to do with this. Plus, he simply wouldn't hide a dead body, especially Mama's!"

"You don't—" began Douglas, turning on her. She stared him down. "Well, all right, you're right. He wouldn't. But then who?"

Liddy said, frowning, "I don't know. But now that they know it was an allergic reaction, the sheriff will know it was a natural occurrence, Dad didn't kill Mama—no one killed Mama."

Doogie said, "You're right, I agree, not murder, never murder. Maybe the autopsy report will show what she was having a reaction to." He asked Betsy, "Is that possible?"

Betsy said, "I don't know. We'll have to wait and see."

Douglas asked, "If they don't release Dad, who is responsible for taking care of my mother's body? I don't like the idea of her being stuck in a refrigerator somewhere until . . . well, until this is straightened out."

"They've done the autopsy, that's how they found out she didn't drown," said Liddy. "So they have to give her back, don't they?"

Betsy said, "I don't know. I think you need legal advice. It's a crime to hide a body, you know."

Douglas said, "I called Dad's attorney and he said he doesn't handle criminal cases—"

"Doogie!" cried Liddy. "I thought we agreed, Dad didn't do anything wrong!"

"We know that, but who knows what the sheriff will

charge him with? We have to face facts, Liddy. Dad's in trouble with the law, and we have to act quickly. I asked Dad's attorney to recommend someone, and he did, and the new attorney said he'd go straight to Grand Marais. That was last night, so he's probably there with Dad now. I had to wire him a retainer before he would even phone Dad."

Douglas stood and came to a kind of attention, like the soldier Frank called on Liddy to be. Liddy, on the other hand, was drooping with woe.

"Do you have the money to make bail for your father?" asked Betsy.

Douglas nodded. "Yes. Unless it's hundreds of thousands, of course. That would take a few days to round up."

Liddy perked up at Betsy's look of surprise and said with a sly smile, "What, nobody told you my mother was rich?"

"Actually, yes. But it takes time for a will to be admitted to probate—even more time, if there isn't a will. Months." Betsy was speaking from experience.

"No, you still don't understand," said Liddy. "Our mother set up trust funds for each of us when we were born. That's all we get, that's our inheritance. But Mama's no piker; the income from those trusts has kept us in socks and school and sports cars all our lives. What, you thought Doogie works for the Forest Service because he needs the money? No, we work because— Why do we work, Doogie?" Her tone had turned dry and mocking, another abrupt mood change.

"What's the matter with you, Liddy?" he asked, half angry, half concerned. He said to Betsy, "Mother's estate goes to a private laboratory researching allergies. She told us that years ago."

Liddy continued as if he had not spoken. "We work because we want to make a difference, because we want fulfillment, because that's what's expected of healthy young people, because there's satisfaction in having money you earned yourself, because it's hard to fill the lonely hours with idle amusement. But as a happy home-maker, I fill the lonely hours just fine." She looked at Betsy with a strange little smile. "Are the dead lonely?" she asked.

"I think it depends on where your spirit goes after death," said Betsy.

" 'Heaven for the climate, hell for the company'!" quoted Liddy, the smile turning real. "Oh, my God!" she said and began to cry, with loud sobs this time.

Douglas gave Betsy a cold look and went to sit beside his sister on the bed, his hand on her bent back. "I think you should leave now," he said. "I hope you got what you wanted, and I hope you're satisfied. We'll see you at lunch for an answer to our question about our father."

Betsy left the room, and found Carla waiting out in the hall. "How dare you make that child suffer even more than she's already suffering?" she said with a hiss as she reached past Betsy for the doorknob.

"Wait!" Betsy said. "Please? May I talk with you for just a few minutes? It won't hurt, surely, for Liddy to have a bit of private time with her brother."

Carla stepped back to look with cold suspicion at Betsy. "What do you want to talk to me about?"

"About Sharon Kaye."

"I can't tell you more than I already have."

"I think you can. And you can tell me more about Frank as well as Douglas and Elizabeth. Maybe between us we can find the truth."

"Oh?" Carla still glared, but Betsy, remembering how Jill could calm a person with a calm look, accepted her glare, and Carla looked away first. "Oh, what does it matter? All right." The anger vanished into mere annoy-ance, Carla went past Betsy to the head of the stairs.

"Come on, I promised I'd let Liddy know as soon as lunch was served."

"Fine," said Betsy, following her down.

They went into the dining room and sat on the round couch with the pillar. The faded red fabric was scratchy, and the circle was small enough that it was impossible for them to look one another in the face without leaning forward, or hanging halfway off the seat.

Wait people were bringing dishes, flatware and glasses to the counter, further breaking any sense of intimacy.

Carla said, "Sadie told me you investigate crime, so you must know about things like what is going to happen to Frank?" Her interest was obvious, even desperate, though she was not looking at Betsy.

"I don't know what the penalty is for concealing a death, but it can't be as serious as even the least serious charge of homicide. The question is, why did Frank try to hide Sharon's body?"

"He didn't!" objected Carla sharply. "He doesn't know anything about Sharon dying in his room! He didn't know she'd even been there until you and Jill came knocking on his door."

"How do you know that?"

"Why . . . he told me," said Carla, and closed her eyes against Betsy's next question.

Betsy asked, "Did he come to Naniboujou to see you?"

Carla grimaced and opened her eyes. "Cut right to the chase, don't you?" Betsy held her tongue, and Carla said, "He came because he loves this place, and to do a little cross-country skiing—and yes, to see me."

"Did Sharon come here to try to break up the relationship between you and Frank?"

"I don't know. Perhaps. Yes, I think so." Carla paused a few moments, thinking before she spoke. "Sharon

couldn't get along with Frank, but every time he started
to look elsewhere for female companionship, she came
back to him, saying she wanted to reconcile. I'd watched
her do it once before, but I didn't recognize it for the
game it was. Then she found out Frank and I were getting close and she started in again with talk of reconciliation. She was using exactly the same language as
before, and I suddenly realized this was a pattern of
behavior. I couldn't think what to do, but at last I spoke
candidly to Frank about it—and to my utter surprise, it
was like someone turned on a light in Frank's head. Poor
man, he kind of stared at me and said, 'Do you know,
I think you're right,' like he was surprised at my per-
spicacity." Carla gave a halfhearted chuckle, then leaned
forward to confide, "You and I come from a generation
that said the woman must never reveal her tricks to the
man, nor speak of another woman's tricks. Just like we
must never let on we're smarter or stronger than he is."

Betsy nodded. She had started adolescence at a time
when women still held such notions, though some had
started questioning them—and a few had even laughed
at them. But some still took them seriously even now,
in the twenty-first century. She said, "Were you really
angry with her?"

Carla nodded. "At first, when I realized what she was
up to. But I won, you see. Frank wasn't going to take
her back. We talked about it, and he was quite firm on
that." Chin up, she smiled in remembered triumph.

But Betsy thought of the confident way Sharon had
spoken of a reconciliation. Carla might have won, but
Sharon hadn't known it.

"How well did you know Sharon? Were you friends?"

Carla frowned at her. "No, of course not."

"Yet you seem to know her pretty well. Did you see
much of her at needlework functions?"

"A fair amount. I never talked to her about Frank, of

course. Or the children, except to ask her how they were. And she always said they were doing very well, as if she knew, or even cared. Her treatment of them was totally self-serving. Yanking them this way then that, saying she was coming home for good, then smashing their joy with an indifference that was shocking in its cold-bloodedness."

"Did you talk to Liddy and Douglas about this?"

Carla hesitated, then said, "Yes, I did, once they knew about Frank and me."

"Knew what?"

"What happened was, Frank and I were having dinner at his house and they walked in on us. That was last summer. We'd thought they were gone for the weekend, sailing on Lake Michigan, but they came back Saturday night because the weather had turned bad. It was embarrassing, but—" Carla smiled again, this time in a way that let Betsy understand it might have been even more embarrassing if the two had come in an hour later than they did.

"What did they say when you talked to them about Sharon?"

"That was a few weeks later, after they got over the shock of learning their father had a girlfriend." Carla laughed. "At first, they defended her to the uttermost, poor things. But I could tell they were hurting, her behavior was—what's the word? Whipsawing, that's it, whipsawing them."

Like I am doing to Jill, thought Betsy. "Are they close, the brother and sister?"

"Yes, very. Their mother's . . . 'inconstant love' is the term Frank used, and isn't that the most poignant thing you've heard in a while? Anyway, she'd been behaving like that for years, so Liddy had taken over parenting Doogie. Frank allowed that, which I think might have been a mistake. I think that's why she's still living at home, so Doogie can feel they'll both be there for him, his father and his sister. Of course Doogie's twenty-one, so it's past time Liddy started thinking of her own future. I'm doing what I can for him, and I consult with Liddy about what Doogie likes and needs, which makes both of them happy. I think I'll be as good for them as I am for Frank. At the very least, I can relieve Liddy of responsibility for Doogie."

"What do they think of the relationship between you and their father?"

"Oh, I'm sure they approve. Naturally they want their father to be happy."

But Betsy knew that children who "defend their mother to the uttermost" were not normally pleased to find another woman in her place. There could be all sorts of cruel angles here. Carla might be angrier than she had said she was about Sharon trying to come back to Frank, and not so sure as she had appeared to be that she had won the battle for Frank's heart. Douglas and Liddy might like Carla much better than their own inconstant mother—so much that they saw their mother as a threat to the stability Carla could bring. Or as a threat to their father's happiness. Or perhaps only Douglas hated his mother—how Freudian! Or, had their father at last come to hate her and, his eyes opened to her perfidy, try to hide her body because he had murdered her?

"You knew about Sharon's allergies, right?"

"Oh, yes; everyone knew."

"Yet she smoked."

"I know, and not some delicate, low-tar brand, but something extra long and dark, very exotic." Carla's lip curled slightly.

"I heard she was trying to quit."

"I know she still smoked. Well, she did cut back, but . . ." Carla shrugged.

"Did you also know she carried an EpiPen everywhere she went?"

"Yes, she showed several of us how to use it after that one time she had a severe reaction at a meeting and none of us knew what to do. She came to the next meeting with one in her purse and showed it to us and demonstrated how to use it. Not difficult, fortunately. And even more fortunately, we never had to."

"She carried it in her purse, or her sewing bag?"

"It was in a plastic bag in her purse. Easier to find than in a project bag. You could dig for ten minutes in her project bag before you'd find something that size. And of course time is important when you need to use that thing."

"My bag hides things, too," said Betsy with a wry smile. She hadn't even owned a knitting bag—project bag, that was a better name for the thing!—as recently as September, and already hers was a jammed mess. She sold two kinds of needlework carriers in her shop, but it hadn't occurred to her to buy one for herself. "What do you use?"

"I'm not one of those ultra-organized fanatics. I roll my canvas up into a plastic tube, and I carry everything else in a big plastic box. I use ZipLoc bags for my silks, and the box has compartments for my scissors, needles, laying tool, dololly, and any other oddments. I had Frank hot-glue a magnet to the inside of it for my needles. The box itself is light, so it's easy to carry. I don't use a frame for any but the biggest projects, and I don't travel with those. Since I have two homes, I keep a Dazor light at both places, because I have projects I'm working on in both, too."

"You do a lot of needlework?"

"A great deal."

"After Sharon, isn't Frank a little leery of getting involved with someone else who does needlework?"

Carla said, with perfect seriousness, "Well, I hardly think someone who does trame is in the same class as someone who does counted, don't you think?"

Betsy got to hide her smile by turning her head at the sound of footsteps. It was Jill. "What did he say?" Betsy asked.

"He's on his way."

"Who?" asked Carla, eyes lighting up.

"Sheriff Goodman." The light went out. Jill explained, "Betsy found something and the sheriff wants a look at it."

Carla looked at Betsy. "What did you find?" she asked, and the fear was back in her voice, now colored by anger that Betsy hadn't said anything about a find.

"An EpiPen I think is Sharon's."

"Why does the sheriff want Sharon's EpiPen?" She seemed genuinely puzzled. "And how do you know it's Sharon's?"

"Do you know anyone here besides Sharon who carries one?"

"Well, no. But is finding her EpiPen important?"

"Maybe," said Jill.

Carla said, "Well, if you want to know who else might have one, ask Isabel. She's handling lost and found, she would know if someone is missing one."

"Yes, of course," said Betsy.

She went in and found Isabel, who was all but finished with her roses on linen pattern. Betsy watched her for a minute, as Isabel, caught up in the excitement of finishing a project, was stitching very rapidly. Her tongue was just showing between her lips, its tip moving a little in rhythm with her stitching.

"Ha!" Isabel said, an exclamation of triumph, and turned her work over to run the end of the floss under several stitches and snip the remainder off with a tiny pair of gold scissors. "Ahhhh," she said, relaxing and

turning it back again to regard it happily. The pinks
glowed against the snowy linen, and Betsy suddenly realized there were realistic drops of dew in the pattern of
petals.

"Very nice," said Betsy, and Isabel, startled, looked
up.

"Oh, hello, Betsy."

"Isabel, does anyone else here carry an EpiPen?"

Isabel blinked, changing gears from stitcher to person-
in-charge. "Why, no, not that I know of. In fact, I think
Sharon was the only person bothered by anything more
serious than hay fever. Why?"

"Because I found an EpiPen and I wondered who
might have lost it." Betsy showed it to Isabel.

Isabel took it and looked at it. "No one's asked about
one of these," she said, and stood. "May I have everyone's attention for a moment?" she called, and slowly
the lounge quieted as faces turned to her. "I have here
an EpiPen," she continued, waving it over her head.
"Did anyone here lose this?"

There was a silence, broken when Nan said, "It's
Sharon's, of course. Where did you find it?"

Isabel said, "It was found here at the lodge," glancing
at Betsy and getting a nod of confirmation. "So none of
you claims it?"

No one did, though two women wanted to know if
Jill was coming back to finish her lesson on the Amadeus stitch. Betsy said she didn't know.

Isabel sat down again, and Betsy took the EpiPen back
from her. "Is there something significant about that
thing?" asked Isabel.

"Yes, but I'm waiting for the sheriff to come, so I can
tell him about it."

"Is it that it hasn't been used?"

"You noticed that?"

"Sharon showed us how to use it, so yes, I noticed

that it's still full of whatever the medicine is called. I take it that means Sharon didn't have an allergic attack after all."

"Ladies?" said a man's voice. It was James, standing at the other end of the room. "And, gentlemen," he added with a little smile. "Lunch is served."

Everyone began to put things away, except those who just had to run out the last two inches of floss, or finish a row of stitches. The quiet murmur of the room grew a little louder with anticipation: Naniboujou's meals had been a delight so far.

The room had nearly emptied when Betsy, who had forgotten where she left her project bag, finally found it and was making sure everything she had with it was there. She heard, "Ms. Devonshire?" in a gruff voice. Betsy looked up to see Sheriff Goodman standing not far from her.

She followed him to the tiny lobby, where she quietly described finding the device and showed the sheriff where it had been sealed shut.

"This pen does not belong to anyone working at the lodge, or anyone here for the stitch-in, so it has to be Sharon's. And it could not have been sealed like this by accident. I believe it was done deliberately by someone hoping for just what we have: Sharon Kaye Owen dead of an acute allergic reaction."

"The first test on that string you gave me came back one hundred percent cotton."

"So it wasn't a blend substituted for the cotton. Then you'll find it's been sprayed or dipped in peanut oil or powdered latex or something equally lethal to Sharon. Because why sabotage the EpiPen unless you know she's going to need it?"

Goodman stared at her, seeming for the first time to take her seriously. He asked, "What time did you see the body in Mr. Owen's room?"

"I'm not sure. It was dark, and they were serving dinner in the dining room, which would make it after six but before seven-thirty."

The sheriff nodded once, sharply, and went to the lobby. James handed over the phone behind the desk and Goodman dialed. "Gimme the jail!" Goodman barked when someone answered. There was a pause, then: "I want you to put a hold on one Francis Arvid Owen till I get back there." Another, shorter pause. "What? Oh, hell! Oh, dammit to hell! Where'd he—yeah, yeah, yeah, damn all lawyers. Did you eyeball the car? Well, dammit—Yeah, yeah, I know, I know. Hell, he's probably taking him to the nearest airport! All right, put out an APB, wanted on probable cause murder. That's right, murder! I've got the evidence right here in my hand!"

14

The sheriff left. Betsy saw him barking orders into his radio as he fishtailed one-handed up the snow-packed lane to the highway. Remembering Frank Owen's mild manner, she thought Goodman's ferocious attitude a bit overdone.

On the other hand, whoever was responsible for that sealed EpiPen certainly deserved a bit of ferocity. Considering the blue-lipped woman lying cold and still on Frank Owen's bed, maybe a lot.

Betsy returned to the dining room. Liddy and Douglas were sitting with Jill and Carla. Liddy took one look at Betsy's face and stood. "What's happened? What's going on?" she demanded as Betsy approached.

Heads turned, so Betsy raised a hand to request silence and, on arriving, at their table said, "Let's go into the lounge."

Jill, Carla, and Douglas came, too. Betsy said, "I showed Sheriff Goodman an EpiPen I found in the office. It had been tampered with. I thought perhaps someone was using it as a prop in a first-aid class, but no one will claim it. So it's probably Sharon's."

"Tampered with?" echoed Carla. "How?"

"The cap was sealed shut. With superglue, I think. The sheriff called the jail, but Frank has already been released on bail, so he ordered an all-points bulletin for him. Have any of you any idea where he might go? I think someone should call and warn him about this."

"Yes!" Liddy exclaimed. "Let's call—"

But Jill interrupted, saying, "That's a very bad idea, Betsy. You don't help a wanted man get away."

"No, no, not to help him get away, to tell him to turn himself in. I don't want him to get shot by someone trying to apprehend him."

"Oh, my God!" said Liddy, lifting her arms as if in surrender. "Oh, no, Doogie, we have to do something! Call someone, tell them! Have that search called off!"

Douglas frowned at her. "I suppose we can try to contact Dad's lawyer—"

"That may take too long; there must be something—" Carla said, her voice high and frightened.

Liddy turned to Jill, arms forward now in appeal. "Please, you're with the police, for the love of God, stop them! Don't let them shoot my father!"

People in the dining room were falling silent, watching and listening through the French doors that separated the lounge from the dining room.

"Keep your voices down, please!" begged Betsy. "You'll have everyone asking questions."

Jill took Liddy's hands in her own. "Take it easy, your father is in no danger." She shot a cool glance at Betsy, then continued in the same soothing voice to Liddy, "No one is going to shoot anyone. Your father doesn't carry a gun, right? Answer me: Right? Or wrong?"

Liddy, trembling, tears spilling out of closed eyes and running down her cheeks, nodded. "R—right. Right."

"And when I talked to him, I thought that I have rarely encountered a more laid-back person—and I've lived in Minnesota, land of the staid, all my life."

Despite herself, Liddy smiled. "That's t—true."

"So when a police officer comes up to him and says, 'Mr. Owen, will you come with me?' what is your father likely to do?"

Liddy's eyes opened and she said with an odd, choked laugh, "He'll say, 'Sure, you bet.' "

Douglas said, "That's right, that's exactly right."

"See? No shooting."

"Yes, yes, no shooting." Liddy nodded again and Jill released her. Liddy collapsed onto a couch and put her hands over her face.

"Here now, what's all this?" said a quiet voice, and they all turned to see Frank Owen coming toward them. With his Sorel boots, down jacket, ashen hair, and thick, drooping mustache, he looked quintessentially Minnesotan. Walking behind him was a slender man of medium height in an exquisite gray suit, a gray overcoat hanging off his shoulders. He had an expensively shaped mane of salt-and-pepper hair, gold-rimmed eyeglasses, and an unlit cigar tucked into a corner of his mouth. All that, plus his extremely self-assured manner, announced that here was a high-priced attorney.

"Daddy!" shouted Liddy, jumping up to run over and hug Frank.

"Gosh, Dad, you don't know how glad we are to see you!" said Douglas, going to stand near him. His manner was both diffident and protective.

"Oh, I think we have a pretty good idea," said the lawyer, giving Liddy and Frank some room. "But once they found there was nothing funny about the cotton floss"—he cast a sharp look in Betsy's direction—"they decided they had to turn us loose."

"Sorry to disappoint you, sir," said Jill. "The sheriff

left here just a couple of minutes ago. He's putting out a want on Mr. Owen, on a charge of murder."

"Murder?" echoed Frank, disentangling himself from his daughter's embrace. His shaggy eyebrows raised high, he said to Liddy, "Explain this to me."

"It's too awful, they're all so stupid, they won't listen!"

Douglas said, "This woman"—he gestured toward Betsy—"found Mother's EpiPen in the lodge office. Someone had super-glued the cap on. Mother couldn't use the pen when she had an allergic reaction, and that's why she died."

Liddy interjected, "So the sheriff is charging you with murder. I know, I know, that doesn't make any sense! But that's what he's doing. And so—and so everyone is looking for you, and they have guns, so you'd better call them."

"Call who?"

The lawyer said smoothly, "The Cook County sheriff is the person to contact, since he put out the want. I'll call him, Mr. Owen. But we don't have to do that immediately. They aren't likely to let you out on bail on a charge of murder, so you'll need to make some arrangements about your job and your house. We can do that before I call Sheriff Goodman to arrange for your surrender. But more than that, you and I need to talk. We'll need some privacy. Do you still have a room here?"

"The only phone for guest use at Naniboujou is a pay one in the lobby," warned Jill.

"That's why I have one in my pocket," said the lawyer, pulling out a tiny cell phone.

Frank had pulled one from his jacket pocket as well, Douglas was reaching into his shirt pocket, and Carla was reaching for her purse. There were smiles all around.

"We've been up in your room, so I suppose it's still yours," said Douglas.

Liddy said, "I think now I really ought to go home. The police will come there, and may break in if no one answers when they ring the doorbell." Her voice took on a note of pleading. "I can't bear staying here, especially in that room. Mama died in that room. I can do whatever you want done from home, make phone calls, arrange with work for you to get a leave of absence. Right? Doogie can do whatever needs doing here."

"Yessir, of course I can," said Douglas.

But Frank eyed him coolly. "You've got a job of your own to go to, son," he said. "Besides, when I really need someone I can rely on, Liddy has always come through."

Betsy exchanged a glance with Jill. Douglas was turning back into a little boy right in front of them under his father's remarks.

Frank said to Liddy, "You'll get a different room tonight, soldier. But since they'll keep me in Grand Marais, I need someone who is not a long-distance phone call away."

"Oh, God, please," said Liddy, and it was a prayer.

"Hey, now, hey now, who's my brave soldier?" he said, looking a little surprised at this display of weakness.

Carla said, "Honestly, Frank, if you could see how brave your son has been through all this, you'd be very pleased. He's the brave soldier, not Liddy."

Douglas spoiled it by whining, "Come on, Dad, I can call the station and tell them I need some time off. That job's nothing important, after all."

"Every job's important."

Liddy found a remnant of backbone somewhere and said tiredly, "It's all right, Doogie, I'll stay."

"Good girl," said Frank.

Carla said, "I don't think—"

The attorney interrupted, "We'd better get started, Mr. Owen."

But as they turned to go, Betsy said, "Douglas, Liddy, you don't by some chance have a set of keys to your mother's car, do you?"

Liddy stared blankly at Betsy. "No."

Douglas shook his head. "I don't even know what kind of car she was driving."

"Why do you ask?" asked the lawyer.

"There are some items missing—her coat, her purse, her project bag. They're not here in the lodge, and we can't see them through the windows of her car. We were wondering if they're in a wicker basket in the backseat."

The lawyer frowned. "Who are you?"

"My name is Betsy Devonshire. This is Officer Jill Cross. She's with me," Betsy said with the same authority Jill had used making the same explanation to Frank. The attorney nodded and led Frank away, Douglas and Liddy following.

Carla called, "Frank, is there anything I can do?"

Frank stopped, hesitated, then said, "Will you come sit with me while I make arrangements?"

She hadn't expected that. "All right."

Betsy watched them all go, then said to Jill, "Now what?"

Jill shrugged. "Is there anything left to do? You found the body, you found the EpiPen, you've got the authorities interested in conducting a serious investigation. Frank is in the hands of an attorney who will make arrangements for him to turn himself in. You've done your part, and you didn't have to accuse anyone of murder. Aren't you satisfied?"

Betsy looked at the group, which had stopped again to talk near the door to the lobby. "I suppose I should be." But she wasn't.

"Come on," said Jill, "let's get some lunch while there's still a selection."

Thus encouraged, Betsy tried again to break the binding cords of curiosity. She went with Jill to the dining room, where people were lining up for seconds. Jill was greeted by several women impatient to talk of their success—or lack of it—with the beautiful but difficult Amadeus stitch. Two of the women wanted Betsy to come and sit with them, too, obviously goggling with curiosity about what had gone on in the lounge.

But Betsy didn't want to talk anymore about the Sharon Kaye murder. She waved at the women to go ahead, filled a plate with salads, and found an unoccupied table near the kitchen door, where the constant passage of wait people bringing refills made it undesirable.

She sat down and began to pick at the cranberry–apple salad. She had barely gotten two bites when Sadie wheeled up. "So, who did they arrest for murder?" she asked cheerfully.

"Nobody," said Betsy repressively.

"Why not? Did they decide it was some kind of accident? She fell into the waterfall?"

"No, she was taken to the waterfall after she died. Mr. Owen was charged with moving her body and released on bail."

"Yes, I saw him come back. Did he say why he did it?"

"No."

"Do you think he murdered Sharon Kaye?"

"I don't know."

"Come on, you've been sleuthing, you must have an opinion. Are you seriously saying you don't know?"

"Yes, I am. I don't know. I really don't know."

So Sadie huffed—the exhalation could hardly be called a mere sigh—in disappointment and wheeled off.

Betsy finished her lunch in peace, then went back to the lounge.

Jill was sitting with the women she'd had lunch with. They were asking her about the cashmere stitch now, though when Betsy walked up, they all stopped to listen to what she might say.

Betsy said, "I'll be down at the other end of the room."

Jill nodded and immediately caught the attention of the women by saying, "Now here's the real catch to that stitch."

Betsy went first to find her project bag, and then to a place at the far end of the long room. The little love seat there was empty and facing a door to the parking lot. She sat down, her back to the room, a position which suited her mood very well.

She got out the black Aida cloth and tried to concentrate on the pattern. She checked and found the error in the previous wedge. She'd have to frog both wedges.

Wait, no she wouldn't. All she had to do was frog the last one she'd done, make a very slight adjustment in the pattern—leave out two stitches here, add a stitch there—and that last wedge would fit right in where it belonged. It wouldn't make a very noticeable change in the shape of the wedge. She smiled to herself. "Real" stitchers often spoke of adjusting patterns, changing colors, or even removing whole elements, and here Betsy was doing the same thing. Her smile broadened. She was catching on to this stuff!

With increasing confidence Betsy quickly undid and restitched the wedge, and held the hoop out to admire her work. The change she had worked in it was barely noticeable, not bad at all.

She outlined it with Kreinik and was well into the last wedge when a secondary shadow fell across her pattern, blocking the light from the door, rather than the still-brilliant windows. She looked up to see Linda Savareid bent over from a polite distance, trying to see what she was doing.

"Like it?" asked Betsy.

"Very nice. Kreinik gives such a pretty sparkly effect. And an unusual pattern, too, kind of asymmetric."

Betsy frowned at her black Aida cloth. "It's not asymmetric, it's a circle. See? It just looks crooked because I'm not finished with it." She handed the pattern to Linda, who turned it around for Betsy to look at. At this distance, it was easy to see the adjustment she had made did not disguise more serious errors in placement. Instead of a circle, the wedges outlined an egg shape. She bit her lip to keep from groaning out loud. Her anxious, placating brain said she could use that, make it an egg-shaped rose window; it would be pretty, all she had to do was continue making constant adjustments as she went along.

Which was not remotely possible. First of all, it looked ridiculous shaped like that. Secondly, if she'd botched the stitching with a pattern to guide her, how could she make adjustments to a pattern as she went along?

Linda, trying to keep from laughing, said, "So why should you be different from us mere mortal stitchers?"

"Mere mortal—! Look at the beautiful work everyone else is turning out! I make a little adjustment to the pattern because I didn't want to frog almost all of what I've done, but I only made it worse. I don't know whether to go ahead and frog, or just toss the thing away." She sighed. "Am I ever going to stop being a beginner?"

"Sweetie, we're all beginners somewhere in the needle arts. Each of us learns a little more over time, but only a very few master this craft. There's just too much to learn. How long have you been at it? A couple of years?"

"Four months."

Linda stared at Betsy. "Four months?"

"Yes. I inherited a needlework shop from my sister—"

"Crewel World! That's who you are! Margot Berglund's sister, right? I've heard about her—and you!"

"Sadie Cartwright talked to you, huh."

"No, no, this was before I came to this stitch-in. Anyway, I don't listen to Sadie, her tongue's dipped in acid."

"Unlike several other people I could name."

Linda laughed. "Guilty, at least as far as Sharon Kaye Owen, Ms. Escapade Design, goes. Now there was a witch!"

"Please—after all, she's dead."

"Why does that matter? I never did get that business about not speaking ill of the dead."

"There's a very old belief that the ghost of a dead person hangs around for a while, and making him angry by saying bad things about him causes him to wreak havoc."

"Good heavens! And you believe that?"

"No, of course not. But that's how it got started, not speaking ill of the dead."

"How do you know that?"

"My ex-husband was a history professor. Thanks to endless dinners and parties with his peers, I picked up scads of useless bits of information like that."

Linda laughed. "Has any of it helped solve mysteries?"

Betsy threaded her needle through the edge of her fabric and released it from the hoops. "No. If my ex-husband had been a science professor, I might have had something I could use."

"Like what, for example?"

"Well, like what kind of allergen is odorless and tasteless, and won't show up in a lab test, but that nevertheless causes a fatal allergic reaction."

Linda sat down. "I can't help you there. But is that what you think happened? Something was deliberately put on her floss?"

"Yes. Because when I first saw her, she was fine. She wet her floss before she threaded her needle, said something I now think was, 'I've got to go get my EpiPen,' and when I saw her again, she was dead."

"So it also has to be something that doesn't wash off easily."

"What do you mean?"

"You said she wet her floss. Did she wet her fingers and run it down the floss, or use a sponge, like I do?"

"She wet it with a sponge. But what I meant was, she stuck the end of it in her mouth. That's how she . . . ingested the allergen." Betsy sat back frowning.

"Oh, a floss licker." Linda nodded. "People who are making heirlooms don't do that; saliva eventually damages the floss."

"It does?"

"That's the argument against it I've heard. But I figure by the time my work is old enough to be a treasured heirloom, if it ever is, which I doubt, they'll have figured out a way to reverse saliva damage. Not that I've ever noticed any on my grandmother's work, and she licked every piece of floss that went through the eye of her needle."

Betsy laughed, Linda laughed and went away, and Betsy, after sighing for another minute over her spoiled pattern, decided it was definitely a CASITA, not to be stood anymore. She folded it, put it into her project bag, and got out her knitting.

15

When Betsy would sit down to rest, or watch television, or just think, her mind would prod her
with lists of things she ought to be doing. But knitting
was doing something. Knitting, especially a simple pattern, didn't take much brain power, so her mind was
free to compare and ponder. And for the first time since
she had come to Naniboujou, Betsy wanted to really
think.

She went to work again on the sleeve of her sweater,
working on the last rows of the cuff. But this was not
like the last time she sat in this lounge, going knit, purl,
knit, in the deep and sunny silence. Now, distractions
abounded.

First, a monologue from Isabel caught her attention.
"When Liddy broke her engagement to that nice man
last Christmas, he was just devastated—and so was
Frank. He was beginning to think she'd never move out,
but Carla started encouraging her to try for that position
at Nordstrom's as a buyer. Carla says Liddy has the most

exquisite taste, and she should know, Carla's degree is in clothing design—it's been kind of a bond between the two of them. She's really very good for Liddy. And, of course, if Liddy gets the job, she'll be traveling constantly, and that will give Frank and Carla the opportunity they need to form their own bond."

"Only if one of them doesn't go to prison for murder," Ingrid said, lofting selected words for emphasis.

Betsy pulled her attention away, but it was caught by Nan saying, "She was a good person, so generous with her time." This was amusing, compared to the last time Sharon Kaye was the topic of discussion, but all that came back was someone else saying fervently, "Yes, yes, that's right."

Betsy pulled firmly on her attention as she began to concentrate on switching from the knit–purl of the cuff to the rice stitch of the sleeve. Here she had to add stitches to create fullness.

Who had the best alibi? she asked herself, knitting a stitch, but not taking it off the left needle. She knitted it again, adding a stitch to the total. Who had the most to gain from Sharon Kaye's death?

She went back and forth three times, doing the rice stitch, and then began the complication of a twist of cable that would run up to the shoulder.

Betsy had been surprised to discover that the cable stitch was formed by actually twisting the yarn where the two rows crossed one another. She had been sure it was an illusion, like the one that looked like woven strips of knitting. She got out the short plastic needle with the hump in its middle and knitted four stitches onto it, then moved the needle behind the sleeve while she knitted four more, then picked up the little needle and knitted the four back onto her big needles, then went back to the rice stitch. Four rows later, on her way back across, she did the same thing, only this time she put the little humpbacked needle in front while she knitted four stitches.

She remembered when she was learning the cable stitch, how extraordinarily satisfying it was to look down and see the twist of lines running up the knitting. It wasn't hard to do, not once you knew how. You just had to remember, this time in front, this time in back. Otherwise you had the curious illusion of the cable on top somehow coming from below, even though it had crossed on top last time, too. Like an Escher drawing. To look real, it had to be two lines crossing under and over one another.

"Betsy," said a voice.

"Hm?" There, she had recaptured the hanging stitches.

"Betsy," it said, more firmly.

Betsy looked up. It was Jill.

"What's up?"

"The BCA is here to process a crime scene."

"What's 'BCA'?"

"Bureau of Criminal Apprehension, a state organization that investigates crimes. Particularly useful to small local law enforcement agencies that can't afford the expense of a first-rate crime lab. Wanna watch?"

Betsy bent down to put her knitting away. "Will they mind?"

"Not so long as we keep our distance. But that's not why I came for you. Guess where they're going first?"

"Well, I dunno. Frank's room, I guess. Oh."

Jill's smile had a hint of malice in it. "I want to see that criminal attorney's face. Come on."

There were four of them, two men and two women, none in uniform. They were carrying black, heavy cases and mounted the stairs behind James with heavy, patient tread. Jill and Betsy braved the cold to run around the lodge without coats, coming up the back stairs to enter the hall just as James was knocking on the door to Frank's room.

The door was answered by the attorney, who managed to overcome his stunned silence at the sight of their badges to say that he was that very minute going to call Sheriff Goodman and arrange for Mr. Owen to surrender.

The lead investigator said, "Uh-huh."

Beside Betsy, Jill sniggered softly.

A deputy came out to collect Frank and his attorney, and the BCA crew went to work. They spent about an hour in Frank's room, and then went down the back stairs. Betsy and Jill had come closer, standing outside the room to wait for results, but the team refused to say anything. Still, they could not prevent them from observing at a distance, and when Betsy, standing on the landing, saw them pluck a tiny bit of something from the back door frame, Jill murmured, "Fibers, probably. With luck it's from her sweater, because that will be easy to compare."

They went out the back door and Betsy asked, "What are they going to look at next?"

"Her car, I'd guess."

"Can we watch that, too?"

"Too cold to stand out there long. Let's ask Amos if we can stand very small in his kitchen and look out a window."

The kitchen staff was busy clearing the counter and the tables, bringing things into the kitchen. Carla, Douglas, and Liddy were still sitting at a table, using the excuse of not-finished desserts to remain there.

In the kitchen, a dishwasher was making grinding noises. The aromas were of applesauce and roast pork; dinner preparations were already underway.

Through the window Betsy and Jill could see Sharon Kaye's sky blue Volvo with the team of four BCA investigators standing around it. They wore the heavy gear of people who spent a lot of time outdoors in a Minnesota winter. One had a video camera and was walking sideways around the car, camera to one eye. He went over every inch of the car, from door handles to license plates to tire tread to the splash of freeze-dried road slush on the roof.

When at last he was done, he said something to one of the women standing beside a very large black tool chest. She replied, nodded, and opened the chest.

She reached confidently in, then with a look of surprise looked inside, moving things around. Still squatting, she asked something of the man who wasn't videotaping. He turned from a conversation with the other woman to gesture at the box, and she looked again. When she still couldn't find it, she called to him again. He came over in that way men walk when they're exasperated. He stooped to reach into the box. The exact same surprised look crossed his face when he, too, couldn't put his hands on whatever they were looking for.

The two of them began taking things out of the box, little things that looked like dentist tools and tweezers in clear plastic holders, and big things like pry bars and hammers, and medium things like spatulas and little paint tins and small glass jars full of black or silver powder, and a throwaway camera. But not what they were looking for. The man, naturally, left the woman to put the things back in the tool chest. He went back to the other woman, who appeared angry, and he apologized and for some reason glared at the man with the video camera, though he wasn't doing anything at all right then.

"Wait here," said Jill.

"Uh-uh!" said Betsy. The two hurried up to their room, Jill moving with the swift grace of the athlete,

Betsy panting behind. They grabbed their coats, went down the hall to the back stairs, and outside, Betsy still fumbling with her buttons.

"Need a shim?" asked Jill as she approached the quartet.

"How'd you know?" asked the woman who had been angry with the man. She was tall and dark, with suspicious eyes and a mouth thinned by authority.

"We were watching out the window." Jill gestured toward the kitchen, and the woman turned to look at the window set in the black shingles of the lodge as if she suspected it of larceny.

"You got one?" asked the man with the video camera.

"Yes, it's in my kit, in my trunk, right there." Jill pointed toward her big old Buick three cars away.

"What are you doing with a shim?" asked the other man in a voice with handcuffs in it.

"Opening doors of cars with the keys locked inside. I'm Officer Jill Cross, Excelsior PD."

"God, you guys still offering that service?" said the woman, finishing fitting things back inside the toolbox.

"Oh, it's sweet little Excelsior," said the man with the video camera. "What else are they gonna do to justify their existence?"

"You want the shim or not?" said Jill, and they all four looked at her. But her amazing poker face absorbed their looks like a desert floor sucks up water, leaving no trace behind.

"Yes, thanks," said the tall woman.

Jill went to her trunk and returned with a flat bar cut into the shape of a hook at either end. She handed it to the woman beside the box, who took it to the driver's side of the Volvo and worked it down behind the rubber seal on the bottom of the window. She moved it around experimentally, and finally hooked something, and on the second try, the door lock button lifted.

Betsy, careful not to catch the eye of any of the investigators, watched while the big wicker basket was searched. No coat, no purse, no project bag, just two smaller baskets. One held a collection of plastic containers of evenweave cloth, cardboard bobbins wound with varying colors of floss, and stapled sets of graph paper, some blank and some with simple patterns; the other a collection of sets of more coarsely woven cloth, small scissors, white cotton floss in two thicknesses and stapled sets of instructions. In the bottom of the basket was a large tablet of blank paper and a ZipLoc bag of markers. Sharon's materials for her two classes.

In the glove compartment were maps, a flashlight, and an EpiPen. *A spare, surely,* thought Betsy. Liddy had said she carried several.

The trunk was opened from inside the car. The matching canvas suitcases contained gray, navy, and black slacks woven of a material that was probably silk, half a dozen hand-knit sweaters, three cotton blouses, a nice silk dress, gorgeous silk underwear, an open carton of More cigarettes, and a large makeup case with a mirror that lit up. In the makeup case was another EpiPen.

Betsy waited until they were finished searching, then approached the woman not responsible for the big black tool chest—who was busy dusting for fingerprints inside the Volvo—to say, "May I make a suggestion?"

The woman turned. "Who are you?"

"My name is Betsy Devonshire, and I'm a friend of Officer Cross, who loaned you her shim. I'm the one who saw Sharon Kaye Owen's body here at the lodge, and it was Jill and I who discovered that the Devil's Kettle was blocked with Sharon's body. I also found the EpiPen in the lodge that was sealed shut with superglue, which I believe was a factor in Sharon's death. I see you found two more of the EpiPens. Are they also sabotaged?"

The woman went to the big paper bag into which she had been putting smaller paper bags marked with evidence tags. She found and ripped open two of the smaller bags with the authority of one who is allowed to do that sort of thing, and pulled out the EpiPens.

"Don't seem to be," she said. "How was it done on the first one?"

"The cap was super-glued in place."

The woman tried the cap of one, and it started to turn. She screwed it back down. "Nope, this one is fine." The second one appeared to work properly as well. She went to the little stack of brown-paper evidence bags—which looked a lot like lunch bags—on top of the Volvo—and put each pen in one, stuck new Evidence labels on them, and said to Betsy, "Come over here," and led Betsy out of earshot.

She introduced herself as Investigator Michelle La-Pere, and pulled out a notebook. "So you're the one who thought we'd find something on that floss that Ms. Owen was violently allergic to?"

"Yes, ma'am," said Betsy. "I saw her put an end of a piece of that floss into her mouth to thread her needle, and soon after that I believe she started to have an allergic reaction. I wonder how thorough the test was, because I really think that's what induced the attack."

"Well, I'm sorry to poke a hole in your balloon, but the floss is one hundred percent cotton and there appears to be no foreign material on it. That's two strikes against you, one on the floss and now this one on the pen."

"Okay, I struck out on the floss. But I'm sure that attack was induced somehow, deliberately, by someone who wanted it to look like an accident. I think that's why these EpiPens are in good working order, so people might conclude Sharon forgot to move one from her car to her purse. I've been told she carried several."

"I don't understand why they all weren't sabotaged."

"I think the one I found was supposed to be taken away, hidden, or destroyed. Someone carried some of her things to the furnace shed to burn them, and dropped that lavender floss. Her coat and purse, a canvas bag with her stitching in it are all gone. I think the sabotaged pen would have gone, too, but it rolled under a locked door and he couldn't get it back."

"He?"

"Or she. I don't know who yet."

A tiny smile quirked in the corner of the woman's thin mouth. "The floss you gave Sheriff Goodman. Was that the floss someone dropped out by the furnace?"

"Yes."

"And you think it was the murderer who did that."

"Yes."

A small, patient sigh escaped the BCA investigator. She asked, "So how was the attack induced, if not by the floss?"

"I don't know. Something on her needle, perhaps, or on something else she handled. In fact—" Betsy stopped, thinking.

"What?"

"I can't help but think there are two separate crimes involved here. Sharon Kaye died of a severe allergic attack. There's nothing suspicious about that, considering that she was allergic to just about everything. So why hide the body? And though some of her things are missing, her car is here. It's like—"

"Like what?"

"I don't know. But it's murder, it's got to be."

"There are so many odd things about this case that I'm inclined to agree something illegal was going on. How about you tell me what you know, from the start."

Betsy explained what she knew and what conclusions she had arrived at while LaPere listened carefully, asked sharp questions, and took a lot of notes. Before they were finished, Betsy was sure most of her toes were frostbitten, though not that she had convinced the investigator of anything. LaPere's face could give Jill lessons in impassivity. At last LaPere looked over at the man without the camera and said, "Bobby, go find out what they do with the wood ash from that furnace. Arrange to bring it to Grand Marais. I want it sifted for sewing needles."

Betsy thought to correct her—hardanger needles and counted cross-stitch needles were not the same as ordinary sewing needles—then thought better of it. It didn't matter. Steel needles wouldn't burn in a fire, and their presence in the ashes would prove what had become of Sharon Kaye's project bag.

LaPere dismissed her, and Betsy went back into the lodge, looking for the maintenance man. She found him taking thin birch logs out of a canvas carrier and stacking them neatly in the holders beside the fireplace.

His name, he said, was Dan—actually, what he said was, "I'm Dan, the maintenance man," accompanying the rhyme with a wry smile, having apparently discovered that using rhyme himself preempted others from doing so. He was a wiry young man with an open face and the restless air of someone who has a lot to do.

"That furnace out in the shed," said Betsy, "do you burn trash in it?"

His eyes rounded, as if he were being accused of some crime. "Oh, gosh, no! Only wood and paper. We never burn trash in the furnace."

"So if they find sewing materials in the ashes, it isn't because you emptied a wastepaper basket into the furnace."

"No, ma'am."

"Thank you," said another voice, and Betsy turned around to see Michelle LaPere waiting her turn to talk to Dan. "Doing my job for me, I see," she added.

"I apologize," said Betsy. "But while I was talking to you, I thought of that question and couldn't help asking it."

"How about I go get more wood while you two talk?" suggested Dan.

"Fine," said LaPere. "But don't be long."

When he was out of earshot, Betsy asked, "Do you think Frank Owen is guilty of this murder?"

"I came into the game too late to know that for myself. As I investigate further, I may come to that conclusion. Though I will tell you his alibi is pretty solid; he was in Grand Marais most of the afternoon, shopping and skiing, seen there by several people. On the other hand, the town is only sixteen miles away. Do you think he's guilty?"

"No. It's interesting, I think everyone involved is lying about something, but obviously they're not all guilty of murder."

"Do you have any idea which one is guilty?"

"Not a clear one. You might talk to Carla Prakesh. She and Frank were romantically involved, and Sharon was trying to break them up. And the children, Elizabeth and Douglas, need to be looked at closely. It's not for the money; their mother left a lot of money, but not to them. But Elizabeth's behavior especially is . . . hinky. Do you use that word, too?"

Again the tiny quirk. "Yes. May I ask why you've involved yourself in this?"

"Actually, I've been trying to stay out of it. But things keep nagging at me."

The lobby was full of suitcases, but the women were all back in the lounge. By checking out ahead of time, they could stitch uninterrupted until they were shooed out the door for home. Betsy wound her way through the luggage to the pay phone. She called the ranger station in Grand Marais and asked three questions.

Then she called Sheriff Goodman.

After talking with him she found Linda and asked to borrow the blue sponge she used to dampen floss to smooth its kinks and keep it manageable while doing cross-stitch.

Then she went to find Jill.

The two filled mugs with coffee and went to the table where Carla, Douglas, and Liddy still sat, looking sad.

"Do you mind if we join you?" asked Betsy.

Liddy and Carla looked about to mind very much, but while they tried to think of a less rude way of saying so, Douglas said, smiling, "No, not at all. Sit down. Maybe some cheerful company will cheer Liddy up."

Jill and Betsy sat and tasted their coffee while Betsy tried to think how to begin this conversation.

Carla threw etiquette aside and said directly, "I don't know how you have the nerve to sit here. After what you have done to me and these young people, taking their father and my dear friend away from us, to sit down and expect us to be polite is the sheerest gall I have ever encountered."

"I didn't arrest Frank Owen," returned Betsy. "I reported the finding of a dead woman to the police, and things followed from that. The sheriff is the one who decided Mr. Owen murdered her. As a matter of fact, I don't think he is guilty."

"You don't?"

"Oh, I'm so glad!" said Liddy, with a faint hint of sarcasm in her voice.

"Why not?" asked Douglas, tossing a frown of censure at Liddy.

"He has an alibi, for one thing. He was in Grand Marais and the Pincushion cross-country ski trail during the time the murder happened."

"I thought the sheriff had concluded it wasn't murder. I certainly don't think it was," said Douglas. "Our mother was extremely allergic to all kinds of things. She'd had serious reactions before, so it's no surprise that she had another. It was just horrible luck that she had one here at a time when there was no member of the staff around to help her. I'm sure she went upstairs to ask Father to call an ambulance, but he wasn't here, either."

"What about the EpiPen?" asked Jill. "That was no accident."

"Sure it was, in a way," said Douglas. "Factory defect, obviously. Or a demonstrator model that got shipped accidentally."

Liddy looked at Douglas as if seeing the light at the end of a dark, sad tunnel. "I hadn't thought of that!" she said. "But of course, that must be what happened."

"No," said Betsy. "Long ago I worked for a manufacturer and I assure you, demonstrator models are never mixed with working models, for exactly the reason you're talking about, a consumer might get hold of a nonworking model. No, someone deliberately sealed the cap onto that device. Just as someone arranged for your mother to come up here, and then arranged for her to have a severe allergic reaction."

"Now wait just a minute," objected Carla. "Are you saying that *Charlotte Porter* is responsible for Sharon's death?"

"No, of course not," said Betsy, surprised. "Oh, I see what you mean. No, if you talk with Charlotte, you'll find that Sharon volunteered rather than that Charlotte asked her. Sharon found out Frank was going to be here, and decided she had to come. You told me how Sharon Kaye reacts to any woman getting close to her ex-husband, so I don't imagine you were the one who told her he was coming up here the same weekend you were."

"No, of course not. I told him about the stitch-in and

he said he'd been wanting to come up and do some cross-country skiing, and now he could see me as well. I certainly didn't see any need to let Sharon know that her ex-husband was courting me."

"Who did you tell?" asked Jill.

"No one. Well, Liddy and Doogie, of course. I mean, I don't want them to think their father and I would do anything clandestine."

"Then Dad must have told her," said Douglas.

"No," said Betsy. "Because he also knew Sharon's pattern of breaking up any relationship he formed with another woman, so he would have been very careful not to let her know about Carla."

"That's right," said Liddy. "Mama still loved Daddy, in her own way. And she loved us, too. But she didn't want any other woman to take her place. So nobody told her. It was a coincidence, her coming up here."

"But why would it matter if she knew?" asked Jill. "Didn't she have her own boyfriend?"

"Oh, Tony Campanelli didn't matter," said Douglas. "She was always getting boyfriends, and then leaving them again."

"No, this one was more serious," said Jill. "I heard that Sharon and he had talked about getting married."

"That would never have happened," said Liddy. "Tony has two young children, and Mama's life is complicated enough without adding young children to the mix. I talked to Tony myself, and warned him not to get too serious, because Mama had an intricate medical problem with many foods and that might complicate things for the children."

Betsy said, "Yes, those poor children. Didn't you tell me that those youngsters are about the age you two were when Sharon Kaye left your father for another man? And that's what this was really all about, isn't it? Saving two small children the grief you and your brother suffered?" And Betsy reached into her lap for the small blue sponge, which she put on the table in front of her plate.

All the color left Liddy's face.

"No," said Douglas at once.

"Why did you do that?" asked Carla, staring at the sponge.

"Because I thought someone did something to Sharon's floss to induce an allergic attack, but she didn't. The floss is just fine, as pure as the day it was purchased. But somehow someone induced an allergic attack in Sharon Kaye. I was present at the start of it. It could have been put on the needles, but why, when there was something even easier at hand? The allergen was put on the sponge Sharon used to dampen each length of floss as it was cut, to make it more manageable. If that length she cut and dampened hadn't been burned, we could prove it."

"I didn't do any such thing," said Liddy, reaching for the sponge.

"They have some really amazing tests nowadays," Jill remarked, very deftly sliding the sponge out from under Liddy's fingers even as they began to close on it. "Finding even trace amounts of things like latex powder or milk solids." She held it under her nose and inhaled.

"No!" screamed Liddy, lunging across the table at Jill, sending silverware, food, and crockery flying.

"Stop it, stop it, stop it!" shouted Douglas, grabbing his sister by an arm and shoulder to pull her back. "Sit down, for God's sake! Can't you see she's bluffing? It's not possible that is Mother's!"

Jill, Douglas, and Carla picked up fallen chairs and the bigger pieces of crockery, and shoved the wet tablecloth around on the table to sop up spilled liquids.

Women filled the doorways and windows of the lounge, staring.

A wait person slammed out of the kitchen, but Jill waved her away.

"Why not?" asked Betsy, who had not moved, as if the incident had not happened.

Douglas gave his sister a final push to make her stay in her seat and sat down himself with a thump. "What?"

"Why can't it be her sponge? How do you know we didn't find your mother's purse and project bag in the trunk of her car?"

"She didn't keep them in the trunk," replied Douglas, never taking his eyes off Liddy, who was watching Jill put the sponge away in her purse.

"You don't know that," said Liddy, surprised, her head coming around. She said to Betsy, "He knows that isn't Mama's because he burned everything, the idiot. I told him to burn just the sponge and the EpiPen. Mama carried spare EpiPens, so who would miss one? And who would notice the sponge wasn't there? They'd notice if the floss was gone, or the needles, but not all stitchers use sponges. I had it all planned out, I told Mama about Dad going up to the lodge, and talked about him and Carla, and I brought a box of dried milk and sprinkled just a little on her damp sponge and put it back in the little poly bag. Mama's not allergic to polyethylene."

"When was this?"

"I had her over for brunch Friday morning, just before she left to come up here. I sealed her EpiPen, the one she keeps in her purse, when she went to the bathroom. There was plenty of time, she has to use the bathroom off the back bedroom, way upstairs, where there's no perfumes or shampoo, no potpourri, nothing that she's allergic to, and I got out the little hepa filter to run, like I always do when she visits." She sighed. "All those rules. We were always having to be so careful, changing our clothes when we came home from visiting a friend who had cats, never using fabric softener, or hair spray, or perfume. I know everything she's allergic to, there was a long list of things to choose from."

"Liddy! Elizabeth!" Douglas groaned, but she continued as if he hadn't spoken.

"I planned it all very carefully. I even arranged to be at work when it was going to happen. I asked her to phone me when she left so I could check to be sure she arrived, then I phoned Doogie that she was on her way."

"Oh, my dear child," said Carla, "do you realize what you are saying?"

"Of course she doesn't!" said Douglas. "She's having a nervous breakdown, anyone can see that. For heaven's sake, Liddy, stop making a fool of yourself!"

Liddy smiled at Carla. "But it wasn't because of you, dear Carla. I like you, and Dad likes you, and we all want Dad to be happy. Sharon made him so miserable, and she made Doogie's and my life a living hell, coming home to say she loved us, then walking out, over and over. We kept thinking it was our fault, but no matter how good we were, she'd just leave again. And Betsy is absolutely right, she was talking about marrying Tony, who has two young children. I like to think I got over Mama, but poor Doogie, he's never been a brave soldier like me, he's got a broken heart from Mama treating us like disposable diapers. I did what I could for Doogie, but after all, I'm only sixteen months older than he is, and I'm not really his mother." A sob escaped her, and she waved a hand in front of her face in apology.

"Please stop talking, Liddy!" groaned Douglas.

She went on. "Mama told me how Tony had introduced her to his children, and how they were two darlings, sweet and good, and I'm sure she was being so charming and nice and kind to them, just as she was to us. Over and over, every single time, she broke our hearts, until we didn't have real hearts anymore, just little bags of broken rocks. It wasn't fair. I couldn't bear it. All of us so messed up, Daddy, Doogie, me—and now she was starting in on Tony and poor little Benjamin and Annie. I couldn't let that happen, could I? Well, could I?"

Into the silence that followed, Betsy said, "I saw the snowmobile tracks on the lawn. I suppose skimping one grooming of the Pincushion mightn't be noticed, Douglas."

"What are you talking about?" he said.

"When I called the ranger station in Grand Marais, they told you were assigned to groom the Pincushion cross-country ski trails last Friday. That's done on a snowmobile. They gave you the key to the shed where the snowmobiles are kept. You're familiar with the Pincushion and the trails through Judge Magney State Park, aren't you? You're the apprentice who goes through the park looking for stranded or injured tourists. So you noticed, didn't you, that it's the same key that opens the shed in Grand Marais and the shed across the highway. It even opens the station over there, too, where there was a spare uniform, which you borrowed. The ranger in Grand Marais says they always keep a couple of spare shirts and trousers and even a jacket there, because ranger work can be messy, and you can't meet the public in a messy uniform."

"No," agreed Douglas.

Betsy continued. "You put on the uniform, and you sat in the dining room and sipped that dreadful overcooked coffee until she arrived, didn't you? You watched while she sat down in the lounge to talk to me and work on her new design of a Victorian doll. And she had an allergic attack. What did you tell her, that Frank was in his room with a cell phone?"

Carla said, "What—Doogie, too?"

"Oh, yes," said Betsy. "It took both of them. It was

Liddy's idea, and she used Douglas as her cat's paw."

Douglas said, "What cat's paw? I never was here, I never saw my mother until—until they made me come and identify her body. I never touched my mother's body."

"Oh, Doogie, never mind, she knows everything." Liddy's eyes, huge and shadowed, turned to Betsy for confirmation.

But Betsy could not lie, not now, when truth was the most important thing. "I don't know everything. What I don't understand is why Douglas tried to hide the body. Sharon died of an allergic reaction, which anyone might think was an accident or even, for her, a natural death, to be expected since she was so violently allergic to so many things."

"Yes, you did it all wrong, Doogie," said Liddy. "Not like I told you at all. Why did you do it like that?"

Douglas turned on her ferociously. "Because, you silly bitch, she didn't die of that allergic reaction! I smothered her!"

The silence this time was electric, then Douglas exhaled noisily and pulled at the wet and rumpled tablecloth as if to straighten it, but quit after the one pull. "I know you said it couldn't go wrong, Liddy, but it did, big time. First, when that doctored EpiPen got away. I watched it roll under the door and it scared me, but I thought maybe we could do it anyhow. I said I didn't have a quarter to call an ambulance, and she said she'd left her coat and purse up in Dad's room. I said his cell phone is probably up there, too, and I took her and her canvas stitchery bag up there, but of course Dad always has his phone with him, so I said I'd find someone to call an ambulance and get her spare EpiPen out of the car. I went down the back stairs and hung around outside for fifteen minutes, and no one saw me. But when I went back up there, she was still breathing. She was suffering—it was horrible, I had to end it for her, she was hurting . . . And anyhow I couldn't wait any longer. Dad might come back, or someone out in the hall might hear the noise she was making. So I put a pillow over her face and held it down for a really long time, till I was sure she was dead."

"Oh, my God, Doogie!" cried Liddy, horrified. "You poor thing!"

Jill and Carla looked at Liddy wide eyed. Betsy was sure she'd never heard anything more cold-blooded in her life.

Douglas said, "Well, I've read they can tell when someone's been suffocated, so the original plan to make it look like allergic reaction was shot to hell. I ran back up the lane and across the road to the shed and got the snowmobile and brought it around to the back door, not knowing Miss Nosypants had already walked in on Mama's body. I went up and put her coat on her, and got her purse and that canvas thing her sewing stuff goes into. The scariest part was taking her down that hall and down the stairs. I could hear women talking in the rooms. But no one came out and saw me. I was going to put everything down the kettle and come back to drive her car away, but by the time I got just out to the high- way I had stopped three times to pick up the bag and the purse and coat, so I put the coat on her and hid the bag and purse in the ditch, and went up the long back trail in the near dark to the river, a ride from hell I assure you, and carried her down the falls and dropped her in. She went right down out of sight and I ran back to my snowmobile and drove it back to the ranger station. Then I had to walk up and down in the ditch for what seemed like an hour before I found the purse and bag, but be damned if I could find the car keys. I finally walked over to the shed, where there was a light, and I opened the door and dumped everything out of the bag and her purse, and they just weren't there."

"So you didn't fall," said Betsy.

"Fall?" he said, looking at her politely. "No, I didn't fall."

Liddy said, "You don't pay attention, Doogie. Her keys were in her coat pocket, she always puts her keys in her coat pocket, didn't you ever notice that?" She began to giggle, an eerie, high-pitched sound, and Douglas slammed his hand on the table to make her stop.

He continued. "So I picked up everything and put it in the furnace, went back to the station for my car, and drove like hell back to Grand Marais, where I clocked out and went home scared to death." He sighed a long sigh and said quietly, "It started unraveling when the EpiPen rolled under the door. I should've known right then we were screwed. But I thought we might still get away with it when they said she died of an allergic reaction. I suppose being knocked around in that kettle covered up what happens to smothered people's eyes. But I was right after all, it was the EpiPen that tore it for us."

"What about the eyes?" asked Betsy.

Jill said, "He means petechial hemorrhages, tiny marks in the eyes of someone who's been smothered. But I suppose once they examined the lungs and saw such strong evidence of an allergic reaction they didn't look any further. Anyway, I suspect the symptoms of smothering might be hard to tell from someone dying of a severe allergic reaction, which also stops the breathing."

"You only had to be patient," said Liddy mildly. "She would have died by herself, if you'd just waited awhile."

He turned again on his sister. "And have this snoop walk in on me hovering like a buzzard over her? No way! But if you'd kept your crybaby mouth shut, we'd be going home about now anyhow!"

Liddy scolded him, "So what if somebody walked in, even Dad? They'd've just found you trying to help Mama. So it isn't my fault, it's yours, Doogie, it's all your fault!" Her tone was that of a big sister who has been found with little brother rooting around in the Christmas presents hidden in a closet, and it would have been funny if it hadn't been so wildly inappropriate to the occasion.

Betsy looked at Jill, who had the look of a cop being handed an extremely unlikely excuse for speeding. *Ah,* thought Betsy, *she's getting a head start on her defense.*

"Douglas Owen, Elizabeth Owen, I am placing both of you under arrest for murder," said a rough voice, and everyone looked up to see Sheriff Goodman, accompanied by the quartet from the BCA. "You have a right to remain silent," he continued, and everyone sat quietly until the ritual warning was completed. "Do you understand your rights as I have explained them?"

"Yessir," said Douglas, "and I wish to speak with Dad's attorney."

Goodman looked at Liddy, who, eyes very wide, whispered, "Yes."

Goodman asked Jill, "They say anything incriminating?"

"Oh, yes indeed," replied Jill. "I suppose you want us all to come by to fill out a report."

"That's right. Finish your . . . meal first." He frowned deeply at the wet rubble they were sitting in. "Well, anyhow, I'll be waiting for you." He included Carla in his sweeping glance, then had Liddy and Douglas stand while they were handcuffed and led away.

"My word," said Carla, after they'd gone. "I was going to marry their father."

"No reason why you shouldn't," said Jill, brushing a shard of coffee cup off her lap.

"Oh, no, it's impossible now. In a few years everyone will halfway forget who murdered whom, and I might find myself included on the wrong list. I can't believe they murdered their own mother—and not for the money, but to protect two little kids they didn't even know."

Betsy said, "Most children work their way through the pain and anger of divorce. It leaves a scar, of course, but most children recover and lead productive lives. But Sharon kept renewing the wound. Because she was a vicious, selfish person, they were never allowed to get over it. Liddy says she did it to save Tony's children, but I wonder if this might have been an attempt to reach back in time to save herself and her brother, doing what she wished someone had done for her all those years ago. I think she both loved and loathed her mother. And worse, she planted and nurtured that hatred in her brother."

"So you think Liddy was the prime mover in this," said Jill.

"Don't you?"

"Actually, I do. Though with a good lawyer and the lack of a money motive, there might be trouble proving it. Doogie, after all, was the person on the scene with the pillow. But of course there are the incriminating statements we just sat through. What an odd way for Douglas to behave! If he'd simply aborted the plan and just helped his mother, brought her the spare EpiPen out of the car, no one might have been the wiser, and they might have had another chance down the road to try it again. Or if he'd just walked away into the sunset, left his mother to die in Frank's room, who knows what trouble poor Frank Owen would still be in?"

"That's why I called him a cat's paw," said Betsy.

"She told him what to do, and it never occurred to him not to struggle on through with the plan."

"How awful!" cried Carla. "And I would bet those two would have let their father go to prison for it, don't you think? Oh, poor Frank! Those were his children! Oh, what is he going to do?"

"Seek comfort from a woman who loves him?" suggested Betsy. "Who would promise to stand by him for better or worse?"

Carla looked at Betsy, and very slowly a little smile formed. "That would be generous and kind of me, wouldn't it? And I really do like him very much, you know."

Two wait people came to tidy up the floor and table, spreading a new cloth. "If you would like something to eat," said one—Billie, the woman with the braids wrapped around her young, freshly scrubbed face—"I'll see if the cook can make you an omelet."

"Thank you, no," said Carla, and Jill and Betsy shook their heads. They all stood. "I think I'll drive into Grand Marais alone," Carla said. "In case Frank wants me to run any errands." Her dark face pulled into a grimace. "Or bring the children something, I suppose."

16

Coming back from Grand Marais and the lengthy and tiresome completion of reports, statements, affidavits, and other paperwork, Betsy sighed and squirmed in the passenger seat.

"What's the matter?" asked Jill.

"I don't know. I just feel restless. It's late, I should be sleepy—God knows I tried, but I couldn't seem to get enough sleep; it must be the air up here or something—but now I feel like, oh, I don't know, like a long walk up the lakeshore, or even putting on those skis and heading up the river again. If I were home, I'd be cleaning out cabinets or scrubbing the bathroom tile."

Jill asked, "Are you pregnant?"

"For heaven's sake, why do you ask that?"

"Because I had a cousin with four kids, and with every single one of them, the day before labor began, she was up all night cleaning. 'Nest building,' she called it."

"Humph. No, I am not even a little bit pregnant, much

less nine months gone. Say, what's that light up ahead? Like a glow on the horizon. Is there a big city north of here?" Betsy was leaning forward, looking out the windshield.

Jill immediately pulled over. "No," she said, "it's the northern lights. Sometimes they're like that before your eyes get fully adjusted to the dark, kind of a very faint gold." She turned on the flashers and opened the door. "Come on, let's take a walk."

Betsy climbed eagerly out, and they walked up the shoulder of the road. It was late, dark, bitterly cold. The sky was spattered with stars. The farther they walked away from the flashing lights, the darker it got. As their eyes adjusted, more and more stars appeared. A few minutes later, the strange gold light shifted subtly, and then turned colors and began to dance.

"Listen," whispered Jill, coming to a halt.

Betsy, walking in front, froze and looked around in alarm, fearful a wolf or moose was coming. Then she heard it, the faintest possible crackle, as of someone a mile away wadding up cellophane. "What's that?" she whispered.

"Sometimes you can hear the northern lights."

"Aww—!" scoffed Betsy.

"No, I'm serious. It happens more often if you're up near the Arctic Circle. But it can happen here, too."

Betsy listened some more. "Wow," she breathed. She looked around the sky. "Look," she said, "the Milky Way. And the Big Dipper. And Orion—he's my favorite, I don't know why. I remember the first time I saw Orion from San Diego, and it was strange to be sitting on grass, surrounded by blooming flowers, because he's the winter constellation." She began to walk again, stamping her feet hard because they were getting cold.

"You miss San Diego?"

"Sometimes. But this"—Betsy stopped to gesture at

the black shapes of evergreens lining either side of the road, visible in the faint reflection of starlight on snow—"is amazing. It's beautiful, but so harsh, so unforgiving. How did people live up here before furnaces and Thinsulate?"

"Beats me."

"And Naniboujou. I thought that was such a silly name when I first heard it, but now . . . Now I wish he were real, that you could court his good will with a pinch of tobacco. I'll never look at wild geese flying in formation the same way again."

They walked a little farther, then Jill said, "We'd better start back. It's late and I'm getting cold."

"You? I don't believe it! You love winter!"

"Yes, I do. But I'm feeling a little blue, thinking about Mr. Owen. He's been living a nightmare, and to escape it he lost both his children."

"Yes," said Betsy, suddenly a little sad herself, and turned to follow Jill back up the road. "Jill, what makes some people turn to murder and others not? You hear people saying, 'No wonder that kid turned to crime, he never knew his father, his mother was a drug addict in a bad neighborhood, he went to a bad school, had nothing but bad companions.' But you hear about another kid from the same neighborhood, same school, no parents, surrounded by the same bad companions, and he somehow turns out great. Why?"

"Beats me."

"Douglas and Elizabeth. Those two had a bad mother, but a good father, and every other advantage. Yet they did a wicked thing. Why?"

"It's not my job to know. It's not your job either. Not to find them out, or figure out why they did it. I think I'm feeling what you feel after you've solved one of these mysteries, as if you are looking into a terrible, meaningless abyss that swallows the innocent along with the guilty."

"Yes," said Betsy, remembering.

"So if you still want to, call it quits. I won't try to change your mind. I suppose you can knock down that impulse to investigate for good if you keep trying."

They were at the car. They had left it unlocked. They climbed in, Jill started the engine, turned the heater up high, shut off the flashers, and hit the headlights. The road was completely empty and she pulled out. "Shall we start for home in the morning?"

"I suppose so. No, wait a minute. You've still got the whole week off. No need for you to go back. You can run me into Grand Marais and I can catch a bus. Is there bus service from there?"

Jill laughed softly. "A bus ride all the way back to the Cities? That would be a long, serious trip, with a stop at every wide place in the road. It'll take you fourteen hours, probably. No, I'll drive you home."

"But that wouldn't be fair to you. How about I stay on? I want to work on that rose window pattern, and I've got a lot to do. Frogging, then restitching."

"I thought you'd quit working on it."

"Oh, I can give it another chance, I guess. If I give it enough chances, I may get it right."

"Stubborn, aren't you?"

"I prefer to think of it as determined. Just like I prefer to think that I'm curious, not an incorrigible snoop. Nothing wrong with being curious. And maybe, like Carla with her trame, and the geologist Parker, a little obsessed. I start wondering about things, and once I start wondering, I just have to keep going until I have the explanation." She chuckled. "That doesn't sound like nosy Miss Marple, it sounds more like driven Hercule Poirot."

Jill said, "It's neither. Your ability to ferret out crime

and make the perps confess is a blessing to the innocent."

And with a rush of something like pleasure, Betsy realized Jill was right. But Betsy was right, too. She had somehow become driven by questions, unable to leave the unexplained alone. But being a blessing to the innocent—she had never seen it from that angle. She smiled to herself, then at Jill, and settled comfortably in her seat. "If I go home, I'll have to start coping with that leak in the roof, and repairing the ceiling of the shop, and finding some part-timers who aren't planning on going away for the summer. I need this break. You need it, too. The stitch-in is over, the stitchers have gone home. We'll have the whole place to ourselves tonight. Maybe all week, unless James gets his wish and the travel editor of the *New York Times* drops in. Tonight we can get what we came here for in the first place—a little peace and quiet, and a good night's sleep."

Denise E. Williams

Design Count: 42w x 42h
Design Size: 3.5 x 3.5 in, 12 Count

Key: + DMC 320   Pistachio Green-MD
      ● DMC 326   Rose-VY DP
      ❑ DMC 725   Topaz
      ★ DMC 740   Tangerine
      ❂ DMC 824   Blue-VY DK

Stitch on 12-count canvas using DMC Perle
Cotton #3. Design may be worked in continental
stitch, or in bargello fashion using long vertical
stitches.